ORPHANS of WAR

MICHAEL REIT

MICHAELREIT.COM

PART I

AMSTERDAM,

7 FEBRUARY 1941

CHAPTER ONE

Christiaan Brouwer waited as the last passengers disembarked at Victorie Square. An elderly lady made her way down the steps, giving him a little wave as their eyes met in his rearview mirror. It's why he'd applied to become a tram driver straight out of high school four years ago—he loved interacting with his fellow *Amsterdammers*. No day was ever the same, even if the routes were.

He pushed his tram into gear and crossed a small bridge over the Amstel Channel. Traffic on the other side had come to a standstill. Another tram blocked his path, its driver standing outside, smoking a cigarette. Christiaan stepped out of his own tram and walked toward his colleague, whom he didn't recognize.

"What's going on?"

The man shrugged. "Some kids getting into a fight, I guess." He pointed at a gathering about 100 meters ahead of them and took a drag from his cigarette. "I hope they clear it up soon, I want to go home."

A bone-chilling cry pierced the air, followed by a woman's wail. Christiaan didn't hesitate and sprinted up the street. Something was off. He quickly covered the distance. His heart sank when he spotted the black uniforms of the *Weerbaarheidsafdeling*, the WA. They were the paramilitary arm of the Dutch National Socialist Movement, the *NSB*. The organization had seen a surge in membership recently— people were keen to pledge their support to the Nazi oppressors, to which the NSB was closely aligned.

He pushed through the crowd to see two Blackshirts on either side of an older man lying face down on the cobblestones. One of the thugs viciously kicked the downed man in the ribs. He doubled over, coughing violently. A woman in the crowd let out a cry, while another shielded her child between her skirts.

"There, you Jewish piece of shit! That'll teach you to get out of the way the next time!" The Blackshirt couldn't be older than twenty.

Christiaan felt the blood rush to his head. He scanned the crowd and saw another half a dozen Blackshirts looking on. The other people looked terrified: they were mostly women and children. A few elderly men wearing kippahs stood in the back, looking on help- lessly. When the other Blackshirt used his boot to lift the stricken man's face off the ground, Christiaan couldn't stand it any longer. He broke from the crowd.

"What the hell are you doing?" He squared his shoulders as he approached the Blackshirts. Their eyes showed surprise as they turned to him. "Feeling big beating up an old man?"

The man groaned in pain as he turned his face to meet Christi- aan's. He was shocked to see the man was even older than he expected—he was well into his seventies. Dark patches were already forming around his cheeks and eyes. Christiaan felt his temples throbbing with anger. His eyes went back to the nearest Blackshirt, and without another thought, he swung a fist at the man's face. It connected with his jaw and Christiaan felt a sharp pain radiate through his hand and arm. It was quickly suppressed as adrenaline kicked in. The man reached for his jaw, and Christiaan swung again, this time hearing the satisfying crack of the man's nose breaking.

The Blackshirt went down howling in pain, blood gushing from his nose.

Christiaan turned to the other man, whose eyes now burned with fury. "You should've stayed out of this." He growled, then came at Christiaan, his fists up like a boxer's. Christiaan stepped back, avoiding a flurry of jabs. *This one is better trained.*

"Come on! What are you waiting for!" The man roared and attacked again, grazing Christiaan's cheek as he managed to avoid full impact. The man grinned as he paused. "You're mine. And when you're down, we're going to finish you." He nodded at the other Blackshirts in the crowd.

Christiaan's eyes went between the group and his opponent. He knew he didn't stand a chance against all of them. Then he looked at the old man on the ground, his face turned toward the fight. He was shaking, there was defiance in his eyes. The man balled his fist, stoking a fire inside Christiaan. *Might as well take down as many as I can.*

He returned his focus to the Blackshirt, and for a moment, neither of them moved. Then Christiaan let out a roar and charged forward. The move surprised the Blackshirt, and they tumbled onto the ground together. The crowd gasped and moved back as they wrestled on the ground. The Blackshirt was now on top and struck Christiaan in the face twice. Christiaan lifted his hands and caught one of the man's wrists. Locking it with both hands, he pushed himself sideways, twisting the man's wrist as he turned onto his stomach. There was a sharp crack before the Blackshirt howled in pain. He rolled away clutching his limp, broken wrist. Christiaan breathed hard, a numb pain building around his eye. With an effort, he got to his feet, in time to see the other six Blackshirts surrounding him like a pack of wolves circling their prey.

Christiaan gritted his teeth. For a moment, nothing happened as they decided who would attack first. From the corner of his eye, Christiaan saw the glint of a knife. His blood ran cold. He wouldn't stand a chance. He swallowed hard and looked at the men's faces. All he saw was pure hatred. There would be no talking his way out of this.

The man with the knife slashed at him, but Christiaan stepped back, deftly avoiding the attack. Adrenaline rushed back as the world appeared to slow down. He focused on the man with the knife, then felt a blow to the back of his head. Stars clouded his vision, but he forced himself to stay on his feet, keeping his eyes on the knife-wielding Blackshirt. The man thrust this time, but Christiaan stepped aside, the knife narrowly missing his groin. On instinct, Christiaan reached down for the man's arm. He grabbed his elbow and squeezed with all his strength. The knife clattered to the ground, and Christiaan kicked it away. It disappeared into the crowd. Still holding onto the Blackshirt, he crashed to the ground, landing on the man's chest. The sound of distant whistles filled the air, but Christiaan hardly noticed. He furiously rained down punches, turning the man's face into a bloody mess. Suddenly, he felt strong arms gripping his arms and shoulders. As he felt his strength ebb away, he knew this was it. The other Blackshirts would finish him off. *At least I took down three.*

He waited for the inevitable flurry of punches as he was dragged from the unconscious man. Then he spotted two of the Blackshirts on the edge of the crowd, looking on impassively. Christiaan was confused. A deep, baritone voice shocked his senses back to the present.

"What the hell were you thinking picking a fight with them?"

Christiaan looked into the face of one of the police officers hauling him away. His head was swimming and felt his right leg throbbing. He looked down. His pants were torn and soaked in blood.

"You're lucky we got here just in time. They got you good."

Christiaan wanted to say something, but his tongue felt too thick to talk. His eyes felt heavy as the world started spinning. The last thing remembered was being pulled into the ambulance. Then his world went black.

CHAPTER TWO

Nora Brouwer rushed through the wet streets, carrying the day's meager harvest in a small bag on her shoulder. *Floris won't be thrilled.* She'd arrived at the market early enough, when the sun was still out, but she'd been disheartened to find the queues for most stalls snaking through the narrow passages. She gambled on her favorite vegetable stall, most people were queuing for meat, but when it was finally her turn, there was little left to choose from. She decided she'd make the best of it tonight; carrots, onions, and potatoes would make a nice *hutspot*, even if she didn't have any sausage or ham to serve alongside it. She shook her head, unable to remember the last time she tasted ham. Besides, Floris would probably be home too late to enjoy whatever she prepared anyway.

The raindrops increased in frequency and she pulled up the hood of her coat. It didn't help much, only delaying the rain seeping through to her long black hair underneath.

As she left the Nieuwmarkt behind her, she noticed people loitering around in the streets. This area of the city had a lot of Jewish citizens, and even though they were banned from patronizing the market, they were still allowed to go outside. They would often find non-Jewish Amsterdammers to go to the market for them—still the best place to find the freshest produce, even though the supply had dwindled dramatically. People would entrust their precious ration coupons to these food runners—often in exchange for a share of the produce. Nora looked at the faces of the people shivering on the side of the street. Some looked nervous, most were praying. She knew the risks they took. A food runner could easily disappear, leaving them with nothing.

She hurried on, anxious to get home and out of the rain. A few hundred meters ahead of her the road was blocked by several trucks. She sighed. *Perhaps it was just a checkpoint?* As she neared, German soldiers were ushering the people ahead of her away from the main thoroughfare. Nora stopped in front of the blockade to see what was going on.

"Move along, ma'am," one of the German soldiers said in a stern voice. Nora met his eyes and even though he looked intimidating in his full army outfit—including a sidearm—his face wasn't unfriendly.

Nora decided to risk it. "I need to get to the Weesper. Is there no way through here?"

"Afraid not." The soldier shook his head. "You'll have to take the long way around. We're doing some checks in the Jewish quarter. All the streets to and from are blocked."

As the soldier motioned for her to move on, Nora felt discouraged. This would not only add at least half an hour through the now-pouring rain to her journey but would mean she had to pass through De Wallen, an area she tried to avoid at all costs.

She was shaking as she followed the small procession. Everyone kept their eyes focused straight ahead. These random checks appeared out of nowhere, especially around the Jewish neighborhoods—you never knew when or where. Whenever she was asked to show her papers she was always waved on quickly.

Nora neared the water and, as the soldier had predicted, her route directly south was blocked, forcing her to cross a small bridge. She took a deep breath as she reached the other side, where people went their separate ways. Nora decided she'd try the shortest route, following the water south, and then cross one of the bridges to make her way home.

She kept her pace fast and her eyes down as she navigated the quiet streets. She was startled by laughter as one of the doors of the many cafes opened and a couple of men stumbled out. They seemed oblivious to her as two scantily clad women followed them and helped them up. They soon disappeared into an alley farther down the street.

Nora continued along the water until she found her path blocked by a group of men some 50 meters ahead. There were at least twenty of them, talking to a number of police officers. Even though it was Nora's shortest route home, she decided to give them a wide berth. She turned into one of the side streets, its cobblestones slick with rain. Nora hurried on, anxious to return to the main thoroughfare alongside the canal. As she navigated the alleys, a familiar building loomed up ahead. Nora stopped in her tracks, her heartbeat shooting up. The red lights above the front door hummed softly as Nora took a deep breath.

The building had been her home for almost three years. She closed her eyes as the memories came flooding back. The heavy make-up and perfume that made her feel well beyond her eighteen years, the endless stream of strange men: touching her, using and discarding her after they'd sated their carnal desires. But worst of all, living in constant fear of the woman running the brothel. Madam Nel had taken her in when she was no longer welcome in the orphanage. At first, Nora had been grateful to the woman giving her food and shelter. That quickly changed when Nel told her she had to earn her keep.

The door opened and a man stepped out, quickly scanning the street before scampering away. The smell of cigarettes and sex snapped Nora back to her senses. She shuddered and hurried away.

Clasping her small bag tighter, she returned to the main thorough-fare, the sound of the rain clattering on the canal providing some comfort.

"Rosa, is that you?"

The words came like a punch to her gut, and Nora reluctantly turned to find a heavily built man following her. *Where did he come from?* There was recognition in his eyes, and she felt her chest tighten. She had trouble breathing, but still managed to croak, "I think you have me mixed up with someone else."

The man's eyes narrowed, looking her up and down, and she instinctively wrapped her coat tighter. "No, I'm pretty sure—" the man started, but Nora was already walking away. *Keep going, don't encourage him.* She took large strides as she prayed he would leave her alone.

It wasn't to be. Heavy footsteps caught up with her easily. "I don't forget a pretty face like yours, even if I haven't seen you here for more than what, two years? Nah, probably even longer. Four years, surely. You haven't aged at all. You still look the same as the last time I had the *pleasure* of seeing you."

Nora didn't stop and looked at the water to her left as she tried to block out his words. It was impossible. Mustering up all her courage, she stopped and turned. "Please leave me alone. I'm not who you think I am, I'm just trying to get home." She recoiled when she saw the lecherous look in his eyes.

"You know, why don't you stop lying and we can go and have a good time," the man said, stepping closer to her. "For old time's sake."

Nora took a step back, edging closer to the canal. There was nowhere to go, no way she could fight off this man twice her size. He sensed her fear, which only aroused him more. He grabbed her hand, his grip strong, making it clear she wasn't going anywhere.

There was only one thing left to do.

"Help! Help!" she shouted at the top of her lungs, dropping her bag, a carrot rolling out and into the canal.

The man's face contorted in rage, and he readjusted his grip on her wrist. He tightened it so much it hurt, and she felt the tips of her fingers tingle. To her horror, there was nobody to come to her rescue; the street was abandoned.

"You little whore," the man hissed as he pulled her away from the water and toward one of the alleys across the street. "You just have to make this difficult, don't you."

Nora struggled to free herself from his grip, but it was no use. He dragged her across the cobblestones, twisting and turning, the world turning hazy from her tears.

Then, just before the man entered the alley, she saw the door to a cafe down the street open. With everything she had left, she screamed across the empty street one more time, praying whoever exited wasn't too drunk to hear her. "Help! Please, somebody!"

She was pulled into the darkness of the alley, the man muttering at her. "Think you're too good for me now all of a sudden, don't cha'. I remember you, even if you've forgotten about me."

Nora tried to control the terror washing over her body. *Don't make him even angrier. It'll only make things worse.* Even though she tried to look calm outwardly, she felt hot tears rolling down her cheeks. With her free hand, she wiped them away.

The man's eyes shot up and down the alley, confirming what they both knew: they were alone. Satisfied, he loosened his grip for a moment, only to lower himself on her, grabbing both of her hands and holding her down.

Don't give him the satisfaction. Nora tried to control the urge to fight—fearing it would only arouse him more—and for a few seconds, she managed to stay completely still as he fumbled around. Then, as one of his hands released hers and gripped her breasts, she snapped.

"Let go of me, you piece of filth!" she shouted in a voice she didn't recognize. Her fury erupted from deep within as she lashed out, scratching at his face. Blood appeared as her nails made small cuts, and he seemed taken aback for a moment. Nora continued clawing at his face and throat. She kicked out but hit nothing but air. She was breathing hard and screaming at the top of her lungs.

"Get off me, you bastard!"

He relaxed his grip for a moment and Nora lunged forward, biting his hand with so much fury she thought she'd break his fingers. The man roared in pain as he punched her in the head with his other hand. The force of the blow was devastating as Nora's world flashed bright white before she slumped onto the cold ground.

"You bitch!" he hissed inches from her ear, and the alcohol on his breath made her nostrils flare in disgust. "You shouldn't have done that."

Nora groaned in pain, her head pounding as all strength was sapped from her body. The man unzipped his fly, his hands now pulling at her skirt.

"Hey! What the hell is going on?!"

At the end of the alley, four or five tall figures approached. She was so relieved she could cry. She called out, but only managed a whimper. She tried again, this time with a bit more strength. "Help!"

The men didn't immediately move, and Nora's heart skipped a beat. *Are they not coming?* They stood there for what felt like an eternity until everything happened at once. The pressure on her body eased as her assailant got off her and ran in the opposite direction. Heavy footsteps passed as the men gave chase. She took a deep breath and was startled to see an outstretched hand in front of her. "Are you all right, miss?"

She recoiled from the hand, then looked up to see a young man—he couldn't be older than eighteen—with soft eyes looking at her inquisitively. She took his hand and he helped her up. "Any injuries? Did he hit you?"

She rubbed her head. "You got here just in time."

At the far end of the alley, a triumphant cry was followed by a howl of pain. Nora turned her head to see the younger men had caught up with her would-be rapist. He was on the ground, the men mercilessly beating him.

"He won't be bothering you anymore," the man next to her said, holding Nora's bag. "I suppose this belongs to you?"

Nora reached for the bag but failed to grab it. Her hands were shaking, and she suddenly felt very cold. She trembled, her teeth chattering. The man looked at her with concern.

"Maybe we should go inside, get you some water? You've been through a lot. See if we can get the police?"

Not the police! Nora shook her head. "If you don't mind, I must be on my way. I'm sure my husband is wondering what's keeping me."

She thought she detected a flash of disappointment in his eyes, but he recovered quickly, shaking his head. "You're not going anywhere." Nora raised an eyebrow, and he quickly continued, taking a step back, raising his palms. "Sorry, I didn't mean it like that. Please let me take you home."

"That really won't be necessary." She took a step toward the street when her knees buckled and she lost her balance. He caught her just in time.

"I'm afraid I won't take no for an answer. You're in no state to go home alone."

Her head was spinning and she rubbed the spot where the man struck her earlier. A bump was forming. She decided the young man was right. She gave him her address.

"Please take me home."

CHAPTER THREE

It was well past sunset when Floris Brouwer adjusted his cap and pulled up the collar of his blue uniform. He glanced at his partner, Hans de Vugt, next to him, who looked just as keen to get off the street and back to the station.

"Pretty chilly now that the sun's gone, won't you say?" Hans said in his thick, drawling Amsterdam accent. Floris' partner was born and raised in the Jordaan, one of Amsterdam's predominantly blue-collar neighborhoods, and proud of it. It annoyed Floris, who preferred to speak clearly and eloquently, as his position as a police officer required.

"You forgot about the rain earlier already?" Floris said, curling his lip. "It's been a miserable day."

"Yeah, well, at least it was nice and quiet. I love days like these, when people stay inside and don't cause too much trouble," Hans said.

Floris hardly heard him. "Say, do you want to join me at De Bever? We're meeting up with some of the others from the station."

Hans frowned and avoided Floris' eyes. "I don't know. I told Maja

I'd be home in time for dinner. She left early this morning. Apparently, a butcher in De Pijp got his hands on some bacon."

Floris frowned, and his younger colleague looked mortified. "All right, maybe I'll join you for a quick one. Let's get back to the station and clock out."

Floris slapped him on the shoulder. "That's the spirit." He looked forward to meeting his colleagues—who were also close friends—tonight. Despite the German occupation, life had carried on much like before, albeit with some restrictions. Sure, there were food shortages, but this was to be expected in wartime, with the Germans procuring a lot of the produce for their armies. For most Dutch people, life carried on almost as usual, with businesses profiting from the increased German demand.

Life had perhaps gotten slightly better for Floris and his fellow police officers. They had kept their jobs and carried on much as they did before. *Except for those arrogant clowns who think they're too good to work with our German colleagues. I wonder where they are now. Probably—*

"That doesn't look good," Hans said, interrupting his thoughts. Floris followed his partner's gaze and gritted his teeth in frustration.

Only 50 meters up the street, a crowd had gathered. People had their backs to them, their attention drawn to what was happening in front of a cigar store. Floris could hear raised voices.

"I can bloody well decide for myself. You don't have the authority to do this."

As they neared, Floris looked over their heads to find a small middle-aged man gesticulating wildly in front of the store. He was surrounded by five young men wearing black uniforms. *That man doesn't know what he's up against.*

The store owner glowered at the fascist thugs. "Get out of here, you bastards!" He yelled.

Floris considered his options. Nobody had noticed him. He gauged the situation—nothing had happened yet. He decided to hang back just a little longer; perhaps this problem would resolve itself. He looked over at Hans, who hadn't moved either. Floris shook his head, and Hans nodded. *Good. He understands.*

Floris scanned the faces of the people crowding around. Most looked on disapprovingly but made no effort to get involved.

"You know what you're doing is illegal," one of the Blackshirts said, taking a step closer to the shopkeeper. Floris noticed all five Blackshirts were young—none older than twenty, a good five years younger than him. "Do as we say, and we'll be on our way. You don't want us to hang around much longer, right?" The young man spoke calmly, but the threat was clear. Tension rose as the people at the back of the crowd inched forward, some standing on their toes to get a closer look. All eyes were on the shopkeeper.

Floris was tall enough to see the man's eyes darting between his store and the Blackshirts, looking at the crowd for support. Nothing. He opened his mouth, and at that moment, he spotted Floris. His eyes lit up, and he appeared to grow slightly taller.

"Officers, I'm so glad you're here. These men are blocking the entrance to my store," he said, extending his arms in front of him. "Look, all these people behind you are unable to come inside. They're quite intimidating, the five of them." There was a hint of sarcasm in the man's voice, which was lost on the young Blackshirts.

The crowd, including the Blackshirts, turned to Floris and Hans, and one of them addressed Floris: "We're just making sure this man upholds the law." He sported a blocky mustache, not unlike that of the Führer himself.

"What law is he breaking?" Floris asked while Hans shifted on his feet.

"He's selling cigarettes to filthy Jews," one of the other Black-shirts spat.

The shopkeeper stepped forward, his face now red with rage. "It's not the law because you say so, you stupid boy."

Floris moved forward, the crowd parting. He kept quiet as the same Blackshirt from earlier responded, his voice now full of contempt. "Why are you helping them? You're not Jewish. If you were, you wouldn't be running this shop anymore. So why don't you fall in line and stop selling to them? Put up a sign like the other shops in the city." Two Blackshirts made their way into the little store, jumping over the counter and opening drawers.

The shopkeeper rushed after them. "Get out! What are you doing?" He turned back and, with an effort to control his frustration, said to Floris, "Are you going to let them get away with this? Now they are breaking the law!"

"We're helping you. Let us put up a sign, and then we'll leave you alone." One of them said mockingly.

Floris slowly entered the store, Hans following nervously. *A little longer. Let's see what happens.*

The Blackshirts shifted their attention to the exclusive cigars behind the counter. "Boys, why don't you step away from the cigars now? I'll take it from here," Floris said.

Holding a box each, the young men stared at him for a moment. Floris raised an eyebrow, and Hans—finding his nerve—took a step forward, hands on the baton hanging loosely from his belt. The youngsters dropped the expensive-looking cigars and joined their friends outside.

The shopkeeper sighed in relief. "Thank you so much, officer. You're going to make them pay for those broken—"

"Shut up," Floris said with a harsh tone. "We're not done yet."

The man looked confused. The crowd had fallen silent, and Floris felt twenty or so pairs of eyes following his every move. The Blackshirts crowded around the door.

"You brought this onto yourself," Floris started, and the shopkeeper's face fell. "You should know what's good for you, and continuing to sell to Jews certainly isn't."

The man looked crestfallen, and for a few seconds, everything was silent. Then, one of the Blackshirts spoke up. "So, are you going to make him follow the law, officer?" Floris cringed as he turned to him.

"I can't make him do anything. He's right about one thing. It's not the law. Yet. But I think you've made it clear to him what will happen if he doesn't put up a sign." Floris kept his face neutral as he turned back to the shopkeeper. "You'll take care of that, right?"

The shopkeeper looked up, meeting Floris' eyes. He was surprised to see a hint of defiance—hidden from the people standing outside—as he slowly nodded. "I don't think I have much of a choice."

Floris nodded, pleased with how he handled the situation. He was ready to break up the crowd when Hans spoke up.

"Gentlemen, just one small thing before you go. You are going to pay for those, aren't you?" He picked up one of the cigar boxes and placed it on the counter. He then purposefully picked up two broken cigars. "How much were these?" he asked the shopkeeper.

The man appeared surprised at the turn of events and took a moment to respond. Then, Hans turned back to the Blackshirts when he named the price. They looked back in surprise as their eyes went between Floris and Hans.

Floris cursed inwardly. *Why did Hans have to make a big deal out of a few cigars?* It was the shopkeeper's fault for foolishly continuing to sell to Jews. Before the situation could escalate further, he said, "Why don't you boys get out of here? He promised to put a sign up." He felt Hans' eyes burning into the side of his face but ignored him. "If I hear about you coming back here and causing more trouble, you will pay for more than a few cigars. You got that?"

The Blackshirts looked relieved, all mumbling assent before scrambling away through the dispersing crowd. The excitement quieted as people returned to their regular business.

Floris turned to the shopkeeper. "I'll be back tomorrow. Make sure you don't give those boys a reason to do the same."

"Yes, officer. Thank you, officer," the man said, his face now set in hard lines.

Without another word, Floris stepped out of the shop, Hans in tow. When they were clear of the shop, his younger colleague opened his mouth, but Floris raised a hand. "You were pushing it. The shopkeeper was foolish standing up to them; a few broken cigars are nothing compared to the beating he would've gotten had we not shown up."

"You think this is okay?" Hans countered as he struggled to keep up with Floris, who was keen to clock out. This little altercation had delayed him longer than he cared for.

"I think sometimes people need to sort things out themselves," Floris said. "And we stopped it before it got much worse."

Hans wouldn't let it go that easily. "So you think those boys can terrorize anyone who disagrees with them? You know as well as I that this nonsense about not allowing Jews into stores is just NSB propaganda. Nazi bootlickers."

Floris felt his cheeks burn and abruptly turned. "Careful now, Hans. Before you say something you'll regret."

Hans looked at him. "Sorry. But I believe we're still police officers that follow the actual law."

They reached the station without another word, and Floris used the short walk to calm down. It wasn't Hans' fault for not seeing the sense of the NSB party line—the approach of the Blackshirts wasn't for everybody. *He'll come around. He needs a bit more time.* Floris needed to keep his partner on his side and stopped at the station's door.

"Look, sorry about earlier. You're right. We can't have those boys roaming around like that." Hans looked unsure but slowly nodded, and Floris opened the door. "How about we clock out and grab that beer, huh?"

Hans didn't follow him inside and, to Floris' surprise, said, "Actually, I think I'm going to head home. I'm sure Maja is waiting for me with dinner. Maybe next time."

"Sure, no problem. See you tomorrow," Floris said. Then, as he went inside to get changed, he smiled as he imagined telling his friends about the afternoon's events. He was sure they'd agree he did a fine job.

CHAPTER FOUR

Nora sat in the kitchen, a small candle illuminating the room. She looked at the clock—almost nine. *He should be home soon.* She stood up and checked the large pot on the stove, the small gas flame keeping it just warm enough. When she lifted the lid, the strong smell of onions hit her nostrils. *At least it'll still taste decent.*

She sat again and picked up her lukewarm mug of tea. Her body convulsed violently—she could still feel the man's strong hands pinning her to the ground. She could smell his foul breath again. She'd taken two showers since getting home, scrubbing until her skin went sore, yet the man's smell still lingered.

Nora took another sip, stood up and peeked through the curtains. Their flat faced a small canal, and in the summer she loved standing by the window and watching the merry procession of vessels—from homemade rafts to fancy little boats—cruising by. Now, the only light dancing off the water was from a weak crescent moon. The streetlights had been disabled long ago, as the Germans introduced a full blackout policy. She stood for a moment and enjoyed the silence of the night, until she saw a familiar figure making his way down the street.

She closed the curtains and hurried toward the stove, turning up the heat. She hoped Floris would be in a good mood. He'd finished his regular shift around six, and she never knew which version of her husband would show up. She checked her reflection in the mirror in the hallway. Her hair was down, hiding the bump on the side of her head. She could feel it, but Floris wouldn't be able to see it. Unless he caressed her, but that was unlikely.

The building door opened, followed by the sound of heavy footsteps echoing through the stairwell as he climbed the two flights of stairs to their second-floor apartment. Nora sighed and braced herself as she heard him fumbling with his keys. She held her breath as he struggled to find the keyhole. *He's drunk again.* Her chest tightened as the door creaked.

He took off his shoes, dropping them in the hallway with a loud thud. Nora considered her options—stay near the stove or sit down and hope he'd pass through the kitchen and leave her be. She sat at the kitchen table just before Floris stumbled in. His cheeks were puffed, his eyes bloodshot and glassy. Nora gripped the edge of the table.

"Hi, honey," she said, forcing her sweetest smile. "Did you have a good day?"

Floris looked at her with little interest, grunting something before heading straight for the stove. He lifted the lid off the pan and immediately dropped it, the lid landing on the floor with a loud clang.

"What the hell!" he shouted, quickly turning on the tap and holding his hand under it. He shot Nora an furious look. "Why didn't you warn me it was hot?"

Nora struggled to keep the smile on her face. "I thought you might want something to eat. It's late, and you look like you could use something."

He turned off the tap, ignoring her as he inspected the pan's contents. He wrinkled his nose. "Hutspot? That's the best you could do? You know, Hans was telling me his wife went out early to get them bacon earlier today. Bacon." He shook his head as he snarled at her: "I'm hungry, but this is garbage."

Nora's eyes stung. She swallowed hard.

"You're so useless," Floris said as he took hold of the pan and, in one quick swoop, flung it off the stove. The food spilled across the kitchen floor, and Nora could no longer contain her tears. She held her head in her hands, hiding her face from him as she sobbed.

"Oh, come on, not this again," Floris said in a harsh voice she knew all too well. "Stop crying." He stepped closer to her, but Nora hardly cared anymore. She felt a stab of pain in her heart. Her chest heaved up and down, and she struggled to breathe, drawing in quick gasps of air.

"Nora, stop making such a show!" Floris now stood next to her, practically shouting. "Who are you trying to impress? Not me, I hope. I'm not falling for your act!"

The words hit her like punches as her chest further constricted. "Floris," she said in a croak. "I ... can't ... breathe ..."

She looked up at him, his unfocused eyes meeting hers. She had hoped to see some compassion, some understanding from the man that was supposed to be her partner. Instead, the red eyes looked back at her without emotion. No, worse than that—it was contempt. *Why does he hate me so much?* She already knew the answer, and it hurt even more. *It's not my fault.*

"Are you going to clean that up?" His voice was muffled and distant, and she blinked hard, returning to the present. Floris stood pointing at the mess on the floor, now tapping his foot—an annoying habit he picked up, which only became more prominent after he'd had a few drinks.

Nora didn't immediately respond, and this only angered him further. "Stop crying, Nora. Are you deaf?"

She stood up in a daze, using the kitchen table for support. She slowly walked toward the sink, but before she got there, Floris caught up with her. He spun her around, then slapped her in the face with blinding speed. Her cheek burned and her ears rang as more tears sprang into her eyes.

"You brought this on yourself, you know." Floris looked at her contemptuously, slurring his words. "That's for making me burn my hand." He brought his arm back again, but this time Nora saw it coming. Floris hit nothing but air and lost his balance. He growled in anger, "You stupid cow!"

Nora faced him, her cheek burning, but no longer caring what would happen next. With surprising composure, she said: "Touch me again and I'm leaving you."

Floris' eyebrows shot up. He cocked his head, then started laughing. "And where would you go? Nobody would want you! Look at yourself. You can't even bear a child."

Nora clenched her teeth, fighting the urge to reach for one of the knives on the counter. "Imagine the outrage when people hear about the police officer whose wife left him? For slapping her around, at that?" She turned the cheek he'd just struck to him. It was glowing and she knew it would turn into a bruise overnight. "How would that look?"

There was indecision in his eyes. Even in his drunken state, Floris understood Nora's threat. The mocking snarl on his face disappeared as he held up the palms of his hands.

"You know what, you're not worth it," he said coolly. He took a step closer to her, but Nora held her ground. "It's been a long day. I'm sure we'll both feel better in the morning." His eyes shot to the remains of dinner, now reduced to a mess on the kitchen floor. He stepped past her and toward the stairs. She kept her eyes on him as he made his way upstairs. She heard him crash onto the bed, and then the house became quiet. She didn't move until she heard the first snores coming down the stairs.

As her pulse slowed, the pressure in her chest eased and she took a deep breath. She stepped to the kitchen counter and started filling a bucket with hot water and soap. She'd never stood up to Floris before, and she smiled. It had felt good. Plunging her hands into the hot water, she retrieved a sponge and started scrubbing the floor. She thought of the men coming to her rescue in the alley—they hadn't hesitated for a moment. No one was going to rescue her from Floris. She looked up at the window across the room and caught her reflection. If anything was going to change, it would be up to her. Nora squeezed the dirty water from the sponge with force and clenched her other hand into a fist. She wasn't going to be pushed around any longer.

CHAPTER FIVE

F loris looked at the clock in his small office. It was almost four —still a good two hours before his shift ended. He sighed and grabbed another file, already bored with what he'd find. Hans was off today, and Floris had been assigned to go through this week's arrest reports. Most of them were for petty crimes, and he'd soon grown bored. He flipped through the file. Some stupid cow complaining about her man slapping her around. Floris had it in mind to go slap the woman himself, just for wasting his time.

His thoughts went back to a few nights ago. Nora had surprised him. Even though he doubted she would carry out her threat— where would she go?—he'd decided he wouldn't risk it. The scandal would blemish his career and progression on the force. They had hardly spoken in the past few days, and that was fine with Floris. *She'd only rile me up.*

He reluctantly started reading the file, and he thought about the evening ahead. He was looking forward to it. A few of his friends had organized a rally at De Bever, and it was rumored there might be some higher-up NSB party officials attending. Although Floris wasn't slated to speak, there would be a chance to talk to some of them after the speeches. There were rumors that Mussert's second-in-command might even make an appearance, and he was keen to speak with the man—De Bever wasn't the largest of venues. The NSB was growing, and Floris wanted to make sure he was seen for what he was. Someone who'd stuck around, even when it was illegal a few years ago. *I don't care for all those May beetles joining now that it's back in fashion.*

He closed the file. She had it coming, even getting the police involved. *Waste of my time*, he thought as he leaned back and stretched his legs. He stared through the window, dusk was setting in. Another look at the clock. Only ten minutes had passed. Floris sighed and picked up another file when he heard excited voices down the hall. Intrigued, and with little motivation to continue his mundane task, he decided to find out what was happening.

The voices were in the main room, and he marched down the hall, other colleagues peeking their heads out of their offices, some joining him.

He entered the room to find two street uniforms surrounded by their colleagues. They looked flushed, and the station chief stood next to them.

"Are you sure that's what you saw?" he asked as the other voices faded.

One of them nodded. "They're marching through the city center. We're pretty sure they were headed in the direction of Waterloo Square."

"And you're sure they're WA?"

"No doubt about it. They were wearing their black uniforms, chanting their usual songs," the other officer added.

The station chief thought for a moment. "How many?"

"Around forty at first, but more were joining."

Floris leaned against the wall and felt a flutter of excitement. *I need to be a part of this.*

The chief's voice boomed from across the room. "If they're heading for Waterloo Square, there's bound to be trouble." He looked around. Theirs was a small station, and most of the officers were out on patrol. There weren't more than twenty of them at the station, and most were desk staff. The chief's eyes fixed on Floris, wearing his street uniform. "Brouwer, why don't you go take a look. If anything happens, do whatever you feel is necessary to keep this under control. We don't need more trouble after the past few days. I've already got the Germans breathing down my neck."

Floris suppressed a grin. This was perfect, and he couldn't wait to see what the WA were up to. "Certainly, sir." *Don't appear too eager.* "Perhaps we could get some backup to the square?"

The chief stroked his chin and nodded. "Sanders, why don't you join Brouwer."

Floris followed the chief's gaze and saw Jan Sanders standing next to him, in full uniform. He nodded at the older man, keeping his expression neutral. *I didn't know Sanders was on duty today. Great!*

"Shall we?" Sanders said evenly, not waiting for a reply as he turned to the exit. Floris hurried after him and they stepped out into the street. When they were well clear of the station, Sanders turned to Floris. "Do you know what's going on?" His clear blue eyes bored into Floris's, but he didn't flinch.

"I don't. I was just as surprised as the others in there to hear about it. Did you?"

"No, and to be frank, it annoys me," Sanders said as he set off down the street, without looking at Floris. "If I'd known, I would've joined them."

Floris smiled. He liked Sanders, who was just as loyal to the NSB as Floris was but hid it very well. Floris hadn't known until they'd met each other at one of the rallies a year ago. When Floris approached him, surprised to see him there, Sanders told him he'd seen Floris at other events, but wasn't sure if Floris was made of the right stuff. But then Sanders explained a lot of the party's members had recently joined the party, right after the Germans took over. Floris had been happy to share his membership card, which dated back to 1935. Since then, Floris and Sanders had become silent allies, never drawing attention to themselves at work.

They were a few streets from Waterloo Square when they heard singing and chanting. Floris felt his pulse quicken and they increased their pace.

"Hurry, we may be too late," Sanders said, his face flushed. *He feels it, too.*

The tension on the square was palpable, and Floris felt the hairs on his arms stand up. What he saw was even better than he'd hoped for.

On their side of the square, only a few meters away from them, stood the group of WA men his colleagues had spotted marching through the streets. They had overestimated the size of the group; he counted only thirty WA men. Not all wore the black uniform, some had probably joined on the spur of the moment. They hurled abuse at a group about 50 meters opposite. These men, none of them wearing any kind of uniform, clutched leaden pipes, pieces of splintered wood, and a number were holding bricks. A Jewish *knokploeg*. These fighting squads had formed all over the city, as young men gathered to protect their communities and businesses.

"How many do you think there are?" Sanders asked, seemingly reading Floris's mind and not waiting for an answer. "Must be at least sixty. They look ready for a fight." Floris turned to see Sanders scanning the square, his brow creased. Floris followed his gaze and saw why Sanders was worried. *How did they gather so quickly? These WA boys are in trouble.*

"They're outnumbered," Floris said. "And so are we. What do you want to do?" He still felt the adrenaline in his body and eyed the WA men. They, too, were armed and had slightly less crude weapons. Most of the men carried baseball bats, and he even spotted one or two wielding knives. Floris felt woefully ill equipped with just his baton.

Sanders responded calmly, patting his baton. "We're not going to do anything. You know these boys are well trained, right?" He nodded at the Blackshirts. "Those Jews don't stand a chance."

Floris scanned the WA men, looking for familiar faces. He didn't recognize any.

"What are you doing here, fascist scum?" someone from the other side yelled. "We don't want your kind here. Get away from our square!"

As he spoke, something was launched from the group of Black-shirts. A half-empty beer bottle shattered inches away from him. The WA men laughed and jeered. "Take that, you filthy Jews! Go back to your holes!"

For a moment, nothing happened. Then both sides stormed forward, covering the short distance in impressive time. Sanders stepped back, and Floris did the same.

As the groups clashed, the square quickly turned into a battle-ground. The first line of WA men was overrun, and their friends stumbled over each other to beat back the Jewish fighting squad.

Within thirty seconds, the scent of blood was in the air, and Floris took a few more steps back. He was now a good 30 meters from the carnage and watched as men fought with savage enthusi-asm. Knives flashed, lead pipes and baseball bats collided as the men swung through the air. A small Jewish man held his hands in front of his face as he tried to block a knife-wielding Blackshirt. The next moment, he was on the ground, his hands a bloody mess. The WA man stood over him, bringing back the knife before he was pummeled with a piece of wood in the back of the head. The man with the slashed hands was quickly carried away, his agonizing cries echoing between the buildings on the square.

After a minute, more people started to retreat. Some clutched their bloody heads, while others dragged fallen comrades away. As the number of fighters quickly dwindled, Floris was disappointed to see the battle turning into a stalemate. Then, his attention was drawn to someone lying motionless in the middle of the square, away from the remaining scattered skirmishes. He elbowed Sanders. "Do you see that?"

"That's not looking good at all," Sanders said, concern on his face. "One of ours?"

Floris saw the man's black uniform. *Shit.*

Whistles sounded on the opposite side of the square. Floris saw at least twenty of his own men make their way over, batons drawn. He was even more relieved to see several dark gray uniforms in their wake. Their comrades of the German *Sicherheitsdienst*, or SD, armed with pistols and automatic weapons.

The remaining fighters spotted the police and SD as well, and they fled into adjacent streets and alleys.

Floris rushed to the man on the ground, as black uniforms now crowded around their fallen comrade. "Coming through, police," he said with authority as he knelt next to the man. The man lay on his back, his face ashen white, contrasted by a puddle of blood forming around his head. He didn't recognize the face. Floris held his ear to the man's mouth and checked his pulse. The man was still breathing, and he noticed this man was an *Opperwachtmeester*, the WA's highest rank for noncommissioned officers. *We need to save him.*

He looked up to find he was now surrounded by WA men. He recognized a few of them, and they did him. "Is he dead?"

Floris shook his head. "No, but he's in really bad shape." He noticed Sanders, and asked, "Did you call for an ambulance yet?"

"They're on their way."

Floris stood and looked around the square. The fight had taken no longer than a few minutes, but the square was littered with bricks, abandoned weapons, and patches of blood. The man at his feet looked to be the only serious casualty.

An ambulance arrived, and Floris watched as they carefully loaded up the stricken man. As the car sped away, two of the others approached him.

"You saw what happened, right?" He looked familiar, but Floris couldn't place him. The man lowered his voice. "You're one of us, right? I've seen you in De Bever."

Floris looked around; they were well out of earshot. He slowly nodded. "I saw what happened, sure."

"You were here from the start, I saw you and your partner looking on. Are you going to report it?"

"I have to."

"Then you agree that they provoked us, right? We were just standing here, minding our own business when they attacked. They can't get away with it. They may well have killed Koot, the man who was just sent to the hospital. You saw that, right?"

Floris swallowed, feeling a trickle of sweat roll down his forehead. He wiped it with his sleeve and looked at the two men. Their faces betrayed no emotion, but they held his stare. "Right?"

The man in the ambulance was barely alive, and what for? For standing up for what he believed in. No, for what they all believed in. He balled his fists. *It's not right that those filthy Jews get away with this again.* It might well be the perfect opportunity to show everybody at the station—no, in the city—what scum these Jews and their fighting squads were. He looked back at the men—now looking impatient—and smiled.

"Don't worry. I'll make sure everybody knows exactly what happened."

CHAPTER SIX

Christiaan slowly mounted the stairs, the cut on his right leg aching with every step. Despite that, he was excited to see Nora. *She's going to love this surprise.* He clutched the package a little tighter. Reaching the top, he knocked on her door, and it didn't take long until he heard muffled footsteps on the other side.

There was fumbling with the lock, but then it clicked and the door slowly opened. Nora peeked through, hesitantly at first, but when she recognized him, it swung open and her face broke into a big smile.

"Chris, what a lovely surprise!" She winced when she noticed the gash on his cheek. "What happened to you?" She stepped aside to let him in.

"Ran into some Blackshirts the other day. I got three of them before the police broke up the fight."

Nora took his coat, looking him up and down as he limped into the kitchen. "Looks like they got you pretty good. Are you all right?"

He waved his hands. "It's just a small cut, I'll be fine in a few days. It was worth it."

They stepped into the kitchen, and now it was Christiaan's turn to wince when he saw Nora's face. *He's done it again. That bastard.* The area around her left eye was swollen—and even though it wasn't completely black anymore, it was clear something had happened.

Nora caught his look and rubbed her eye. "Oh, this? It's not as bad as it looks. It was my fault. Tea?" She put the kettle on the stove before turning back to him. "I was cleaning the cupboard and, silly me, when I reached down and up again, I bumped into one of the open doors."

Christiaan sat at the kitchen table, placing the brown bag prominently in the middle. He studied his sister-in-law as she went about preparing their tea and considered whether he should press on. *Why does he do it?* He remembered the day Floris introduced her to their parents for the first time. They had been so in love. Ignoring his parents' objections to Nora, Floris married her only six months after he rescued her from the brothel. They had moved into a small apartment and all appeared fine. Until the bruises appeared a year into the marriage. Christiaan had asked her about it, but she had made it clear, on a number of occasions, that she didn't want to talk about it. That was now well over a year ago. The beatings appeared to have become more common these past months, and Christiaan's resentment toward his brother was growing.

"So, what did you bring?" Nora's voice interrupted his thoughts as she put two mugs of tea on the table and sat opposite him. She smiled, her large green eyes twinkling. He remembered why he came, and decided to let the matter rest for now.

"What do you think?" he said, pushing the bag across the table, just out of her reach.

She puffed, feigning impatience. "Oh, come on, let me see already!" She reached for the bag, and Christiaan gave it its final push. As she opened it, she squealed in delight. "Where did you get this?" She pulled out a thin book. "Is this Achterberg's newest collection?" She carefully flipped through, caressing the pages.

Christiaan smiled, delighted to see her face light up. Nora loved reading, but books were hard to come by these days. The Germans required authors to register at the newly founded Dutch Chamber of Culture. Unsurprisingly, many were skeptical, and few had done so. Those who refused found their books banned. Thankfully, Christiaan had plenty of connections throughout the city, and when he was offered a copy of Gerrit Achterberg's latest poetry collection, he knew he had to get it for Nora.

"Calm down," he said with a chuckle. "I've only borrowed it, but at least it's something new, right?"

Nora was still beaming as she placed the book on the table. "Thank you so much. I can't believe you got this."

There was a moment of silence as they sipped their tea, and Nora stood up to switch on the radio. The music of the *Nederlandsche Omroep*—the Dutch broadcasting company—filled the room, and Nora remarked, "At least it's another fifteen minutes until the next news bulletin, right?"

"I wonder what great accomplishment from the German Reich they'll have for us next," Christiaan said as the music filled the background. Earlier that year, the Germans had banned all Dutch radio stations, replacing them with one state-controlled broadcaster. Even though most people preferred to listen to the BBC or *Radio Oranje*— where Queen Wilhelmina broadcast her messages from London— Floris would have none of it in their house. He'd even gone as far as to remove the dial from their radio, making it impossible for anyone but him to change frequencies.

The familiar news jingle blared from the radio. Christiaan was convinced the broadcaster somehow upped the volume every time they switched to the news; it certainly seemed louder than the music prior.

"I'll turn it down. No need to hear their propaganda," Nora said as she got up. As she did, the newsreader spoke in excited tones.

"Breaking news from Amsterdam. *Weerman* Hendrik Koot, 54,

has just died in the hospital after being attacked by Jewish criminals"

Nora's hand froze on the volume dial, and Christiaan sat up in his chair.

"The assault took place last Tuesday at Waterloo Square. Koot and his son were taking a walk at the time. Witnesses state that the group of Jews was over forty men and that they were spitting on him as he lay defenseless. The attackers then ran off as they left Koot bleeding on the pavement."

"Did Floris say anything about this?" Christiaan asked, a feeling of dread building in his stomach.

Nora shook her head. "Not much, no. He only told me that there had been an assault on a group of Blackshirts at Waterloo Square and that a few men had been taken to the hospital. He doesn't usually share that much with me."

The broadcaster continued: "Authorities are rumored to be in talks with officials in Germany following the unprecedented events that took place today. Our great leader, Anton Mussert, is reportedly deeply saddened by this turn of events and is asking his German counterparts to intervene. He's also added that whoever is responsible for this will be severely punished." The presenter concluded the announcement by offering his deepest sympathies to the Koot family before the broadcast cut to solemn music.

Nora and Christiaan sat at the kitchen table in silence. Nora looked pale.

"This is bad, Nora. You know what's going to happen next, right?"

"Maybe the Germans won't get involved?" she offered hopefully. "They didn't attack any Germans."

Christiaan wasn't so sure. "No, you heard the broadcaster. They're framing this as a Jewish attack on one of their own. And you know the Germans will always side with the NSB."

"I can ask Floris what he thinks when he gets home," Nora offered. "He may have learned more at the police station?"

"That's a good idea, although I'm not sure how useful it will be, considering he's NSB himself." Christiaan still couldn't believe his brother had joined the Dutch Nazis. *And I thought he was difficult to get along with after joining the police force.* He finished his tea and stood. "But for now, there's nothing we can do. I'm going to head home. That should give you some time to read before Floris returns from work."

Nora handed him his coat and opened the door. She gave him a peck on the cheek as he brushed by. "Thank you for the book, Chris. I appreciate it."

"You're welcome. Take care." He looked into her eyes, again noting the swelling. *I can't keep looking away. I need to talk to Floris.*

As the door closed behind him and he headed down the stairs, he worried about the retaliation of the Blackshirts. Koot's death was the perfect incentive for them to up their reign of terror.

CHAPTER SEVEN

Floris stood on the pavement, eyes fixed on Koco, the ice cream parlor across the street. Even though it was February, that didn't stop people from buying whatever they were selling. *It can't be ice cream at this time of year, surely.*

He looked down the street and was relieved to see two familiar figures appear. He checked his watch—they were late. *But not too late.*

"Hey, Floris, how's it going?" Daniel stuck out his hand. "All quiet, still?" He nodded to the parlor, where a middle-aged woman exited carrying a small bag.

Floris was too excited to remark on their tardiness and shook his hand. "No, it appears we're here just in time." He glanced at the other man. "Hey, Japie, how's the family?"

"Very good. Maria is pregnant again," he said, beaming.

Floris stiffened and felt his chest tighten. *If only I'd known, I would never have married her. Just my luck.* He controlled his breathing and gathered all his strength to mutter, "That's great, Japie. I'm really happy for you both. Give my best to Maria, please."

Daniel changed the subject, his eyes still on the parlor. "Flo, you're sure today is the day?"

Floris nodded, exuding more confidence than he felt. "That's what I heard at the station. They finally made a mistake a few nights ago, when they ambushed those boys on Waterloo Square."

"So they were part of that group, were they?" Japie said, surprise on his face. "How did you find out about that?"

Floris smiled. When he came to work the next morning, he learned some of the WA men had come forward. They recognized some of the faces in the Jewish squad. Even though Floris knew their statements were sketchy, his colleagues had quickly gone out and arrested the men.

"Two of them sang when we told them their friends had already admitted to being part of the squad. After that, it was easy to get them to talk. We found out that they were both part of the Koco fighting squad." He nodded at the ice cream parlor. "When we told the *Grüne Polizei*—the German police—they were more than interested in what else those boys might have to say."

"So you handed them over?" Japie asked, his voice trembling with excitement.

"We did. They took good care of them, and that's when our German colleagues decided to take action. They should be here any moment."

They watched the traffic go by, people casually doing their shopping on the busy street. Even though they were wearing their regular clothes—Floris was off duty and his friends weren't with the police —he still felt conspicuous. *Nobody cares about us standing here. I'm being paranoid.*

"So they've been running their operations out of here for how long? Did they find out?" Daniel asked, his eyes following a young man entering the shop.

"At least a few months now," Floris said. "The boys they arrested joined only recently."

"I'm glad we're finally getting some backup from the Germans.

I'm sick and tired of those Jews attacking us everywhere. And it's not just the WA," Japie said. "I heard they broke into an NSB meeting a few weeks ago and trashed the place."

Floris clenched his jaw. "They're in for a nasty surprise."

There was a low rumble farther up the street. Floris turned and felt a tingle of excitement as a large German army truck bundled down the street. *Here we go.*

The truck slowed to a stop just before Koco, and the men of the Grüne Polizei disembarked. There was a heavy thud from across the street as the door to the ice cream parlor was closed. A frenzy of movement began behind the shop window. *They know.*

The dozen uniformed—and more importantly—armed police officers gathered around, their squad leader barking instructions in German.

"What's he saying?" Japie asked Floris in a low voice.

Ah yes, he still doesn't understand German. "They're going to move fast, not to give the Jews any chance," Floris translated with enthusiasm. He could feel his pulse quicken—he could still picture the pale face of Hendrik Koot a few nights ago. *This will be our revenge.*

Floris kept his eyes on the Germans as they turned toward Koco —the briefing over. They looked up and down the street, but traffic had already stopped. Whenever a German truck showed up, people made sure to get out of the way.

As one, the group stormed straight at the ice cream parlor. They made for an impressive sight, decked out in their sleek green uniforms, wearing their round army helmets for the occasion. Floris inched forward, barely able to contain himself. *I want to be part of that raid.*

The Germans reached the barricaded door. People passing by had stopped to see what was happening.

"Last warning!" the squad leader yelled. There was no response, and he beckoned to one of his men, who sprinted back to the truck and returned with a sledgehammer. Without another word, he moved to the door, lifting the hammer. The other officers drew pistols and stood in a semicircle.

After the first swing, the wooden door cracked, splinters flying around. On the second swing, the middle of the door split in half. The German police inched closer, and with a mighty third swing, the door was torn into two pieces, one half limply hanging inward on its hinges.

The police officers poured forward, guns raised, shouting commands. "Nobody move! Get down on the ground, you're under arrest!"

Their commands were answered by the people inside—the place was filled with resistance scum. *"Kom ons maar halen, vuile moffen!—* Come and get us, you filthy Krauts!"

Floris took his eyes off the action for a moment and glanced at his friends. Their faces were fixed on the raid, eyes twinkling, betraying the same excitement he felt.

As the first officers entered the ice cream parlor, there was a loud hissing sound, followed by cries of agony. Floris raised an eyebrow. *What's happening?*

Moments later, three police officers rushed out of the store, coughing violently, rubbing their eyes. Floris was appalled and ran across the street. *This wasn't part of the plan!* As he did, a putrid smell entered his nostrils. He couldn't immediately place it, but as he neared the parlor, it intensified. The police officers were on the ground, their eyes an angry shade of red as they drew short, wheezy breaths. *Gas.* Floris approached them when loud bangs emerged from Koco. Floris instinctively ducked as the Grüne Polizei fired into the store. Within seconds, it became quiet, but for the soft hissing. The police officers stood with their guns raised and waited. The hissing faded.

"Now!" the squad leader yelled, and the officers stormed the ice cream parlor for a second time. This time, there was no booby traps. A few shots were fired, but it was clear the resistance was outnumbered and outgunned. Shouts of surrender filled the air, and within a minute, the resisting Jews were escorted outside, their hands bound tightly behind their backs. A second truck pulled up and one by one the people inside Koco were hauled into it.

The group of bystanders had grown, and Floris found himself surrounded. Japie and Daniel joined him. "That was exciting!"

Floris nodded. "They won't be causing any more trouble, that's for sure. And this will send out a clear signal to the others."

A man standing nearby overheard them and wrinkled his nose. "You think this is a good thing?"

Floris looked up defiantly. The man had the typical upper-class arrogance of those who'd never worked a day in their lives...and he wanted to slap him.

"Why, do you think it's right these criminals attack gatherings of political parties?"

The man scoffed. "Oh, so that's what this is about. Are you NSB?"

"We all are," Daniel said, taking a step closer to the man.

The man wasn't intimidated, and he shook his head, giving them another look of disgust. "Then you know all about where the actual scum is. Maybe take a look at your Blackshirts, instead." Without waiting for their response, he walked away, still shaking his head.

"Let's get him," Daniel said, already on his way, but Floris stopped him.

"No, look around. We've had enough of a victory, don't you think? Look at these people around us. They're all scared; you don't mess with the NSB. If he continues to talk like that, he'll have it coming soon enough. Let's go celebrate."

———

Floris arrived home a few hours later. Even though he would've preferred to stay in De Bever a bit longer, his comrades needed to go home to their wives and families. They seemed happy to be going home.

He threw his coat on the rack and walked into the kitchen, where

Nora sat reading a book. He glanced at the clock—it was only eight thirty but he felt exhausted. Perhaps it was all the excitement of the day.

Nora looked up, a hint of surprise in her eyes, and asked, "How was your day? Didn't you have the afternoon off?"

He didn't want to talk to her but was keen to share what happened at Koco. Maybe this time, he could make her understand, make her listen. He sat down and put his hands on the table. "Oh, there was a tip-off about some problems at Koco. I went to see what was happening."

"That ice cream place in Van Wou Street?" Nora asked, putting her book down.

Floris nodded. "Turns out they were organizing Jewish raids and attacks from that shop. The Grüne Polizei raided the place, and I went to see."

Nora's mouth twitched. *She doesn't approve.* He sat up a little straighter. "The Jews had some sort of gas installed, and they attacked the police officers. They changed their tack when the police opened fire on them. You should've seen them. They gave up right away. And they think they're some sort of heroic resistance. Ha!"

Nora's expression darkened, and Floris felt excitement building in his throat. *Come on, tell me what you think.*

"Sounds like the Germans came in with excessive force," she said, her mouth drawn in a thin line.

"Doesn't matter! They should've come out of the shop instead of barricading themselves in there and attacking them with gas! Gas, Nora!"

"Didn't the German police and the Blackshirts smash up storefronts around that area a few nights ago?"

Floris gritted his teeth. "Well, these criminals were all arrested in the end. I'm sure they'll be sent to Germany. They'll know how to handle them there."

Nora looked at him with disgust. "Whose side are you on? Aren't you supposed to be a *Dutch* police officer? Don't you have some national pride?"

"Don't you dare lecture me on pride!" Floris stood up, his chair clattering on the floor. He leaned on the table as he pointed his finger in Nora's face. "I'm on the winning side! The Germans are winning all over Europe, in case you haven't noticed. The Jews are only stirring up more trouble here, and if it wasn't for them, Amsterdam would be doing as well as Berlin and Munich. It's just a matter of time for the rest of the city—no, the country!—to see this."

Nora returned her focus to the book. Floris' neck burned with indignation. He controlled the urge to slap her. Her words of a few nights ago still lingered.

"You don't understand, do you? Maybe you will in a few months when you're happy to be married to a police officer."

"A National Socialist police officer," she said softly. "Do you have any idea how people in the neighborhood look at me now?"

He slammed his fist on the table. "Then let them! Tell me who they are and I'll set them straight! They'll come crawling to the NSB when they see us rise, when we've taken the Jews out of public life! Just you wait!"

She looked up at him, her eyes glistening. "Floris, can we please—"

"I don't want to hear it anymore. I'm going to bed."

Floris mounted the stairs, and he had to control himself not to go back. *How did she not appreciate what I've done for her?* He saved her, and this was the thanks he got? *If it wasn't for me, she'd still be in that whorehouse.* He picked up his toothbrush, looked at himself in the mirror and smiled. This was a good day. *Those boys at Koco got what they deserved.* Crawling into bed, he wished he could've joined the Grüne Polizei in that day's raid, and then in the interrogations. He'd set those agitators straight.

CHAPTER EIGHT

C hristiaan clanged his tram's bell in frustration as traffic came to a standstill on the Blauwbrug—the Blue Bridge— just before Waterloo Square. He was running behind schedule—he hated being late. Annoyed passengers were impatiently looking at what was going on in the street.

"Sorry about the delay," he said into the simple PA system. "Just waiting for traffic on the bridge to clear up."

He heard grunts behind him, but there was little else he could do. After a few minutes, traffic on the bridge cleared and Christiaan pushed the lever of his tram forward. He felt his frustration ebb away as they crossed the Amstel River, and Waterloo Square came into sight. The market attracted a steady stream of people every day, but today the streets were unusually crowded. Christiaan again had to slow to a snail's pace, clanging his bell to shoo people out of the way. Crowds were moving away from the square, and as Christiaan halted the tram at the stop, he looked at the faces of the people outside. They looked flustered, shocked even. A man jumped on board and shouted, "Get off the tram, the Germans are rounding up people at J. D. Meijer Square!" He disembarked as quickly as he'd come, and some people heeded his advice.

Christiaan closed the doors and continued onward—he had to finish his route, and that meant passing by J. D. Meijer Square, just around the corner. As he slowly moved through the crowd of people —they got out of the way for him, sometimes further motivated by a gentle clanging of his bell—he turned the corner and gasped.

The scene was surreal. German trucks were parked haphazardly across the square, blocking the street. He stopped his tram and counted them—there were ten, maybe fifteen trucks with dark green tarps draped over them. Members of the Grüne Polizei loitered around the trucks, casually smoking cigarettes. But as he looked ahead, he saw something far more shocking. At least thirty German police officers, clad in the same green uniforms as the drivers, were overseeing a group of about a hundred men. They knelt, their hands clasped behind their necks as the Germans shouted at them to sit still and be quiet. Christiaan felt his temples throbbing as he narrowed his eyes. *What the hell is going on?*

Farther up the street, more people were escorted toward the square by yet more Grüne Polizei. Christiaan felt restless in his blocked tram. He opened the doors and stepped out while most of his passengers stayed on board.

A small crowd of onlookers had gathered at a safe distance, and Christiaan spoke to one of the men, who looked to be around his age. "What's going on?"

"They showed up about an hour ago. A couple of trucks, filled with German police. The rest of the trucks arrived later, empty. We should've known something was wrong then, but we didn't know what they were going to do. This is the Jewish Quarter, after all. Everybody's quite used to the constant checks—we all figured this would just be another one of those."

Christiaan noted the man spoke calmly and wasn't wearing any religious markers—he probably wasn't Jewish. "Doesn't look like a regular check to me."

"It's not," the man said, shaking his head. "After the trucks arrived, the Germans entered the New Synagogue and escorted everybody outside. That must've been about half the people sitting over there." His gaze returned to the men sitting on their knees only a hundred meters away. "They then went around to the houses on the square and the side streets, and hauled more men to the square."

As Christiaan followed the man's eyes, he scanned the faces of the men on the ground.

"It looks pretty random to me," Christiaan said, more to himself than anyone else. "There's even some elderly men."

The man next to him nodded. "Yeah, there doesn't seem to be any logic to whom they're picking up. The only thing they have in common is that they're all Jewish, and they're men. They let the women and children in the synagogue go." He pointed across the street. "Some of them stayed behind, probably waiting to see what happens to their husbands and fathers."

Soon there was movement in the square. Voices shouted in German. "Let's go! Get up, to the trucks!" Some of the older men didn't get up quickly enough and were kicked and hit with the butts of the guns the officers carried. The square turned into a hive of activity as the panicked men were hustled toward the trucks. Some of the men tripped over each other and were mocked by the German police as they laughed and shouted at them to get back up.

Christiaan clenched his fists as the first men were loaded into the truck. *What is this madness? And where are the Dutch police?* He watched in disbelief at the people around him; nobody made a move to do anything. They were paralyzed by fear. Christiaan's anger bubbled over and he could no longer control himself. He needed to know what was going on—could this be happening in their city?

Christiaan took a deep breath, allowing his pulse to slow down. He stepped toward one of the German police officers guarding the square.

"Excuse me." He was careful to control his tone. "What's

happening? I'm driving that tram over there, and I'd like to tell my passengers when we could resume our route."

The officer glared at him dismissively. "Well, you're not going anywhere anytime soon. We need to get these Jews away from here first." The first trucks were now full, the drivers getting behind the wheel, revving their engines. More than half the men still waited to board the other trucks. The Grüne Polizei were prodding them along impatiently, telling them to keep moving.

Christiaan gritted his teeth. "Did these men commit a crime? I've never seen so many arrested at the same time."

The German's eyes narrowed. "Have you not seen what's happened in the city the past few weeks? The Jews are making trouble everywhere. It was only two weeks ago when they murdered that man in cold blood only a few streets from here, remember?"

The NSB and the German command had milked Hendrik Koot's death, even giving him a formal funeral—including a parade through the city. *Propaganda bullshit.*

"And only a few days ago, they attacked my colleagues with acid," the man said, furrows appearing on his forehead. "So yes, they committed a crime, and we'll make sure they receive proper punishment. Did you have any further questions, or are you going to mind your own business?"

Christiaan held the man's gaze for a moment. He wanted to lash out, but realized there was nothing he could do at this point. Another word and he could very well find himself in the back of one of those trucks himself. He swallowed hard and turned away, slowly walking back to his tram.

He climbed the steps and noticed more people had boarded. He informed them he didn't know how much longer it would take, but that they were welcome to stay in the warmth of the vehicle for as long as they wanted.

Christiaan sunk into his chair and looked out the window. The crowds dispersed, the excitement of the raid wearing off. The last men were hauled into the trucks, and with the Grüne Polizei closing the tarps, Christiaan caught a glimpse of the faces inside. Scared, confused, and utterly defeated eyes looked out from the semi-darkness.

Meanwhile, the Grüne Polizei stood around, relaxed, smiling, and smoking their cigarettes while they chatted. For them, this was just another day; one where they could tyrannize random citizens at will. No, not random, Christiaan corrected himself. Jewish citizens.

The trucks bounced away over the cobblestones of the square. The street cleared, and the remaining German police boarded their trucks. When they turned the corner, life on J. D. Meijer Square returned to normal and traffic slowly started moving. Christiaan put his tram into gear, and they crept by the square. Passing the New Synagogue, he spotted the group of women and children. They hadn't moved from their spot after witnessing their beloved husbands and fathers rounded up like cattle. Now, they stood on their own, alone as the world around them returned to normal.

Christiaan felt a sharp pain in his chest but knew there was nothing he could do. He prayed the Jewish community would rally around the women. He clanged his bell and pushed the tram's lever forward as he crossed the bridge taking him south to Weesper Street. As the tram surged ahead, he suddenly felt exhausted, and couldn't wait to finish his shift.

CHAPTER NINE

Nora carefully set three plates on the table, adjusting the cutlery before turning back to the stove. *Good, the quiche is coming along nicely.* She was excited and a little proud of her quiche—it was a bit of a treat as she'd managed to find some bacon at the market that morning. When she also secured eggs and milk, she was glad she could prepare something out of the ordinary for a change.

Floris hadn't laid a finger on her since she stood up for herself two weeks ago. Despite that, the tension had been palpable, and he came home late—and drunk—most nights. They hardly spoke unless it was absolutely necessary. Their argument about the raid on the ice cream parlor had been one of their more meaningful interactions. *And then we disagree on everything.*

After the brothers' parents had died—now more than two years ago—they had agreed they needed to see each other at least once a month, and Nora had suggested Christiaan should come over for dinner. Even though the evenings were often tense affairs, Nora felt some form of control by being able to cook something she knew they both liked. She hoped the good food raised both brothers' spirits enough to keep things civil. She could use an evening where everything appeared somewhat normal.

There were footsteps in the hallway, and her ears perked up. She was slightly disappointed to hear the lock click, and Floris appeared. *At least he seems sober*, she thought as he walked in, his cheeks a little red from the cold. His eyes scanned the table and narrowed. "Is Christiaan joining us?"

"Yes, I told you last night, remember?" Nora said as she stood up and checked the oven again. Floris grumbled something as he sat down, his back turned to her. She focused on the string beans on the stove.

There was a knock on the door, and she breathed a silent sigh of relief. Floris didn't make any move to open the door, so she hurried to do so.

"Hey, I hope I'm not late," Christiaan said as he brushed some water off his coat in the hallway, wiping his shoes before entering. She took his coat and gave him a quick hug before they stepped into the kitchen. Floris got up and shook his brother's hand.

"How's my baby brother?" he said in a mocking tone. "Still enjoying life on the rails?"

Christiaan sat down, ignoring the quip. "Yeah, I like being around people, staying in tune with the mood of the city. You know what that's like, right?"

"When I get to go out, sure," Floris said. "I'm spending more time in a chair than I care to."

Nora opened the oven and took out the quiche. Both brothers looked on as she placed it in the center of the table.

"That smells delicious," Floris said, surprising her with a rare compliment. "Is that bacon?"

"I was lucky at the market. Dig in, you two." They scooped food onto their plates, and for a good few minutes, everything was quiet as they enjoyed dinner.

"So, Flo, I wanted to ask you something," Christiaan said as he put down his fork, wiping his mouth with a napkin.

"Sure, what's that?"

"You said you're spending a lot of time in the office, so I guess you're also picking up on what's happening around the city?"

Floris nodded. "I'm reading all the reports, and when something happens nearby, we usually hear about it when the officers return to the station. Why?"

Christiaan had a dark look on his face, and Nora felt the hairs on her neck stand up. *Something's not right. They hardly ever talk about work.*

"So you know about what happened at the J. D. Meijer Square this morning, right?" Nora felt the tension rise as she looked at her husband, who put down his cutlery.

"What do you mean?"

"You don't know what the Grüne Polizei did this morning?"

Floris wrung his hands, and Nora intervened. "Tell us what you saw, Christiaan." She looked at him pleadingly, hoping he would choose his words carefully.

"They were arresting people on the square, blocking all traffic," Christiaan started, and before he could continue, his brother interrupted him.

"Well, that's nothing new. The police are always checking papers. It *is* the Jewish Quarter." Floris waved his hands as he spoke and returned his eyes to his plate.

"I haven't finished yet," Christiaan said coolly. "They weren't just arresting *some* people. They cleared out the whole New Synagogue, took all the men and loaded them up in trucks. I saw them on the square, forced to kneel like criminals."

"That's because they are." Floris said in a flat tone.

"They even took men from nearby houses at random, more than a hundred people. Are you telling me you didn't know about this?" Christiaan's eyes burned with indignation.

"This is the first I heard of it," Floris said calmly, leaning back and stretching his hands behind him. "But I'm sure the Grüne Polizei had a good reason to do what they did."

"What good reason could they possibly have to arrest more than a hundred people off the streets? Some of these men couldn't even walk on their own anymore. How were they a threat to anyone, especially the Germans?" Christiaan looked ready to explode.

A grin appeared on Floris' face. "The Grüne Polizei know what they're doing. Perhaps they thought enough was enough with the Jewish violence." He sat back up, the grin dissolving as he pressed his lips into a thin line. "The Jews have been causing trouble all over town; they attacked the Grüne Polizei the other day with gas."

"Only in retaliation to those thugs you've given some weird official responsibility to," Christiaan countered.

Nora held her breath—this was escalating fast.

"Are you referring to the Weerbaarheidsafdeling? Let me remind you they're keeping order in the streets. I suggest you tread carefully, brother," Floris said.

"To hell with that," Christiaan shouted, his face red. Nora took a deep breath to calm herself. "Your Blackshirts are a disgrace to the country, committing their violence in the name of defending your despicable party. The Jews aren't provoking anyone. They've been driven into a corner by the Germans and the NSB. Aren't you in the least bit ashamed?"

"The Jews had it coming!" Floris raised his voice as well. "You're too blind to see it, but they've been taking the wealth from the good people in this country for centuries now. It was high time we did something about it. You're wrong about the party. The NSB is the future."

"It's nothing more than a collection of fascist thugs. Not to mention Mussert." Christiaan paused and Nora saw Floris bristle, his eyes shooting fire. "He's nothing but a puppet to Hitler."

"That's it. Out!" Floris jumped from his chair and moved to the other side of the table.

Christiaan stood up and grabbed Floris' collar. "You know what you are, brother. If you think the Germans' actions are justified, you're a traitor to your country."

Nora sat frozen, her knuckles white as she grasped the side of the table. Christiaan was considerably taller than Floris, but there was nothing her husband enjoyed more than a fight.

"Floris! Christiaan! Stop!" Both men turned, shocked by Nora's shriek, Christiaan still holding his brother's collar. They looked at her, and Christiaan let go, the anger dissipating from his eyes as they met hers. Floris looked at her with a sneer before turning back to his brother.

"Out. Now," he repeated. "You're not welcome here anymore."

"Gladly," Christiaan said as he stepped toward the hallway.

Nora remained seated, motionless as Christiaan took his coat and left the apartment. She listened to his fading footsteps as he descended the stairs, the front door slamming shut moments later.

Floris sat back down, picked up his fork, and took another bite of cold quiche. He stared at his plate, grinding his teeth between bites. They sat in silence until he cleaned his plate.

"He doesn't understand, Nora," he started. "He's always been naive. It's because our parents always coddled him. He has no idea of what's going on."

Nora remained silent, surprised at his even tone. She'd expected another lecture or fight. *Does he just want to talk?*

He looked at her with the clear brown eyes she'd once fallen in love with. "If he saw what I see every day, he wouldn't speak like that. The Jews are the problem, Nora. And we let it happen."

Not this again. She had no energy left to argue. It was easier to nod in agreement.

"But Hitler, Nora, Hitler saw it. He saw it in Germany, and he saw it in the rest of Europe. And now, finally, we're doing something about it in Amsterdam. Those arrests Christiaan spoke of today, I didn't know about them. But you know what? I'm glad they happened. It's justice. It's our time."

Nora bit her tongue, and Floris stood up. He tucked in his chair. "I know you don't always agree with me, but thank you for choosing my side today."

I didn't. She stood up and silently cleared the table.

Floris headed into the hallway, and returned with a copy of *Volk en Vaderland—People & Fatherland—*the NSB's party newspaper. He sat down in the living room and started reading.

Nora plunged the plates into the scalding hot water and started brushing them, letting the water burn her fingers until they went numb. She glanced at Floris and wondered how much longer she could keep up this charade...

CHAPTER TEN

I t was still dark when Christiaan locked the door behind him. He rubbed his hands—winter weather was closing in. That would be a welcome change to the monotony of recent weeks. He remembered when he was younger, when the first snowflakes were greeted with enthusiasm—enough snow meant there would be no school. He walked through the streets and looked at the canals— they were still open, and he thought back to those winters where they would freeze over and the city's waterways were transformed into an additional glistening, slippery network to skate around. He smiled at his childish thoughts—those felt a lifetime ago, and he doubted there would be much fun to be had were that to happen now.

He ran into a few people who needed to get to work early, nodding to the other brave souls weathering the cold at this hour.

Christiaan kept a brisk pace, and even though he'd preferred to have a quiet moment to himself, his mind had other plans. He worried about Nora. It had been three nights since the fight, and he'd decided he would steer clear of his brother's home. This wasn't the first time they'd argued, and he knew Nora would talk sense into Floris; she always did.

What made this time different, though, was that Christiaan had witnessed his brother's increasingly violent temper. *Perhaps there's something going on at work?* When his parents were still alive, Floris and he would play outside together, and his older brother would stand up for him if anyone ever troubled him. But things started to change when Floris joined the police force after finishing high school.

Floris had gone away for his training, occasionally returning home during the weekends but often deciding to stay with his new friends at the police academy. Floris became more distant, chiding his parents for some imagined infraction of his new worldview. When he returned to Amsterdam, Floris joined the NSB. Floris' new circle of friends and colleagues—the two overlapped—had everything to do with this worldview. The argument at the dinner table had been a long time coming; Floris' casual validation of violence by the Germans had been the final straw. *I need to know Nora's safe.*

He neared the Amsteldijk tram depot. As he turned the corner, he immediately knew this would not be a normal day. A large gathering of his colleagues stood outside the gates—the closed gates—of the depot. He spotted Peter Stassar, the head mechanic. This was odd, Peter should've opened the gates half an hour ago. Peter made sure the trams were ready to go when Christiaan and the other drivers arrived. Christiaan approached the big mechanic, who was wearing a thick winter jacket and holding a thermos. He didn't look like he was planning to go inside anytime soon.

"Change of plans, Chris!" His voice boomed through the cold morning air. "You won't be driving any trams today."

Christiaan looked at the other men milling around and noticed some holding pickets. "Are we going on strike?"

"We sure are! And it's not just us. There will be strikes all over the country. The party sent out pamphlets yesterday. Public transport will shut down in Utrecht and Rotterdam. Hopefully, everybody else will join in once they find out they can't go anywhere."

"Your party organized this? Who else is in on this in Amsterdam?" Christiaan asked, impressed at the Communist Party's resolve and apparent reach.

"We're not taking any more shit from the Nazis," Peter said, his face reddening. "Or that NSB filth. We're no longer taking this lying down! Do you know how many people they hauled off in those *razzias*—raids—a few days ago?"

I can't get those images out of my head. "Last I heard about 200."

Peter shook his head with vigor. "More like 400 and a bit," he said. "And nobody knows where they were taken. I spoke to some of their wives, and they're getting no information from the police, let alone the Germans. Some said they were sent to Germany to work."

Christiaan was appaled. "That doesn't make any sense. There were plenty of elderly men."

"Then you know why we're doing this. You're damn right it doesn't make sense, and something is going on."

Christiaan cast his eyes over some of the pickets. "Equal rights for equal people!" "No more separatist policies!" He balled his fists, his brother's words of the other night still ringing in his ears. It heartened him to see so many of his colleagues standing up for their fellow Amsterdammers.

"All right, let's go!" Someone shouted. "Off to Dam Square!" The men responded in a chorus of cries as they picked up their pickets and hoisted them in the cold morning air. They moved down the street, the Amstel River to their right. The group's chants echoed across the river, the first sunlight making the water sparkle. Christiaan felt his spirits lifted as the energy of the group washed over him, the hairs on his arms standing up.

He looked around and was surprised to see the face of his former colleague Jozias. He had been fired for being a Jew, and Christiaan hadn't stayed in touch. He felt a sharp pang of guilt as he read the text on Jozias' picket: *The Jews today, the rest tomorrow? What happened to me could happen to you!*

Christiaan caught up with Jozias, who walked—no, marched—with his head held high and shoulders pulled back, thrusting his picket high above his head. His face was determined, eyes burning, and his jaw set tight. A thin smile formed on Jozias' face when he recognized Christiaan.

"How have you been?" Christiaan stammered, not sure where to start, his ears burning with shame.

"It's been rough, but we're surviving. After I was fired, I couldn't get a job anywhere. Trust me, I tried, but nobody wanted to take the risk. They were all very sorry, but it was clear they didn't want to employ a Jew and the potential trouble that might come with that."

Christiaan was silent as they crossed into the Jewish Quarter. The group had more than doubled in size, as people emerged from their houses to join the march.

"Can't say I blame them," Jozias continued. "I mean, look at what's happened since. These days, you'll get yourself beaten up for just serving us. We have food coupons, but we can't go into the stores or markets to use them. Thankfully, we know some good people who'll help us out, but not everybody has that luxury. Plenty of people are being robbed and targeted daily, it's awful."

Christiaan's feelings of guilt intensified. "I'm sorry, Jozias, I should've reached out. I abandoned you when—"

"No. You have nothing to apologize for." He stopped and waved his hand at the people walking alongside them. "This is what we need. This will get the rest of the country's attention. I know it's going to make a difference." He placed his hand on Christiaan's shoulder. "And you're part of it. Walk with me, and show the Nazis we won't stand for this. We're all Dutch."

They marched farther into the center, other groups joining them from all directions as they morphed into one large procession. As their numbers swelled, so did their spirits. Dockworkers were talking to teachers who shut down their schools for the day. Bank managers dressed in suits marched alongside factory workers in their blue overalls. The city had never been so united; Amsterdammers from all walks of life came together to stand up for this grave injustice.

Their progress slowed as they filled the streets and soon found themselves deadlocked. As Christiaan turned around, masses of people stretched as far as the eye could see. *It's working. Everybody's joining in.* Jozias still stood next to him, and he looked a little nervous. The fury still burned from his eyes, but there was a frown on his forehead. "Do you think there's trouble ahead?"

Christiaan considered it, but as the people in front of him were all calm, he doubted it. "Probably just a small hold-up at the bridge. We can't all cross at once," he said confidently. "This is unbelievable. If Peter is right, and the other cities are also on strike, the Germans can't ignore this. They can't go on like this if the entire country unites."

Jozias nodded vigorously. "They can't."

Even though they both lived in an occupied country, they lived by a completely different set of rules. A random document check meant a ten, maybe twenty-second delay for Christiaan. For Jozias, it probably meant an interrogation and the constant fear of breaking some new, unknown rule.

Soon, the people ahead of him started moving again. A chant started in the front, and it flowed through the crowd like a wave as everybody joined in. A surge of energy shot through the crowd, as pickets were lifted higher than before—their owners pumping them with new enthusiasm as they sang together.

He looked at Jozias, who looked more confident again, his eyes scanning the masses of people marching with them. As they did, Christiaan felt a shot of adrenaline shoot through his body. *If the whole country unites like this, we stand a chance.*

CHAPTER ELEVEN

Only a few blocks down, Floris stood watching the people stream by, crowding the narrow streets, some dangerously close to the edges of the canals. He stood slightly elevated, having climbed up the characteristic stairs of one of the canal houses. He saw two children looking outside, excitement clear on their faces as they marveled at what was happening.

Floris had to make an effort to keep his expression composed and neutral. Hans stood next to him, enjoying the moment, a hint of a smile on his face. Floris' eyes scanned the crowd, anxious to spot potential troublemakers.

"I didn't think they'd go ahead with it," Hans said, the sun reflecting in his eyes. He looked calm and relaxed. "When the chief showed us those pamphlets, I thought nothing would come of it. Maybe a few communists. But not this."

Floris had thought the same. Their station chief had called all of them to a meeting at the end of their shifts the night before. The pamphlets distributed by the Communist Party appeared amateurish, hurriedly printed, with the ink already fading by the time Floris read them. The message had been clear, though; everybody was urged to down tools in the morning. *Surely only fools would risk losing their jobs over making a statement for the Jews?* How wrong he'd been.

"At least nobody seems aggressive," Hans continued. "Let's hope it stays that way."

Floris grunted a response, still lost in his thoughts. He looked up and down the street and estimated at least 500 people within his sight. *Where are they going?* He spotted a few of his colleagues walking along, casually chatting with the people. A thought struck him. "Come on, let's join the march." He descended the steps, ignoring the children waving from behind the window.

Hans caught up and looked at him inquisitively. "What are you thinking? You don't want to get involved, do you?" He sounded apprehensive. "We're just supposed to keep an eye out."

Floris sighed inwardly. *Why is he always so passive?* "I'm curious where they're going and who is leading them. Besides, it'll be good to speak to them and hear what's going on, don't you think?"

Hans nodded as they merged and stayed on the outside of the group. Floris saw that the people didn't pay them much attention as they walked on. They were too busy talking among themselves and chanting their increasingly anti-German slogans. He bit his lip as the crowd launched into another anti-Hitler chant. Even though it wasn't illegal, it still riled him to hear them mock the great leader like this.

They walked for another five minutes, and as they turned onto Weesper Street, their destination became clear to Floris.

"They're headed for Waterloo Square." J. D. Meijer Square was only a hundred meters from Waterloo Square, and it made perfect sense to go there, considering what had happened recently. It was also in the middle of the Jewish Quarter. "There's not going to be enough space for everybody to fit. They're going to back up all the traffic."

"I don't think we have to worry about the traffic too much," Hans said. "The whole city is out on the streets. I hope it doesn't turn nasty."

It didn't look like it would, but Floris knew any crowd was like a powder keg—a small spark could change the whole situation. He eyed the people around him and noticed a middle-aged man wearing a gray suit walking on his own. Floris caught up with him and tapped him on the shoulder. The man was surprised to find a uniformed police officer in the crowd. "Anything I can help you with, officer?" he asked politely, speaking the accentless Dutch of the upper class.

Floris felt his lip curling up but caught himself, twisting it into something resembling a smile. "Checking to make sure you're all right, sir," Floris said in his most disarming voice. "It's easy to get lost in these crowds."

The man frowned. "No, I'm fine, thank you. I decided to join on impulse. I live up the street, and when I saw them walking by with those pickets, I wanted to see what was going on." His eyes shone, as if analyzing Floris' next move. Then, before Floris could respond, the man asked, "Are you going to break up the demonstration, officer?"

Floris responded coolly: "Not yet. Hopefully, these people won't give us a reason to do anything." *I hope they do.* "I don't suppose you know where they are heading, do you?"

The man nodded. "Of course I do. We're going to Waterloo Square."

Floris nodded and left the man on his own, returning to Hans, who walked a few paces behind him. "Let's follow them to Waterloo Square for now. I'm sure we'll find backup there."

They walked on, and as they neared the bridge crossing to J. D. Meijer Square, the procession slowed down. They couldn't all cross the narrow bridge at the same time. Floris stepped away from the group, keen to find colleagues. Men were slapping each other on their backs, the singing and chanting increasing in volume.

As he watched the people pass, he heard something unusual behind him. It sounded like an engine. He turned to find a small German *Kübelwagen* approaching from farther down the street.

Floris could hardly believe his eyes when he saw the two German *Sicherheitsdienst* men heading straight for the crowd. *Are they mad?*

"They must be lost," Hans said as he stood next to Floris, his eyes wide.

"We need to get them away from here before anyone sees them," Floris said. He looked back at the crowd, who were focused on getting across the bridge, oblivious to the approaching Germans.

Floris ran toward the car, still some 100 meters away. He waved his arms at the driver, but the jeep wasn't slowing down. *Surely they must see the street is completely blocked?*

The car was now only 50 meters from Floris. "Halt! Stop!" Floris shouted at the driver, hoping he'd understand this uniformed police officer was warning them. Thankfully, the jeep slowed down and stopped as Floris made up the last few meters.

The men in the Kübelwagen looked up at Floris as he stood panting next to the driver. "We need to get to the Nieuwmarkt; this is the quickest way?"

Floris looked at them in amazement. *Do they not know what is happening?* He struggled for words as he looked at the stone-faced men dressed in green uniforms.

"With all due respect, I advise you to turn back. There's a protest taking place," he said, glancing over his shoulder.

"They'll have to make way for us," the driver said. "We have urgent business."

The officer in the passenger seat looked ahead, following Floris' earlier gaze, and shifted in his seat. "Perhaps we should listen to him."

"Sir?" The driver shifted the vehicle into neutral. Right at that moment, there were shouts from the crowd. Floris closed his eyes in resignation, then turned to see a group breaking away, heading in their direction. *Damn it! Too late!* He felt for his baton but realized he wouldn't be able to fight off five determined men on his own.

He stood by the jeep—the driver's eyes on the group, but not moving—as the men approached. He saw Hans run after them, apparently trying to reason with them, but the men kept moving closer.

Why isn't he reversing? "Get back!" Floris shouted at the driver. He stepped away from the jeep toward the approaching group. He could now hear them talking amongst themselves—they were only 20 meters away.

"Can you believe these Germans? What do they think they're doing here? They must be lost! Let's go find out, boys!"

Floris moved toward the men, his heart racing. He focused on keeping his face straight and stern. *I am the law.* "Stop right there," he shouted, his voice an octave lower as he spoke in his most author-itative voice. The men stopped, and Floris noticed they were rela-tively young—late teens, the oldest perhaps almost twenty. *They're boys still.* Hans caught up with them, and the young men appeared unsure of what to do next. Floris looked back and saw the Germans looking on from their car. *Turn your car around and leave,* Floris thought, eyeing the small group but nervously checking what was happening behind them. If more people joined, he wasn't sure he'd be able to control the situation.

"Come on, let's go back to the march," Hans said soothingly. "Let's keep things civil."

Floris scanned the faces of the boys. They were wavering, but for one. He looked up, met Floris' eyes, and shook his head. "I don't think you're going to stand in our way if we have a little chat with those Krauts." The other boys found their composure, nodding as he spoke the words. "You're our police, aren't you? You're supposed to be on our side."

The boy's eyes went between Hans and Floris, and he grinned. "We just want to talk to them." He moved a few steps closer to Floris.

From the way he spoke, Floris knew there would be little talking and, without taking his eyes off the advancing group, barked at the Germans behind him: "Get out of here! I won't be able to stop them!"

He took out his baton. The boys were now only a few meters

away from him. "Last warning, fellas, it's not too late to walk away," Hans said, still trying to reason with them.

Then, things happened very quickly. The sound of heavy foot-steps grew behind Floris, and the boys stopped in their tracks. Surprised, Floris glanced behind and saw four police officers next to the jeep. He didn't know where they came from, but he sure was happy to see them. The numbers were now on their side, and the boys appeared to realize it as well. Grabbing the initiative, Floris motioned for his colleagues to join him before turning back to the boys, who hadn't moved, and now stood sheepishly in the middle of the street. "You're all under arrest for threatening an officer."

Hans gave him a look, but Floris ignored him as the other officers stood with Floris. He didn't recognize any of them, but he wasn't in his usual neighborhood. "Can you take them to the station while I convince our German colleagues to turn around?" He walked toward the jeep, where the Germans still sat, the driver gripping the wheel, his passenger calmly observing the scene.

"Now, can I ask that you take a different route? There's a few thousand angry people ahead, and I can't guarantee you'll make it through there." It was only then that he noticed the passenger sported an insignia with four diamonds. Floris gasped—this man was a *Sturmbannführer*, one of the highest ranks in the *Sicherheit-spolizei* in the Netherlands. He couldn't believe he missed that earlier, and saluted the man.

To his surprise, the man smiled, half-heartedly returning his salute. "At ease, officer. No need for these formalities."

Floris didn't know what to say as he put his hands behind his back.

"I appreciate what you did just now," the man continued. "Even though I think we could've handled that together." He patted the pistol hanging on his belt. "Nevertheless, I want to make sure your superiors know of your bravery and handling of the situation. What's your name?"

"Brouwer, sir. Floris Brouwer."

The driver scribbled it down, and the Sturmbannführer nodded. "Now, we'll take your advice and take the longer route. I trust you have this under control?"

Floris looked back. The other policemen were talking to the young men. *Why haven't they cuffed them yet?* He raised an eyebrow, but smiled as he turned to the Germans. "All good, sir. Have a good day."

As the driver turned the jeep around, Floris walked to his colleagues. He smiled, pleased with his handling of the situation, and delighted that it had involved such a high-ranking member of the Sicherheitspolizei. He hoped the man followed through on his promise; he was sure his station chief would be pleased. *But what's going on over here?*

"Why aren't they cuffed?" he said, unable to suppress his annoyance.

Hans looked on sheepishly as one of the other policemen responded, the stars on his uniform suggested the same rank as Floris. "We feel a warning is enough. They didn't know what they were doing and got caught up in the excitement of the demonstration."

Floris felt anger rising but caught himself. His colleagues stood stone-faced, and the young men had their heads bowed, avoiding his stare. All but the one who'd spoken earlier, the oldest, who appeared to be their leader. He met Floris' eyes, a smirk on his face, his eyes challenging him. *He thinks he got away with it.*

Floris took a moment to think. He was outnumbered, and there was no way the other officers were going to side with him. They had decided on their course of action while he was talking to the Germans. Then Floris turned around and saw the jeep turning the corner. He smiled. *It's fine. They can have this minor victory. These boys are small fry anyway.*

He nodded. "All right, that seems fair enough," he said, and the young men raised their heads slowly, their eyes registering surprise.

"But you took down their names, right? Just to make sure they don't take this warning for granted?"

The officer shuffled on his feet, hesitated, and then said, "We were just about to do that, yes."

Floris grinned again. *Bullshit.* "Great, let's do that, and then they can make their way home. Best not to look for trouble in the demonstration, right, boys?"

The young men nodded, looking relieved to get away with this slight reprieve. Then, as the other officers took down their names, Floris motioned to Hans.

"Did you get their names and badge numbers?" Floris said in a low voice, nodding at the other officers.

Hans looked surprised. "I didn't think ... I mean, do you think that's necessary?"

"You and I both know those boys should've been arrested. And you know what they would've done if they didn't show up."

"I suppose so," Hans said, still unsure.

Floris shook his head and took out his notepad. "Give me a second."

The officers had finished processing the young men, who walked back to the procession. *Never mind them.* "Say, shall I write up the report and take some work out of your hands?"

The other officers looked at him in surprise. "I need to report what happened before you arrived as well, might as well do everything in one go." He smiled and held out his hand.

The other officers seemed happy enough to save themselves some time, and they handed over the notes. Floris quickly scanned the papers and casually said, "If you just give me your names and badge numbers, I'll make sure you're included. It would reflect favorably on you when the Germans know who saved one of their officers from a group of street thugs, don't you think?"

To his surprise, they all wrote their names on a piece of paper and handed it to him. "Thanks, fellas. I'll take care of it. Have a good day." He folded the papers with the names and put them in his inside pocket. Floris turned back to the demonstration. Most people had now crossed the bridge. As Hans caught up with him, Floris noticed his partner had an odd look on his face. "Something wrong, Hans?"

"No, no." Hans shook his head and averted his eyes. "All good. Where are we going next?"

"Let's see if there are any more troublemakers," Floris said, rubbing his hands. Today had turned out unexpectedly good.

CHAPTER TWELVE

Nora sat in the kitchen, cradling a large mug of tea. She brought it to her lips and savored the warmth on her face as she took a sip. She looked outside, where a weak sun was battling the drizzle. The streets were still quiet at this hour—it was only eight—but she was anxious to see what the day would bring.

When Floris came home the evening prior, he'd been in high spirits, eager to share the day's stories. Nora had stayed inside as the streets had swarmed with protesters. She looked at them from the safety of her home but had soon noticed there was little malicious intent. It warmed her heart to see the outpouring of solidarity with their Jewish Amsterdammers.

Floris told her about what had happened at Waterloo Square, where a vast crowd had gathered. They'd blocked the bridges connecting the square with the different parts of the city. It felt like the whole city was out on the streets, but there had been surprisingly little violence. Nora sensed Floris was disappointed, but he'd been happy to tell her about his meeting with the high-ranking SD officer.

He left early this morning and warned her he didn't expect the

Germans to accept more strikes, even if the Communist Party had spread more pamphlets urging people to continue. Nora had told him she'd stay at home, but she felt excited about what might happen next. The first day had gone well, and she truly believed they were making a difference. *The Germans can't ignore an entire city protesting, can they?* There were rumors of even more cities joining today after hearing of what had happened in the capital.

She finished her tea and spent some time cleaning the house. She needed some distractions as she kept her eyes and ears perked for signs of things happening outside. She also thought of Christiaan and wondered how involved he'd been. *He can't stand injustice, so he must've been one of the first people to join.* She hadn't seen her brother-in-law for almost a week now, and she missed talking to him—she would much rather have heard how he experienced yesterday.

She put her broom away, then she heard something outside and hurried to the window. At first, she was disappointed to see the street deserted, with only the cobblestones glistening in the ongoing drizzle. But as her eyes scanned farther up the street, a smile appeared on her face. A large group of dockworkers marched down the street, singing and chanting as they called for more people to join them. They were still a good hundred meters away, but Nora felt goose bumps as strong voices echoed across the canal. By the time they reached her window, their numbers had swelled to well over a hundred men, and some women. Nora looked at their hopeful faces as they burst into the chorus of the "Wilhelmus"—the national anthem—and Nora quietly mouthed the words, the hairs on her arms standing up.

Within fifteen minutes, the streets were filled with people as they made their way toward the city center. Nora stood by the window, transfixed by the pickets and activity. These were her people, and they stood up for what they believed in. She caught her reflection in the window and questioned herself. *Why am I inside? I should be out there.*

She saw a mother and a child rush by her window, the little girl holding a small, makeshift picket. *She can't be older than ten.*

Nora turned away from the window and headed for the door. She grabbed her coat and a hat and quickly headed down the stairs. *I can't stay in here any longer.*

She joined the stream of people, searching for familiar faces. She found none, but she did notice those of some of her neighbors peering out of their windows. She turned her head away, hoping they didn't spot her—they might tell Floris later. She then shook the thought—most of her neighbors averted their eyes when they saw Floris. She suspected they disapproved of his NSB membership. She proudly threw her head back and saw the face of Mrs. Landkoop, her next-door neighbor, looking down from her second-floor window and waved. The elderly woman squinted, but when she recognized Nora, she waved back.

As they neared the city center, the crowds thickened, and Nora felt surprisingly at ease amongst the protesters. There was no sign of the Germans, and there was only a smattering of Dutch police, mostly trying to make sure people didn't overcrowd the junctions and bridges.

The march took her past the Albert Cuyp Market, oddly deserted as the market peddlers hadn't bothered setting up their stalls.

"Do you know where we're going?"

Nora turned to look into the inquisitive eyes of a woman. She was probably in her early thirties and a girl of about eight or nine was holding onto her hand. They looked overwhelmed as they struggled to keep up with the pace of the procession. Nora shook her head. "Afraid not. I'm just following along." She remembered Floris said most of the groups gathered around the big squares the day before. "But I expect we'll be going north. That's where most people went yesterday."

The woman nodded and stroked her daughter's hair before asking, "You mind if we walk with you? We're a little lost."

"Of course, no problem." In truth, Nora was happy to have

another woman alongside her, and she asked, "So, where did you join the march?"

The woman looked a little puzzled. "Well, we didn't plan to join. We were on our way to get some groceries when we ran into all these people. So we figured it would be safer to join them."

"Do you think Daddy is with these people?" the girl asked, her soft voice barely louder than a whisper in the crowd.

Her mother shook her head. "I'm afraid not, sweetheart." She looked at Nora, paused, and then said, "He was one of the people taken a few days ago." Her eyes looked sad, her voice quivered.

Nora didn't immediately know how to respond as her hand went to her mouth. She looked at the little girl, who seemed to have shrunk during the last few seconds. "I'm so sorry," she stammered. "Have you heard anything from him?" She dreaded the answer.

The woman shook her head. "I've gone to all the police stations around our neighborhood, but they didn't want to tell me anything other than that the Sicherheitsdienst took him." She sighed, averting her eyes for a moment. "As if I didn't know that. I heard what happened. I just want to know where they took my Izmael."

They walked on silently, and Nora silently cursed. Floris had told her the men arrested four days ago were taken to a camp called Schoorl, where they awaited transport to Germany. He said they'd be taken to work camps there. Nora had heard plenty of elderly men were taken in the trucks, and she wondered what use they could possibly have for them. When she questioned Floris about this, he brushed it off, saying there would be suitable work for everyone in Germany.

She bit her lip as she looked at the woman next to her. *Should I tell her? What good would it do, though? There's nothing she can do about it.* Nora decided it wasn't her place. "I'm sure the police will let you know what happens soon enough."

The woman nodded without conviction and silently walked on for a few minutes, before she turned back to Nora. Her eyes were soft, but she spoke clearly: "You know, we'd almost gotten used to this.

There's a new rule for us every day, and we just took it in stride. But when they came for Izmael, I didn't know what to do next. And then this happened." She waved a hand at the people around them. "And it makes me wonder whether there is a bit of hope. Maybe they'll let him go?"

Nora heard Floris' words echo in her mind, but she wouldn't destroy this woman's hopes. "Maybe it will make a difference." She had to admit she felt more hopeful than when she left her home an hour ago—it *was* an impressive number of people in the streets. The people around them started another chant of "Jewish Amster-dammers are also Amsterdammers!" as they approached the broad thoroughfare of the Stadhouderskade. It was clear something wasn't right when the people in the front stopped and then tried to turn back, crashing into the rest of the group. Within moments, Nora felt the crowd's pressure as the momentum shifted backward. People started to panic, and Nora grabbed the woman's hand and pulled them into a small doorway to the side of the street. She breathed hard as they squeezed into the narrow opening.

The sound of a not-so-distant engine tore through the air, and moments later, a vehicle turned into their street. Nora gasped. *It can't be.*

People pushed themselves to the sides of the street as a German armored vehicle raced around the corner. A small barrel protruded from the front, and three uniformed Grüne Polizei officers—kitted out in military uniform—sat menacingly on the sides of the vehicle, holding their rifles.

"Disperse! Disperse!" the metallic voice of the officer holding a megaphone blared through the street. "Go home! This strike is over!"

One man didn't get out of the way quickly enough and was hit by the vehicle. He crashed onto the sidewalk as the Germans raced on, waving their weapons at the people scrambling to make room.

As the vehicle continued down the street, there was nothing left of the optimistic, jovial mood of only minutes ago. Instead, people ran in different directions, crashing into each as they hurried to get out of the narrow street.

Most people were running back to where they came from, but they would become stuck at the smaller bridges. *What if it's worse over there?* Nora made a decision. "Come with me," she said to the woman and trembling girl.

She ran in the direction the armored vehicle had come from, to the Stadhouderskade. *There should be enough room there, even if there are more tanks in the city.*

Looking across the water, she saw a smaller group of protesters on the other side, stuck between two groups of Grüne Polizei on either side. The Germans outnumbered the men and women in the group, and to her horror, she saw them approach with weapons drawn. Nora stood frozen as she watched the people inch closer to each other; some brave younger men moved to the outside of the group. The first officers reached the group and started hitting the unarmed men with the butts of their guns. Soon, people were jumping into the water to escape the blows.

Nora looked up and down the street and decided she would risk the shortest route home. She had to, as she didn't know where the rest of the Grüne Polizei were. "Are you coming with me?" she asked the woman, who stood looking across the water, her eyes unfocused. Nora shook her shoulder, and the woman looked at her wide eyed.

"No, we're going back that way," the woman said and pulled her daughter back into the street they came from, disappearing into the crowd.

Nora shook her head and ran down Stadhouderskade, staying clear of the water and close to the houses. People were running in all different directions, and every time she hit a junction, her heart skipped a beat. *No more tanks, please.*

She reached the next bridge, but before she could cross, she was almost run over by four boys racing their bicycles around the corner. They were going at breakneck speed, and Nora jumped out of the way, almost losing her balance. Before she could fully recover, a jeep raced around the corner, and the driver yelled something at her. The other soldiers were focused on the boys on bikes ahead of them.

A loud bang rang out, and Nora threw herself to the ground, covering her ears and closing her eyes. Another salvo, and then another. The sound of squealing brakes. She opened her eyes to see the jeep turning the corner, the whirring of its engine fading. Her heart stopped as she saw the boys lying in the street, the wheels of their bicycles spinning. Her ears were still ringing from the shots, but she could hear the faint cries of the people around her. Nora stood up and approached the boys. Her ears popped and the cries immediately grew louder. As she neared the motionless boys, she blinked hard and realized what had happened. One of them was missing half his face—a bullet had torn right through the side of his head. The other boy was hit in the stomach, a puddle of blood forming around him at an alarming rate.

Before Nora could do anything, she heard more engines behind her and quickly stepped out of the way as more jeeps rushed by. The Germans diverted just enough to not run over the boys, but they didn't give them another glance as they sped on.

More people crowded around the boys and Nora felt nauseous as she quickly walked in the other direction. She felt as if moving in a dream, the world slowing down, barely registering what was happening around her. She left the Stadhouderskade and suddenly found herself standing in front of her house. Closing the door behind her, she sank to her knees and wept in the darkness of the hallway.

PART II

AMSTERDAM,

10 JULY 1942

CHAPTER THIRTEEN

C hristiaan stopped and opened the tram's doors, waiting as passengers disembarked. He looked out his open window, enjoying the warm July air floating in. An elderly couple sat on a bench, sharing a simple sandwich. He caught the lady's eye, and she waved at him, breadcrumbs spilling from her mouth. Christiaan waved back, and then checked his rearview mirror. All passengers had boarded, and he closed the doors.

As his tram gained momentum—softly clattering down the tracks—a girl in her late teens appeared next to him. "Does this tram stop at J. D. Meijer? I need to connect there."

"It does. Which connection do you need?" Christiaan asked, keeping his eyes on the traffic ahead.

"The 40, I believe," she said. "But I don't have a ticket yet." She glanced into the aisle behind her, then reached into her coat, taking out a small envelope. She placed it onto the dashboard between Christiaan and her and took out a few coins. "Will this do?"

Christiaan grabbed the coins and envelope, placing the latter into the storage space next to his seat. He handed her a ticket as they approached the next stop. "This will do perfectly. I'll ask the 40 tram to wait for you at J. D. Meijer."

"Thank you." She sat down as Christiaan opened the doors. A few people disembarked, and as he double-checked the doors, he sighed, then turned in his seat. "Move away from the door, please," he yelled. Someone was trying to board, but three men blocked the door. Other people were getting involved now, and Christiaan stood up. *Why can't they just get out of the way?* He strode to the back, where he overheard some of the other people.

"Just let him board. Look at him. Are you going to force him to walk?" a middle-aged woman said, pulling on one of the young men's shirts.

He slapped her hand. "Don't touch me. This is none of your business. He's not allowed on here."

Christiaan approached the small group, growing more annoyed with every step. Controlling his frustration, he said, "What's going on here? You better have a damn good reason for blocking the door." He couldn't help but glare at the young men as they turned to him, their faces filled with righteousness.

"That *opa* was trying to board just now," the tallest of them said in an upper-class accent. "And he's not allowed to."

Christiaan pushed them out of his way to see a frail man standing near the steps, supporting himself with a cane, just as a light drizzle came down. He looked up, his eyes pleading. Christiaan was about to tell the young men off and order them out of the way, when he saw why they were blocking him. Stitched prominently on his chest was a yellow Star of David. Christiaan felt his heart sink. The older man was Jewish, which meant the young men were right.

It was announced only ten days ago—Jews were no longer allowed to use public transport. It had come quickly after all Jews were forced to wear the Star of David in public, two months ago. Amsterdammers responded by giving up their seats to their star-wearing citizens and even going as far as wearing their own badges, "Christian" and "Aryan," in protest of this latest humiliation of the

Jewish community. The Germans responded by enforcing even more restrictions on the Jews, and this newest ban on public transport seemed to have its intended effect in further dividing society. *Here we are blocking an older man from getting around, forcing him to stand in the rain.*

He looked at the faces of the other passengers: there was compassion and even hints of anger in their eyes. Even though not everybody spoke up—this had become more common, even in Amsterdam, where people were used to speaking their minds—Christiaan sensed the injustice he felt was shared by most, if not all, of his passengers. He decided he wasn't going to let this happen.

"Step aside and let him board." He spoke calmly, moving closer to the young men. They looked at him in surprise, and he seized the initiative, gently but firmly pushing the one closest away from the steps. "Or you can get off yourselves."

The elderly gentleman took a step closer, a trembling hand reaching out for the railing by the door. The young man Christiaan had nudged aside stepped down and slapped the man's hand away before he could get a grip on the handle. The man put his cane down just in time to not lose his balance.

People on the tram gasped—the woman who'd spoken up early now looked ready to punch the young man.

The other two men started to laugh. "You're not getting on here, old Jew. You can walk, just like the rest of your sort."

Christiaan felt the blood rush to his face and, without another thought, pushed the man closest to him down the steps. He caught him by surprise, and he almost landed flat onto the ground, breaking his fall with his hands as he landed on his knees. Christiaan glared at the other two. "Out! Now!"

To his surprise, they stepped off, joining their friend. There was hatred in their eyes as Christiaan stepped down to help the older man board.

"You're not getting away with this," the tall one said as he got to his feet. "You're breaking the law. We're reporting you."

Christiaan did his best to control himself from lashing out, focusing instead on the man. "Where do you need to go, sir?"

"Just three stops down," he said, his voice shaking. "But I don't want to get you in trouble."

Christiaan shook his head and helped him up the stairs. Other passengers had stood up and helped him to a seat.

He turned back to the three men, considered a last retort, and then decided against it. He turned away and quickly made his way to the front and up the steps. Even before he sat down, he'd pushed the button to close the doors.

As he set the tram in motion, he took a deep breath and looked into his rearview mirror. Calm had returned to the tram, with most passengers looking out the windows, lost in their own thoughts. He turned his eyes back to the tracks ahead and wondered if he should worry about the young men's threats. Sure, if a formal complaint was made against him, he'd have to explain himself. But would they go through with it? As he pondered what would happen next, he'd missed the woman standing next to him.

"You know, everybody on board agreed with what you did," she said, startling him. It was the same woman who'd spoken out against the men earlier, and Christiaan smiled.

"Thanks, I appreciate it. I'm not sure that will help me much when they report me, but let's worry about that later," he said.

She frowned and turned to the people behind her, raising her voice slightly. "Look, if you need anyone to back you up, provide an alibi or something, I'm sure most people here would be happy to tell them you did nothing wrong." Christiaan saw a number of them nod. The woman took out her purse and scribbled something on a piece of paper.

"Here are my details. If this gets you into trouble, tell your boss to call me." She handed him the piece of paper and walked back to her seat. Two more passengers came up and gave him their contact details. Not everybody had lost their tongue or courage to stand up against injustice.

———

They never met in the same place twice, and Christiaan found himself in a small room in a house well off the main thoroughfare. It hadn't taken him long to find the house, but he'd felt a little nervous entering, as he always did. He was relieved to find two familiar faces waiting for him inside. He knew them only as Toon and Gerrit.

"You sure nobody followed you?" Toon asked, speaking in his usual gruff way. He never used more words than necessary, and at first, Christiaan had been intimidated by him. After a few of these meetings, he'd gotten used to Toon's way of doing things, and he started to appreciate the man. He didn't waste time, and that was fine with Christiaan—they had important work to do.

Christiaan shook his head. "No, it was pretty quiet, so it was easy to keep an eye on what was going on. Nobody followed me."

"I doubt anybody knows what you're doing," Gerrit said. "You've been very careful."

Even though he knew Gerrit wasn't exaggerating, Christiaan was still happy to hear the more experienced man confirm. Toon and Gerrit had been with the group from the start, and Christiaan had only joined a few months ago.

Gerrit pulled out three envelopes and handed them to Christiaan. They were heavier than he expected.

"We think you're ready for this," Gerrit said, frowning. "It's all well and good delivering messages across town, and we all appreciate it, but we need more help with these." Christiaan knew what was in the envelopes, but he waited for Gerrit to finish speaking as the man paused and took a sip of water. "Now that we have people hiding all over the city, we need to ensure they're kept safe and fed. And the only way to do this is by making sure we pay the people hiding them well and provide them with the food coupons you're holding in your hands."

"This will keep those people alive," Toon added, taking a step closer to Christiaan and taking an envelope from him. He opened it and held out a wad of coupon booklets. *How was the group able to get so many extra booklets?* They were tightly controlled by the Germans, who only provided enough for every registered person in the city. He had an idea but kept it to himself. *Maybe another time.*

"You'll deliver these to three different addresses right now," Gerrit said as Toon handed the envelope back.

Tonight? Christiaan checked the time on the small clock on the wall. It was almost seven, which meant he only had a few hours before curfew. He felt his neck prickle as the room suddenly felt a little warmer. He looked at the men across from him, their eyes registering his every move, and he knew he couldn't show any weakness. *This is my test. This is what I signed up for.* He put the envelopes in his inside pocket and cleared his throat. "I better get on my way."

There was a moment of silence before Gerrit's face broke into a smile. "I knew we could count on you. This is where you need to go." As Christiaan memorized the addresses, he was relieved to find they were all relatively close to each other, and in a neighborhood he knew well. "Don't forget, if you suspect you're being followed, abandon the mission and just go home," Gerrit said as Christiaan opened the door to leave.

"Don't worry, nobody will suspect a thing," Christiaan said before closing the door behind him. He stood in the narrow hallway for a moment, and took a deep breath. The envelopes felt like they were burning in his pocket, and as he stepped out into the street, he did an extra take to make sure nobody saw him exit. When he was satisfied he was alone, he hurried up the street, feeling a tingle of excitement in his stomach.

He steered clear of the center, deciding to take a slightly longer route, hopefully avoiding any of the German checkpoints. It would be impossible to explain what he was doing carrying so many food coupons. *Not sure how I would talk myself out of that.*

He thought about the past months and how things had changed. Last year's strike, where he had initially been so hopeful and excited, had been the turning point in how the Germans conducted themselves. They suppressed the strike with violence and death, and Christiaan had been shocked to hear more than twenty people had died, with hundreds injured. The Sicherheitsdienst had even executed several people, with hundreds more arrested and deported to Germany. Soon after, the restrictions imposed on the Jewish population increased. Although gradual at first, these quickly excluded the Jews from many functions of public life.

Most Amsterdammers thought what was going on was wrong, but they were afraid to speak up, never mind do something about it. Christiaan couldn't look away, and he had reached out to Sjakie, a former classmate, to check on how he was doing. Sjakie told him the problem wasn't necessarily *having* money, but being able to spend it, as most shops and markets were off-limits to Jews. The few shops they were still allowed to go to were often poorly stocked.

One morning, before starting his shift, Christiaan spoke with Peter Stassar, the head mechanic at work, who was still deeply connected within the Communist Party. Much to Christiaan's surprise, Peter told him about the secret network of tram drivers delivering messages and small packages all over town. After that, things moved quickly, and that's how Christiaan now found himself part of one of Amsterdam's resistance cells.

Turning onto Wilhelmina Street, Christiaan glanced over his shoulder and saw no one. He quickly made his way to number 23—a narrow, nondescript house in a row of similar-looking houses. He glanced up and down the street one more time before rapping his knuckles on the front door.

It took less than two seconds for a woman in her early fifties to open the door. "What do you want?" she practically hissed at him.

"Umm ... Toon sent me," Christiaan managed, surprised at the woman's demeanor.

She looked him up and down, then said, "I don't know any Toon."

Christiaan felt a trickle of sweat running down his back. He felt exposed standing in the street. *Am I at the wrong address? I'm sure he said it was number 23.* The woman eyed him suspiciously but hadn't closed the door yet. Christiaan decided to take a gamble. "I think I have something you need." He patted his jacket.

The woman took a step outside, quickly looked up and down the street, and pulled him inside. She hastily shut the door, almost hitting him as she did. She then turned to him, her eyes boring into him. "Come on then, out with it!"

Christiaan hesitated. *Maybe he was in the wrong place?* "Aren't you expecting something?"

The woman didn't immediately answer, her burning eyes still on his. He felt uncomfortable and considered leaving when the woman sighed. She walked a little farther toward what looked to be the kitchen at the end of the hallway. As she did, she gestured at Christiaan to follow.

They stepped into a cramped kitchen with a table too large for the space. She pointed at one of the simple wooden chairs and sat down across from him.

"So, you have the coupons?" she said, lighting a cigarette.

Christiaan felt relieved; he was at the right place after all. He reached inside his jacket, took out one of the envelopes and slid it across the table. The woman opened it, counted the stack, and nodded. "Thank you, and apologies for just now. I've never seen you before, and I wasn't sure anybody would show up today. Everything has been quite unorganized and rushed." She exhaled a large puff of smoke.

"It's the first time I'm doing this," he said, not knowing what else to say. They were silent for a moment, and he looked at the woman. In the light of the kitchen, he noticed she had dark rings around her eyes. *This isn't easy for her, either.*

He was about to speak when a faint sound in the hallway stopped him. He froze, his eyes shooting to the woman. She put a finger to her lips, but he read the alarm in her eyes.

The floorboards in the hallway creaked as footsteps slowly

approached. Christiaan held his breath—had he been followed after all?

He turned to the door, and as he did, a young woman appeared in the opening. He heard the woman at the table breathe a sigh of relief, followed by a grunt of annoyance.

"What are you doing here? I told you, you can't be up here when it's still light outside! And even then, only when I tell you it's safe!"

The young woman looked about a year or two younger than Christiaan. She was unperturbed by the older woman's tirade, calm as she leaned against the doorpost. She smiled at Christiaan, ignoring the woman, and said, "Are you delivering our coupons?"

Christiaan pointed at the envelope on the table and wanted to answer, but the older woman stood up and rushed toward the younger one. "You need to go back downstairs. It's too dangerous for you to be out here now. You're endangering all of us; what if one of the neighbors sees you? Come on, off you go." She looked flustered, and Christiaan realized it wasn't anger driving her—she was worried.

The young woman held up her hands, and as she was almost pushed out of the kitchen by the other woman, she looked at Christiaan and said, "Thank you. My family and I weren't sure anybody was still coming. We're very grateful!"

As the two women disappeared down the hallway, Christiaan shook his head. He heard a door close, and the woman returned a few moments later.

"Sorry about that. You weren't meant to see her, of course," she said. Her face was creased with worry as she headed for the window facing the small backyard. She squinted through the smoke-stained windowpanes that looked like they hadn't been cleaned for a while —probably deliberately so—and then closed the curtains for good measure. She turned back to him. "At least you know who you're doing this for now. That girl and her parents live in my basement. They arrived a few days ago when the father received a letter for work reassignment in Germany. I'm sure you've heard of this."

Their small organization had been hiding people for months now, but the requests had more than tripled in the past week. It was hard to find new addresses quickly enough, and people like the woman across the table were scarce—there were only so many people they could trust.

"I understand she's going a little stir-crazy in the basement, but she needs to understand she can't just come up here like that, especially when there's someone else in the house," the woman continued. She appeared to be talking more to herself than to Christiaan. "I think my neighbors are good people, but who knows, these days? Not everybody carries their NSB badge on their chest, or they might talk to the wrong people."

The small clock in the corner started to strike—it was eight o'clock—and reminded Christiaan he had two more places to go. He stood and excused himself. The woman nodded and walked him to the front door. As they passed the basement door in the hallway, Christiaan thought about the woman he'd just met and how she was living down there with her parents. He realized he'd stopped in front of the door when he heard the woman open the front door.

"Thank you for doing this," he said softly as he left. "I hope we'll meet again."

She smiled sadly. "And you. Just remember to forget what you saw today. I'll take good care of them."

CHAPTER FOURTEEN

Floris and Hans stood near a narrow bridge in the city center. It was early in the afternoon, and it was quiet on the other side, where only a few people sat outside the houses, enjoying the sunshine. He nodded at Hans, and they crossed, a sign above their heads indicating they were entering the Jewish Quarter. Behind them, another six uniformed police officers followed quietly, their faces focused. The only one sporting a smile was Floris, leading the way.

He looked at the people near the water in shorts and loose shirts, their feet dangling over the canal's edge. There were only three of them, and still teenagers at that. He decided he would leave them be, for now. Instead, he led his men toward one of the larger houses farther down the street. He'd inspected the area the day before and knew a large family lived there. More importantly, they were wealthy. And Jewish.

He stopped in front of the house, his men forming a semicircle. He was looking forward to surprising the people inside.

"Hans and I will talk to them, and as soon as we're inside, I want two of you to follow us in without saying anything. If I'm correct, there should be four Jews in there, and we don't know how they'll react." The men nodded, and Floris pointed at the two that would join him, then turned to the others. "Two of you will go around the back and make sure nobody tries to escape. The rest will stay here. We may well have some curious onlookers, and I don't want anybody disturbing us. Any questions?"

There were none, and Floris rubbed his hands as he climbed the steps to the front door. He knocked loudly, straining his ears to hear beyond the heavy wooden door. He waited ten seconds, then twenty, as nothing happened. *Was his information wrong? These people were supposed to be at home.* He banged his fist on the door, shaking it in its frame.

After a few seconds, the curtains moved ever so slightly in one of the windows. He grinned. "Open the door, police!" he shouted, banging the door again. "I know you're in there. Don't make us break this down."

It was quiet for a few seconds until he heard a lock click, and the door slowly opened. A man in his late fifties stood in the opening, and Floris knew this was the house's owner. Without waiting for an invitation, he barged past the man and into the long hallway. "Where's the rest of your family?"

The man seemed perplexed but recovered as Hans entered as well. "What are you doing here? We've done nothing wrong."

Floris was already in the richly furnished living room, Persian tapestries on the walls and a large grandfather clock in the corner. "I'll be the judge of that. You're Harry Wolff, correct?"

"I am," the man said with a hint of defiance. "Now, would you care to tell me what you're doing here?"

"Where's the rest of your family?" Floris repeated, ignoring the man's question. He opened another door and entered the kitchen, where he found three women sitting silently at a table. They looked up wide eyed, and Floris felt a tingle of excitement. Two of the women were in their twenties, and the third looked to be their mother, or Mrs. Wolff. *Four Jews already. Perfect.*

"You're coming with me," Floris said as he casually waved his hand toward the hallway. "Get your things ready. You get to take one bag of clothes and toiletries. You have fifteen minutes."

The women didn't move, instead looking to Mr. Wolff. Floris turned to him and coolly said, "The same goes for you. Get ready."

Mr. Wolff evidently wasn't used to being told what to do, and he crossed his arms as he spoke. "Where are we going?"

"Haven't you heard? You're relocating to Germany. Everybody needs to do their part for the war effort."

The man shook his head. "I'm sure there's a mistake. We've received no such orders." He turned to his daughters and wife. "Don't move. We're not going anywhere."

The other officers joined them in the kitchen and looked on with interest. One of them was gawking at a daughter. Floris felt flustered as none of the people in the room made any effort to move. He was losing control of the situation.

Floris stepped closer to Mr. Wolff—who was nearly as tall as him —and put his face close to his ear. Then, he lowered his voice and whispered, "There are four more police officers outside. Will you come with us willingly, or do I need to ask them to escort you out first? I'm sure they'd be interested in your daughters while you're away."

The man's breathing paused for a moment, and Floris turned his face, meeting the man's eyes. He was surprised to see the man's eyes shoot fire, his cheeks puff and then slowly turn red. "You wouldn't dare. You can't do that."

Floris chuckled. "Would you care to find out?"

The man held his stare for a few seconds, then dropped his eyes and nodded slowly. "All right. We'll come with you, as long as I can stay with my family."

"I'm glad you see sense," Floris said, patting the man on the shoulder. He turned to the men in the kitchen. "Keep an eye on them while they're packing their things. Fifteen minutes, starting now."

The family headed upstairs together, followed by Hans and the other officers. As their footsteps faded, Floris stepped into the living room. He was impressed with the wealth on show—they wouldn't have any use for these things anymore. He walked to a small writing desk in the corner, and tried the top drawer. He was surprised to find it unlocked, and when he pulled it open, he found some writing supplies. There was a small box in the second drawer, the kind often used for storing jewelry. He paused, his eyes shooting to the door. He heard footsteps from the ceiling above as the Wolff family went from room to room, but the hallway was quiet. He quickly opened the little box and found a golden pocket watch. He took it out of the box and held it in his hand—it was heavier than it looked, and he slid it between his hands.

It was a stunning piece of jewelry, and he was sure it was worth at least half a month's wages. *It's so easy, and nobody will ever know.* He held the watch a little longer, until he heard footsteps at the top of the stairs. Without another thought, he pocketed the watch, closed the box, and replaced it in the drawer.

Hans poked his head around the doorpost. "We're ready to go. They're all packed."

"Perfect, let's take them to the station for processing. We have plenty more addresses to visit today." Floris stepped away from the writing desk. He moved into the hallway, where Mr. Wolff came down the stairs last and found his family waiting in the street. He looked at Floris with resignation as he carried a small suitcase. Floris followed him outside and he fingered the watch in his pocket. *This job is almost too easy.*

———

The walk to the station took only fifteen minutes, and the Wolff family was quiet on the way there. Only Mr. Wolff had asked Floris why they hadn't received official orders.

Floris had given him the silent treatment, having been sent out that morning to knock on doors of Jews who weren't on any of the lists. As expected, most of the 4,000 people who had received a summons to report for relocation to Germany hadn't shown up. Now, Floris and his colleagues were arresting a smaller group, to be held as collateral. His chief had told him the others had a week to report before people like the Wolff family were sent to Mauthausen, a camp in Austria. Floris looked at them and suppressed a smile. *If only they knew what awaited them, they probably wouldn't be this calm.*

They arrived at the station on Nieuwe Doelen Street, and Floris clenched his jaw in frustration as a crowd milled around the entrance. Mr. Wolff stopped and turned to Floris, showing surprise, and something else—fear?

"Is this where we're going?"

Floris ignored him and instructed the other officers in his group to keep an eye on the family. "I'll go see what the holdup is." He signaled for Hans to follow him.

The people outside loitered on the steps or sat on their little suitcases, some smoking cigarettes, but most looking anxious. Finally, Floris spotted one of his newer colleagues near the entrance and pushed some of the Jews aside as he made his way up the small steps.

The man spotted him and smirked. "Ha, Brouwer. You're a bit late, we've already got most of our Jews today. This is your first arrest of the day, isn't it?" His eyes went to the Wolff family. "Not the most impressive haul, I'd say." He took a drag from his cigarette and laughed. At that moment, two more officers came out, shouting at the people waiting to come inside. As they obliged, they, too, looked at Floris, fear in their eyes.

"That's our fifth family of the day, Brouwer. Maybe it's time to step it up, yeah? We're never going to reach our quota with you slacking." His colleague laughed as he followed them inside.

Floris balled his fists, barely able to control his fury. *Who does he think he is?* He was about to follow them in when Hans put a hand on his shoulder.

"Let it go. They're not worth it. Let's just get these people processed and be on our way. The chief knows the work we're doing. Plenty of them to arrest in the next few days."

Floris nodded—Hans wasn't wrong. After his intervention with the Sicherheitsdienst officer during the riots last year, he'd joined the *Bureau Joodsche Zaken*—the Bureau of Jewish Affairs. While Floris had struggled to grow within the regular police force, this specialized division had him lead a small squad of policemen. And he was doing something he believed in: he was helping solve the Jewish problem. He was always on hand to make sure infractions of the rules were punished. *What were those other officers thinking? He'd arrested more Jews in his time at the Bureau than all of them combined.*

"It's easy to arrest them when you're given a list." Floris nodded. "Let's see how they do without one. It's not always this easy."

Hans smiled. "Exactly. Now come on, let's go inside. We have more work to do."

As Floris signaled for the other officers to escort the Wolff family inside, he looked out onto the Rokin Canal. Mr. Wolff passed by and muttered something, but the words didn't register. Floris stood alone on the small steps of the Bureau. He took out the pocket watch and inspected it as it glittered in the bright sunshine. Floris smiled: joining the Bureau was the best decision he'd made in a while. He would make a big difference, and he was going to make sure his German friends knew all about it.

CHAPTER FIFTEEN

Nora opened the front door, leaning in a little to keep the creaking to a minimum. She'd seen the curtains of her next-door neighbor move when she left the house; the nosy woman was keeping an eye on what was happening in the street—but she didn't feel like talking to anyone right now.

She mounted the stairs, careful to avoid the noisy steps, and she almost held her breath when she reached her floor. She tiptoed to her door, delicately sliding the key into the lock. She opened the door and quickly shut it. As she stood in the hallway of her small apartment, she shook her head and let out a chuckle. *Look at me stalking around like a little girl.*

She opened a window in the living room, and as the warm summer air streamed in, she took a deep breath. She loved the smell of summer in Amsterdam. In the canal below, two boys paddled in a makeshift canoe. She waved at them, and they smiled, both keen to impress her with their paddling skills. *It almost feels like a normal summer day.*

Nora stood by the window for a few minutes, watching the world go by. She heard familiar voices down the street, and she saw more neighbors returning from the city. Mr. and Mrs. Schalken were both retired, and they'd lived in the larger house next to them for over forty years. They had always been friendly to Nora, at times providing her with harvest from their vegetable patch in the yard.

As they passed, Mrs. Schalken looked up, and Nora waved at her. "Hello, good evening!"

The older woman gave her a curt nod and then turned her head. Her husband didn't even look up as they quickly entered their home, almost slamming the door.

Nora stepped away from the window, an uncomfortable feeling in her stomach. This wasn't the first time her previously friendly neighbors had given her the cold shoulder. Even though she told herself it was nothing, she knew better. The Schalkens weren't the only people in the neighborhood avoiding her. It had started subtly: neighbors walking by just a little quicker than usual, seemingly in a rush with no time for a chat. But as the weeks went by, the actions became more obvious. When she was out with Floris, people crossed to the other side of the street.

Nora filled a glass with water and sat down, took a sip and sighed. If only her neighbors knew she was just as repulsed by her husband's actions as they were. She wished she could tell them, but she wasn't sure they'd believe her. Leave him if it's that bad, they'd probably tell her. But it wasn't that simple; she had nowhere to go, and Floris would never let her leave. She looked around the kitchen and chuckled. He didn't even want her leaving the house for anything other than groceries. *I'm a prisoner in my own home.*

Her thoughts were interrupted by the apartment door opening. She looked at the clock and frowned. It was only six, too early for him to be home. Nevertheless, Floris appeared in the doorway a few seconds later. His eyes were unfocused, and Nora sighed inwardly. *Drunk already?*

"You're home early," she said, forcing a smile. "I haven't started dinner yet."

He waved at her dismissively. "That's okay. I'm not staying anyway. I have a meeting in an hour. I came home to change."

Nora hid her excitement at having the evening to herself. "What meeting is that?"

"Some of the party coming to talk about the deportations. We need to help the Germans as the Jews aren't showing up for the transports." He smiled as he walked toward the stairs. "The Germans are considering increasing the bounty for finding and arresting Jews now. Great news, don't you think?"

He didn't wait for an answer as he bounded up the stairs and didn't catch Nora's lowered eyebrows. She picked up the bag of groceries and started cleaning vegetables and chopping potatoes to distract herself. Even if Floris wasn't going to have dinner, she wouldn't starve. She chopped the carrots with fury, biting her lip as her mind returned to Floris' words. *Has he really gone that far to only think about the higher bounty he'll receive?* She shook her head, flustered as the blood rushed to her neck. She dunked the potatoes in the cold water when she heard him come down the stairs in a hurry.

"Did you not wash my good shirt?" Floris stood in the stairway, holding a white shirt. He looked annoyed, tapping his foot on the wooden floor.

"I did, it just hasn't been pressed yet," she said as more blood rushed to her head. She caught herself and said, "Shall I do that for you right now? It'll only take a minute." She took a few steps toward him but stopped when she saw his face.

"Nora, what use are you! You're home all day, the least I can expect is to have my shirts ready when needed," he said, his voice rising an octave. "No, I don't want you to do it now. I want my shirt to be ready when I take it from the closet!" He was practically shouting now, small drops of spit flying through the air. His mouth had twisted in an ugly snarl, and she instinctively took a step back.

As she did, she felt anger boiling up inside her. *Why am I taking this from him? It's just a shirt.* She looked up at him and saw his eyes go to her right hand. She followed his gaze and realized she was still

97

holding the knife she used for the vegetables, her knuckles white as she gripped it tight.

"What are you going to do with that?" he said in a mocking tone, taking a step closer.

Surprised, she held the knife out in front of her, the tip pointing at Floris. She felt like she was watching herself from above, not sure what she was doing, both her hands shaking. "Stay away from me! I'll cut you."

Floris kept the smile on his face, but it was an ugly smile. "Really? What's your story going to be? Attacking a police officer? That's a bad idea, Nora. But I guess I should've known this would happen one day ..."

"What is that supposed to mean?" She didn't recognize her own voice as she took another step toward him. Her hands were shaking, and she readjusted her grip on the handle.

Floris didn't move but looked at her with contempt. "You know what it means. I should've never taken you home that night. I should have never made you my wife."

She swallowed hard, her eyes stinging as she knew what he would say next.

"You're no use to me. You'll never make me a father. You're barren. And I know why."

No. Don't say it. She felt tears well up in her eyes, and she wanted to say something, but her throat constricted. He spoke the next words devoid of emotion.

"You'll never be more than the whore I tried to save."

She lost her composure, the tears now blurring her vision, and she turned away in shame, dropping the knife.

As she heard it clatter in the distance, she felt a tremendous force hitting her on the side of the head, followed by the kitchen counter rushing at her. She bumped her head, then hit the floor—little stars further impairing her vision—and covered her head with her arms, pulling her legs into her stomach to mold herself into a ball. She squeezed her eyes shut and braced herself for the beating that was sure to follow.

It was eerily quiet for a few seconds, and nothing happened. Then, a chair scraped across the floor, and she hesitantly opened her eyes. As she peeked through her fingers, she saw Floris leaning on the chair, looking down at her. Her head was throbbing, and she tried to control her sobbing. *Don't give him more satisfaction.*

He stood looking at her, and she didn't dare move. She knew anything she'd say or do could send him back into another fit.

After what felt like an eternity, he picked up his shirt and moved away from the table. With a final look at Nora, he shook his head before mounting the stairs. Nora stayed on the kitchen floor as she listened to him moving around in their bedroom. Her heart was beating fast, and as her vision returned to normal, she noticed the knife next to her. She hesitated only for a second before grabbing it. *If he tries this again, I will cut him.*

She sat up against the kitchen counter, placing her hands on her stomach. *It's not my fault. It could've happened to anyone.* They had never recovered from the miscarriage a year into their marriage. At first, Floris had been understanding. But when Nora failed to get pregnant again, he started blaming her. He'd grown distant, coming home late, drinking excessively. She knew that's when she lost her husband, but she never expected the beatings.

Her headache was worsening, and every step Floris took as he came down the stairs felt like a hammer pounding inside her head. He had changed into semiformal clothing and wore a different shirt —one she had pressed for him earlier.

"Are you going to stay on the floor the rest of the night?" He'd probably taken a few sips from the bottle of *jenever*—Dutch gin—he kept in his bedside cabinet.

She averted her eyes. Whatever she said would only make it worse. He shrugged and crossed the kitchen into the hallway, brushing by her. She considered pulling out the knife and ending it right there, but stopped herself. *What if I don't kill him? He'll kill me.*

She didn't move as he put on his shoes and jacket. As the door opened and closed, she realized she'd been holding her breath, and she exhaled heavily. She pulled herself to her feet—holding onto the kitchen counter for support—and put down the knife. She took a deep breath and composed herself before walking to the window. It was still light outside, but she could see her reflection in the dirty window.

Her eyes were puffy, and as she licked her parched lips, she tasted a hint of blood. Outside, she saw Floris stumble around the corner. *He will have forgotten about all of this by morning.*

Nora balled her fists at the thought. It wasn't the first time he brought her past into an argument, but he had been especially vicious today. The boys in the canoe were now paddling back in the opposite direction, and they looked up at her window. This time, Nora turned away, closing the curtains. She didn't want them to see her face.

She felt a stab of pain in her chest. *Why am I hiding when I've done nothing wrong?* She knew the answer. She was ashamed. Ashamed of looking away while Floris destroyed so many innocent people's lives. Ashamed of letting her past hold her back.

No more.

She turned to the window and opened the curtains. The boys were well up the canal, but Nora smiled nonetheless. The sun crept down the houses opposite, and Nora suddenly knew she needed to get away. She knew where she needed to go. Without another thought, she rushed to the door—not bothering to grab her coat—and down the stairs. The muggy summer air hit her face as she headed for the only place she could go.

CHAPTER SIXTEEN

Christiaan looked at Gerrit across the table. Gerrit had surprised him by knocking on his door that evening, and for a moment, he feared it was the Sicherheitsdienst, ready to take him away. He'd been relieved to find it was his fellow resistance man but wondered how Gerrit knew where he lived. So he made a note to be even more careful.

"So, are you up for it?" Gerrit asked, blowing smoke into the air. It drifted slowly to the high ceiling, and Gerrit put down his pipe.

Christiaan drummed his fingers on the table and pondered the man's proposal. "Is it getting that much more dangerous?"

"Yes, with more people looking for hiding places, our organization is growing. I don't know all the new people, nobody tells me about them, but we can see how many more food coupons are coming in these days, right?" Gerrit gave him a stern look. "And with more people joining us, the chances of someone getting caught increase as well. I've heard leadership wants to ensure we have as little information as possible."

Christiaan nodded. It made perfect sense. It had only been a month since he started delivering food coupons to three houses. Now, he was responsible for seven families.

"Just so I understand. I would no longer meet with you?"

Gerrit took another drag from his pipe, letting some smoke escape from the sides of his mouth before answering. "Having the same people meet is becoming too suspicious. There are too many nosy neighbors. From now on, you will meet different people all the time."

"How will I recognize them?"

Gerrit smiled. "Don't worry, they'll find you. Just make sure you show up at the meeting spots at the right time. We'll make sure you know where you need to go that week." He paused. "The only people you'll see regularly are those you're supplying with food coupons."

"What if something goes wrong?" Christiaan asked.

"If anything goes wrong, we'll take care of it, and be in touch as soon as it's safe again. Stay vigilant and be careful. If you ever suspect you're being followed, or if the SD might be monitoring you, you need to let us know." He reached into his pocket and took out a simple, worn brown cap. "If something is wrong, wear this to your meeting with your contact. They'll see you, and let the leadership know something's wrong. From there, continue your regular life. We'll be in touch."

Christiaan took the cap and placed it on the table. He stared at it, and they were quiet for a moment, but there was no way he would walk away now—even if the work was becoming more dangerous. *This is what I signed up for.*

"I'm in," he said. Gerrit looked at him with an amused look. *He knew I wouldn't walk away.* "What's next?"

Gerrit waved his hand dismissively. "I don't know, and even if I wanted to, they wouldn't tell me. I'll let them know you're on board with the new protocol, and then they'll be in touch, I suppose." He made to get up when there was a faint knock at the door. They both froze, and Gerrit raised an eyebrow. "Are you expecting someone?" he whispered, slowly putting his pipe down and reaching into his jacket. The glint of a knife flashed, and Christiaan locked eyes with Gerrit. *Should I start carrying a weapon as well?*

"No, let me take a look. Stay here." Dusk was setting in; who would be out now? Christiaan walked to the door, and there was another knock, louder and more urgent. He hesitated before opening it. If it were the Sicherheitsdienst or the police, they wouldn't have knocked twice.

He opened the door and was relieved to see a familiar figure standing in the semidarkness.

"What are you doing here at this time? Quick, come in." As Nora stepped into the faint light of the hallway, Christiaan bit his lower lip and reached out to her. Her face was a mess: both cheeks purple, her nose caked in blood, and a mass of disheveled hair on her head. "What happened? What did he do this time?"

Nora looked at him with a vacant stare, her eyes puffy and unfocused. "I ... I don't remember," she stammered.

Christiaan took her hand and led her into the living room, where he sat her down on his couch. She sat meekly, and Christiaan hurried to the kitchen. Gerrit had moved near the door, knife still drawn.

"You need to leave," he said as he filled a kettle. "Don't worry, it's my sister-in-law. We can trust her."

Gerrit put the knife in his back pocket and left without another word. He walked past Nora, who sat staring into the distance, and as Christiaan returned to the living room, he heard the front door close. He grabbed a blanket and wrapped it around her as he sat next to her. "Nora, are you okay? Are you in pain? Talk to me."

She turned her head toward him, focus returning to her eyes. A weak smile spread on her face, and she said, "It's okay, Chris, I'm fine. It's not the first time he's done this." She rubbed her jaw and flinched. "I needed to get out of the house and get some fresh air."

She's not okay.

"What happened?" he asked again.

Nora ignored his question. "Who was that man?"

"Just someone delivering something. Come, we need to clean you up a bit. Let me look at your face. You're bleeding."

In the kitchen, the kettle whistled, and he filled a small bowl with water and soap. With a soft cloth, he cleaned Nora's face. He gently rubbed her mouth and nose, the caked blood slowly coming off. She sat in silence, eyes closed, her breath soft and regular. After a minute or two, her face looked better, but for the bruises. He drained the water and returned with two cups of steaming tea.

Nora had her legs pulled up onto the couch and gratefully accepted the tea. He sat down and studied her while she sipped her tea in silence.

"Nora, things can't go on like this. He'll kill you one day."

She took another sip and averted her face. She was suddenly very interested in a simple painting on the other side of the room.

"Let me talk to him," Christiaan started. "Maybe I can talk some sense into him."

Her face shot back to him as she shook her head, her eyes wide with fear. "No, that will only make it worse."

"Worse than this?" Christiaan said, looking at her intently. "I don't think so."

She put down her tea and sat up. "Maybe I should go home." She flinched and closed her eyes.

"Nora, you should rest." He put his hand on her shoulder and looked at the clock. "Besides, it's past curfew. You're not going anywhere."

"But he'll be wondering where I am when he gets home," she said, her back melting into the cushions.

"We can handle that tomorrow, you're in no state to cross town now. So why don't you get some sleep, and we can decide what to do tomorrow morning. If you don't want me to talk to him, I won't. But it can't go on like this."

"You're right. He probably won't even notice I'm not home until the morning anyway."

Christiaan relaxed a little and allowed himself to settle into the cushions next to her. "I'll take the couch, and you'll sleep in my bed." He reached for her cup of tea and turned to hand it to her. Her eyes were closed and she was snoring softly. He put the cup back on the coffee table and looked at her for a minute. He finished his tea, gently picked her up, and carried her to his bedroom.

———

The following day, Christiaan rose early. Quietly he prepared a simple breakfast with the little coffee he had left—Nora could use it.

As the coffee trickled into the pot, his bedroom door opened. Nora walked out, offering a weak smile as she sat down. She looked a little better than the evening before, her eyes following him as he placed a plate of eggs in front of her. "I hope you like them scrambled."

She picked up her fork and dug in with relish. "Thanks for letting me stay here, Chris. Sorry for barging in unannounced. I'm sure I was quite a mess." She took another bite, washing it down with a gulp of water.

He waved dismissively and grabbed the coffee pot off the stove. "I would do anything for you, Nora. You know that."

She smiled, and her eyes lit up as he poured a generous mug of coffee. "You still have coffee? How did you get your hands on that?" She reached for the mug and brought it to her lips, closing her eyes as she savored the sweet smell.

He sat down opposite her. "I've been rationing it. I'm almost out." He took a sip, the coffee leaving a warm, satisfying sensation as it made its way down his throat. He took a bite of his eggs, even though he wasn't hungry. Nora had almost finished her plate, and he scooped some of his eggs onto hers. She held up her hand in protest, but he shook his head.

"Come on, you're practically starving."

As they finished their breakfast, he cleared his throat. "So, did you think about what I suggested last night?"

"I appreciate your offer." She looked up at him, and he saw the indecision in her eyes. "But I'm afraid it will only make things worse."

Christiaan had expected this, and he calmly responded, "The next time this happens, he may well kill you, Nora. You know that, right? He's not himself when he's had a few." *Or maybe that's exactly who he is.*

"I know. He scares me when he's like that," she said, setting the mug down and putting her hands on the table. Her eyes darted between her plate and mug, before looking up at Christiaan. "Chris, there's something I need to tell you."

He sat up. "What's that?"

"I'm ashamed to be with him."

She paused, looking uncertain, and Christiaan nodded. "Go on."

"When he was a regular police officer, when we got married, he was kind. But these days, or I should say these past three years, I don't recognize the man I married, the man he used to be."

"I know. I remember when you got married. You were both so happy."

Nora sighed. "I want to believe there is still something of that man left in Floris, but I'm finding it harder every day. Just yesterday, he was gloating about how much harder it is to catch Jews in hiding and how he's looking forward to seeing the bounty increased. And worse, I know he's raiding the houses after they've taken people away."

Christiaan had heard the rumors of the men working for the Bureau emptying the houses of deported Jews but had never seen any proof.

"How do you know?"

"Because I've seen his stash. He thinks I don't know, but he keeps his stolen money and jewelry in the house. I'm so ashamed of him, Chris." She hid her face in her hands. "I don't know what to do. I wish I could do something."

"Do something?"

She looked up at him with big eyes and lowered her voice. "I know there are people in the city helping Jews, hiding them and sabotaging the Germans and the Blackshirts. But can you imagine what it'll look like if the wife of a known Bureau man comes knocking at the resistance? They'd never trust me. Besides, I wouldn't know where to start."

Christiaan could see the passion in her eyes as she spoke. "I understand." A silence hung in the air, and he looked at the clock. It was almost eight, and his mind returned to the task at hand.

"Will Floris be home now?"

"It's Saturday, and he doesn't have to work today, I don't think," Nora said. "Although that doesn't mean he'll be home. He likes to go 'hunting for Jews,' as he calls it, during the weekend. But I'm sure he's still at home now, sleeping off whatever he had."

Even if his brother decided to go to work later in the morning, he could still catch him now. *And it's probably better to talk to a sober Floris.* "How about this?" he started. "Let me take you home, and if Floris is up, I'll have a chat with him. I promise I'll be civil. I just want him to know that I know what's going on. He can't keep doing this."

Nora considered this for a moment, then slowly nodded. "Maybe he'll change."

———

An hour later, they arrived at Nora and Floris' house. All was quiet as she opened the front door, and they stepped into the hall. Nora entered the kitchen, and when Christiaan followed, he found his brother at the kitchen table. He caught his brother's glare at Nora before it made way for a look of surprise and annoyance when he saw Christiaan.

"Didn't expect to see you here, little brother," Floris said coolly. He then focused his gaze on Nora. "I guess you were at Christiaan's last night?" His voice had turned icy, and Christiaan felt the hairs on his arms prick up. He wanted to respond, but Nora beat him to it.

"I needed some fresh air, and I found myself near Christiaan's. Before I knew it, it was dark, and the curfew had arrived. We agreed it would be better for me to stay there. I didn't want to get into trouble." She spoke softly, apologetically even.

Floris looked at her for a few seconds as he seemed to ponder his response. Christiaan felt a sense of restlessness growing. *Doesn't he care about how horrible she looks?* Floris got up from his chair and approached Nora. She took a step back, clasping her hands together. Floris was unperturbed as he stepped closer to Nora, putting his hand on her shoulder. "You shouldn't be out that late at night. Things might happen."

Christiaan could no longer control himself and stepped forward. "She doesn't have to go outside for bad things to happen!" he shouted at his brother, who turned to him in a flash and opened his mouth. Christiaan didn't wait for him to speak and continued, the words coming fast. "Look at her face, Floris, look what you did to her yesterday. You did this, not some thug on the street. You!"

"Christiaan, please," Nora said meekly, standing in between the brothers, but it was too late. Floris's eyes spewed fire as he pointed his finger in Christiaan's face.

"You should be careful with your accusations." His previously calm and controlled voice was now making way for a thunderous, menacing tone. "Did Nora tell you I did this?" His eyes switched to Nora, who didn't respond.

"She didn't have to. It was pretty clear when she knocked on my door last night. She was bleeding and barely conscious."

"But did she tell you I did this?" Floris repeated, his eyes boring into him with a mix of fury and hate. *He's lost his mind.*

Nora took a step back, moving closer to Christiaan, and he instinctively put his hand on her arm. She was shaking and struggling to breathe. Then, in a mocking tone, Floris said, "I see what's going on here. Is there something between you two that I should know about?"

"No!" Nora shrieked, startling Christiaan. "I would never—"

"Oh, shut up!" Floris cut her off before returning his focus to Christiaan. "If you believe anything she says, you're a bigger fool than I thought. You know she'll say anything to get her way, right? Now that I think of it"—his eyes shot to Christiaan's hand protectively on Nora's arm—"you probably wouldn't mind getting a piece of her yourself, little brother. With her past, you may well stand a good chance."

Christiaan felt Nora tense as Floris spoke; her face had turned ashen, eyes glistening as tears formed, and she appeared to shrink a few inches. He looked at his brother, who seemed to revel in his words' damage. Something snapped. "You bastard." Before Floris could respond, Christiaan hit him square in the jaw, feeling it move a little as he did. Floris recovered quickly, and as Christiaan retracted his fist, his brother swung wildly at him. Christiaan ducked and dodged the punch, but he heard a dull thud next to him. An instant later, Nora collapsed onto the floor.

Christiaan looked to Floris, who stood in a daze, no longer interested in Christiaan. Christiaan knelt next to Nora. "Are you all right?"

She rubbed her shoulder, grimacing as she did. "I'm fine. It was only my shoulder. I've had worse," she said softly, making an effort to sit up. Christiaan took her hand and helped her sit as she leaned against the kitchen cupboards. "I'm okay, really, Chris. You should leave."

"Nora, I'm so sorry. I didn't mean to do that." Floris had found a soft, almost sweet voice as he knelt next to her. "I didn't mean those things I just said. I was just worried about you."

Christiaan looked at his brother incredulously. *He can't be serious.* All of a sudden, Christiaan felt like the third wheel as Floris fussed over Nora, checking her shoulder and repeating how sorry he was. His brother had his back to him, but Nora was facing Christiaan.

"Thanks for keeping me safe last night, Chris. I'm really fine. You should go home, please." Her eyes were pleading, urging him to leave. He looked at her in confusion, but she gave him an almost imperceptible nod.

He got up hesitantly and moved slowly to the door. Floris helped Nora back to her feet and escorted her to a chair. As Christiaan opened the front door, he looked back one more time. Floris stood at the stove, his face hidden from Christiaan, his back to Nora. She looked at Christiaan, and in that one look, he saw everything was not okay. Despite that, Nora shook her head and mouthed one word, "Go."

Christiaan exited the building, crossed a small bridge, and looked across the narrow canal. The sun was high in the sky, its rays glistening on the calm water below. As he continued home in the Amsterdam sunshine, the kernels of a plan to help Nora started to form.

CHAPTER SEVENTEEN

Nora took the bag of vegetables from the tall man at the market stall.

"See you next week, same time?" he said with a wink.

"As long as you make sure you have some half-decent potatoes for me, I'll keep coming back." She chuckled as she walked away. She loved the cheekiness of the Amsterdam market vendors—they never lost their positive attitude. Nora deliberately slowed her pace as she passed the other stalls. It was the same everywhere. The stalls were half-empty: potatoes, a bit of rice, and simple vegetables.

Nora passed the checkpoint at the market, where three young German police officers looked bored. They let her pass without a word—they were only interested in people going in the other direction.

August had been surprisingly mild—Nora took a small detour through the newly renamed Bolland Park. It was odd to see that name plastered over the entrance—the Germans had renamed Sarpathi Park, as the former Amsterdam city planner Samuel Sarpathi was a Jew. It didn't matter much, everybody still called it the Sarpathi.

Nora strolled past the small pond, normally filled with quacking ducks. With meat in short supply, the ducks had vanished. Nora hoped most of them had escaped to safer places. *I wish I could fly away.*

She sat on a bench and looked around. Apart from a couple walking on the other side of the pond, she was alone. The serenity of the park was a tonic, the silence interrupted only by the occasional chirping of birds.

Nora stood up when the sun disappeared behind a thick layer of clouds. She felt a shiver run down her spine; it soon became chilly without the sun.

She exited the park and headed home, upping her pace as she noticed dark clouds approaching. As she turned into her street, she was surprised to find someone sitting on the steps of her house. Her heart skipped a beat—Christiaan. *What is he doing here?*

She hadn't seen or heard from her brother-in-law since the fight, and even though she wasn't worried about him, she felt terrible about how abruptly she'd told him to leave. He would've understood, though, she thought as she hurried toward him.

He must've heard her footsteps as he turned his head in her direction. She was relieved to see a smile appear on his face as he stood up.

"Chris, what are you doing here?"

Instead of answering, he held out his arms and pulled her in for a hug. Nora felt conspicuous in the middle of the street but quickly decided she didn't care. Her neighbors hated her anyway.

"I needed to talk to you," Christiaan said as they broke their hug. "Floris isn't home, is he?" He then smiled. "Well, I know he's not home because he probably would've come down had he spotted me."

Nora opened the door. "He's not. How long have you been sitting here?"

"Only fifteen minutes. I figured with the rain coming you would be home soon. And if not, I would have come back later." His eyes went to her bag as they climbed the stairs. "Did you manage to get anything decent? Bit late to go to the market, no?"

"I know the guy selling the veggies. He always keeps some for me," Nora said as she opened the door and they stepped inside. She put her bag on the kitchen counter and grabbed two glasses. "Want some water?"

"Sure, but I won't be staying long." Christiaan leaned on one of the kitchen chairs, not sitting down.

Nora handed him a glass and frowned. "You seem serious. What's on your mind?"

"How have you been since I left?" Christiaan asked as he took a sip, inspecting her face. "You look better."

"He said he's going to drink less. Let's see how long he manages that. But for now, I'm all right, thank you." She sat down and motioned at the chair across the table. "Come on, out with it. You're not just here to check up on me, are you?"

"Well, that was part of it, but you're right." His eyes were serious, and he leaned forward. "Some of the things you told me the other morning got me thinking."

"We talked about a lot of things."

Christiaan turned the glass in his hands before speaking. "You said you're ashamed of being the wife of an NSB Jew hunter."

"Wouldn't you be?"

"Of course. But the way you made it sound was like you wanted to do something about it. You said you wanted to make a difference."

"Well, yes. But I'm not sure what you're getting at."

"What if I told you that you can? That it's not impossible to turn this situation into something good?"

"Come on, stop talking in riddles. Out with it, Chris."

"What if you could join the resistance? Would you do it?"

She let out a nervous laugh, catching herself as she covered her mouth. "Who, me? Join the resistance? I told you, they'd never have me. It's absurd!"

He stared at her. *He's not joking.* "It *is* absurd, Chris. You know that, right?"

Christiaan cleared his throat. "No more absurd than me helping them."

Nora's mouth fell open, and she reached out across the table, grabbing his arm. "You? Really?"

He nodded, a twinkle in his eye. "Sorry I never told you before, but it's not something you go around telling everyone."

Nora struggled for words. "But how? Since when? What do you do?"

He held up his hands. "I can't tell you everything. I can't tell you anything. But this is not about me. It's about you."

She sat back in her chair, struggling to process what she had heard. *Chris, in the resistance? How did I miss this?*

Christiaan smiled and leaned across the table. "Do you want to hear my plan? You can say no if you don't like it."

Nora nodded, excitement bubbling up in her stomach.

"When I left the other night, I started thinking, and I can't believe we didn't consider this before," he started, taking another sip of water. *Come on, Chris, out with it!* "But when you said the resistance would never consider the wife of a Bureau policeman, it struck me. Because you're right. If you somehow managed to find someone in the resistance and ask if you could join, they would probably kill you."

Nora swallowed hard. "It was just something I said to you. I never really thought about it. I wouldn't even know where to start."

"I know, but that's the brilliance of it. Of course, you don't have to. But then I remembered you told me Floris often tells you all about what's going on at work, right?"

"When I ask him about his day, he won't shut up." *It's exhausting.* "I hate it."

Christiaan smiled. "Yes, but it's perfect. He is now far enough up the ladder to hear the plans, right? He probably knows about new raids well before anyone else."

"You're right. He told me about that meeting last week when they decided to increase the bounty."

"Exactly!" He spoke a little faster, and Nora could see he was getting excited. She started to feel the same. "You haven't shown much interest in his stories from work so far, right?"

She shook her head. "Not really. I ask him a few questions, just to keep him talking, but I never really listen."

"And that's the only thing you'd need to keep doing, but now, show more interest. Get him to tell you everything he knows about what's happening, what the Bureau and the Sicherheitsdienst are planning. And then you tell us. You have no idea how valuable this information is." He put his hands flat on the table and looked at her, his eyes burning with passion. "What do you think?"

Nora got up and walked to the window. Dark clouds were directly overhead, casting the street and canal outside in a gloomy semidarkness. A few people hurried down the street, no doubt looking to get inside before the rain came down. She looked across the water at the other houses. What if people were hiding inside those houses as well? In a cellar or an attic? Did they know they lived across the street from a man who wouldn't hesitate to turn them over to the Germans to collect his bounty and then send them off to whatever future awaits in the east? She shook her head—there were hundreds, maybe thousands of those people hiding all over the city. And every day, Floris and his colleagues dragged more of them out of their hiding spots.

Tac, tac. The first drops of rain pattered against the window. She followed them as they landed in the dust as small red-brownish explosions. She looked at herself in the window, her pale face contrasting against the darkness outside. Nora took a deep breath, closed her eyes, and—without turning around—asked, "Who do I need to convince to join?"

"No one. I've already vouched for you. Everything's in place. You just need to say the words."

Tac. Tac. Tac. She watched as the rain started pouring down, the water cleaning the dust off the windows, and she knew she could no longer look away. This was her chance to rid herself of the shame, to no longer idly stand by. She turned away from the window, crossed the short distance to the table, put her hands on the side, and leaned forward.

"Okay. Tell me more."

PART III

AMSTERDAM,

18 DECEMBER 1942

CHAPTER EIGHTEEN

The room was buzzing when Floris entered. He thought he'd show up early, but it appeared he wasn't the only one. He scanned the faces near him but didn't recognize anyone. *Lots of people from out of town for this event.* He also spotted a large number of German officers donning their formal uniforms. He squeezed his way through the crowd, nodding politely at the people making way for him. At the bar, he decided to pace himself and ordered a beer. He would've loved something more potent, but there would be enough time for that later. For now, he wanted to keep his wits about him—there would be many important people here tonight. He leaned on the bar, perched slightly higher than the rest of the room, and took a swig from his bottle. There was a great view of the crowd, and—most importantly—of the entrance. More people streamed in, an interesting mix of men wearing black or green uniforms—plenty of high-ranking officers from both the SD and the WA. He was glad to see them standing side by side, talking amiably. *This is how it's supposed to be, all of us working together.*

"Hey, Flo!" He heard a familiar voice and was glad to see the smiling face of his good friend Daniel. He wore no uniform but, like

Floris, had a party badge prominently pinned to his chest. However, as Floris and Daniel both weren't part of the WA, they never wore the black uniforms—Floris preferred doing his bit for the country by wearing his police uniform.

Daniel ordered a beer and turned to Floris. "I didn't think it'd be this packed yet. It looks like everybody's excited about tonight."

"Well, it's not every day the party rents the ballroom at a fancy hotel. Something big is about to happen."

"I've heard Mussert might make an appearance," Daniel said, taking his beer from the bartender. "Do you think he will?"

Floris had heard the same rumors, but it was nothing new. Whenever there was a large party gathering, people liked to build up the hype.

"I doubt he'll show up. I think he's much too busy securing his position with the German leadership. I heard he's recently had a private meeting with the Führer."

Daniel's eyes lit up. "Sounds like good news. Do you think he'll finally be appointed as the country's leader?"

"As long as he swears allegiance to Hitler, I don't see why not. We've been an important ally to the Germans in the past years, and I'm sure they appreciate our efforts. They need Dutch leadership to show the rest of the country we can help govern."

"A bit like a German province, you think?"

Floris drained his bottle and smiled. "Exactly like that." He signaled to the bartender for another beer. "So, how's work? How's the recruitment for the *Arbeitseinsatz* going?" Daniel worked in the municipal office and was in charge of picking people to work in Germany's war industry.

"Mixed results. Last month we received a new quota from Berlin. They need about 35,000 people. Most aren't keen, and we've had a lot of trouble getting them to show up voluntarily. I'm lucky, in a sense, because we still have a lot of students in Amsterdam. It's a good group to pick from because they didn't sign the act of fealty to Germany."

"Ah, yes. And that makes the students unemployed, right?"

Daniel smiled. "And therefore eligible for the Arbeitseinsatz. Problem is, many of them have gone into hiding. You know a bit about that, don't you? How are things at the Bureau?"

Floris took a large swig before answering. "About the same, although the Jews aren't sent east for work. In a sense, all of them going into hiding has only made my job more interesting." He paused as a woman sat down at the bar. "It's certainly made it more lucrative when I catch them."

"And are you?"

Floris was distracted by the woman—her dark blond hair in a bun, a sleek red dress accentuating her features. He found it difficult to look away. "Am I what?"

"Catching the Jews."

"Yes," he said, his eyes fixed on the woman, who ordered a cocktail, seemingly oblivious to Floris' attention. "There are always ways to find them."

Daniel chuckled, his eyes fixed on Floris' wrist. "Hey, fancy cufflinks."

"Yeah, it's pretty lucrative working for the Bureau."

After evicting an elderly Jewish couple who hadn't even bothered hiding, he'd done a quick inspection of the house. When he entered the old man's study, the cufflinks were right there on the desk. He delivered the couple to the SS soldiers at the Hollandsche Schouwburg—the former Jewish theater—himself. They would be well on their way to the east, with a prolonged stop in Camp Westerbork if they were lucky. Either way, nobody would ever hear their complaints.

"Hey, there's some colleagues of mine over there." Daniel nodded across the room. "I'm going to say hi. I'll see you later, yeah?"

Floris nodded, secretly pleased to see Daniel leave. He turned to the bar and sat down on the empty stool next to the woman as the bartender placed her drink in front of her. She reached for her purse, but Floris held up his hand. "Please, let me buy you a drink."

She raised an eyebrow—looking him up and down—but then put her purse away. She smiled and held up her glass. "Well, well. Thank you, although that wasn't necessary. I can afford my drinks."

He clinked her glass. "But you shouldn't have to. I'm Floris."

"Samantha." She took a slow sip from her drink, her eyes locked on his. He felt his heart beat a little faster as he tried his best to remain composed. He took another sip of his beer and looked around the room, feigning nonchalance. The only thing he wanted to do was look into her bright blue eyes and talk to her.

"So, you're not wearing a uniform," she said confidently. "Not black, and certainly not green. What does that make you?"

"Interesting," he said, surprising himself.

She laughed and took another sip. "You're pretty sure of yourself, aren't you? It's funny, because it seems like most people here are either German or part of the WA. What brought you here?"

"I could ask you the same thing."

"Ah, yes. Well, let's just say I was invited."

"Are you a member of the party?"

She shook her head, and he felt a pang of disappointment before she said, "But I certainly don't disagree with the direction Mussert is taking us."

Floris looked at her, not sure if she was serious. Her eyes were playful; she might be mocking him. He decided to chance it. "You mean working alongside the Germans? Did you hear he's about to be appointed leader of the country?"

Her face turned serious. "Of course, I've heard. Why do you think I'm here? I'd love to hear his plans."

Floris relaxed—she wasn't mocking him.

"You still haven't told me what you do," she said, finishing her drink.

"I work for the Bureau," he said as he signaled to the bartender for another round. "My job is to take care of the Jewish problem in Amsterdam." He studied her face intently as he spoke those words, and to his surprise, she didn't flinch. Instead, she nodded, and he thought he saw a hint of admiration in her eyes. *This girl is fascinating.*

"And how is that going? I'm sure it's a tough job," she asked with genuine interest. "Plenty of people in this city disapprove of what you're doing, I guess?"

Floris waved his hand dismissively. "It's no big deal. With the support of the SD, we're catching more and more every day. Of course, they can hide, but we'll find them."

The bartender set down their drinks, and Floris raised his bottle. He was starting to feel a little woozy, and he wasn't sure if it was because of the beers—*How many have I had?*—or the stunning company.

They were making a toast when a young man in uniform approached, heading straight for Samantha. He casually put his arm around her waist, ignoring Floris as he greeted her. Floris felt a stab of jealousy—*Who was this man interrupting their moment?* He opened his mouth to say something when he noticed the insignia on the man's collar patch. The two lightning strikes made him stop. This man was no ordinary police officer—he was part of the SS. *What is an SS Hauptsturmführer doing here?* The man turned to him before he could say anything, the smile disappearing from his face, his dark brown eyes boring into him.

"What are you doing with my girl? Did you think you could get her drunk while I was away?"

Floris looked at the younger man, stunned at the unexpected reproach. Samantha hadn't said anything about a boyfriend, much less that she was with an SS officer. *Who does this guy think he is?*

"We were just talking. There was nothing going on," he said, putting up the palms of his hands.

The German eyed him suspiciously, then shook his head. "No, I don't think so. I saw the way you were looking at her just now. You thought you had a chance." He scoffed, looking Floris up and down with disdain. "A simple civilian, aren't you?"

"I'm a detective in the police force," Floris said, clenching his teeth. "And you and I are on the same side, hence being in this room together."

The SS man grinned, tutting at the same time. "We may be on the same side, but you're nowhere near good enough to talk to Samantha, let alone have a drink with her. So why don't you scurry off. I think you've *entertained* her long enough. I'll take it from here."

Floris felt his neck burning, and he turned to Samantha. She looked at him oddly, pitifully even. *I don't need pity.* He returned his gaze to the SS officer. The man faced him with an amused expression —the way a cat would at a cornered mouse. Floris balled his fists, took a deep breath, and was about to hit out at the German when a voice behind him interrupted.

"Flo, you all right?"

He stopped and turned, seeing Daniel standing there with three other men, wide eyed. Floris stood frozen, not sure what to do next.

"That's right, *officer*, go to your friends, get out of here." The Hauptsturmführer's voice sounded in the distance, echoing in his head. Something in Floris snapped, and he turned back to the German, grabbing him by the collar.

"Don't talk to me like that, you obnoxious little shit," Floris said, shaking the younger man. "You don't know all the stuff I do for the Führer! All these Jews coming from Amsterdam to Westerbork, I take care of that! Me!"

For a moment, the younger man's eyes betrayed a hint of fear, but he quickly recovered. He grabbed Floris's wrists, squeezing them with surprising strength. Floris let go of the collar, and the German forcefully pushed him away. Floris was caught by Daniel and his friends, who held on to him as he struggled to get back to the German. Adrenaline shot through his veins as the German straightened his collar and stepped toward him.

"Try anything like that again, and your career is over," he stated as he jabbed a finger at Floris's chest. "I'll pretend that little tantrum didn't happen, but I suggest you walk away before I report you for assaulting a German officer. Then, you'll join your Jewish prisoners on the next train to Westerbork faster than you can blink your eyes."

Floris found his anger ebbing away with every icy word.

"Come on, let's go," Daniel said, gently but firmly tugging at his sleeve. Floris took another look at Samantha, who seemed horrified. Floris was ashamed of his behavior—it was unbecoming. *I shouldn't have taken the bait.*

He took one last look at the German, who had returned to his seat. *It's not worth it.*

Floris turned to Daniel and his friends. "How about we go get some fresh air?"

The relief in the group was palpable as they crossed the ballroom toward the exit. Floris' anger had faded, now replaced by shame. If he wanted to stand a chance with women like that, he needed to control his temper. He also realized he'd been lucky with the SS officer. Another man wouldn't have hesitated to report him immediately. As they stepped into the cold December air, he vowed to control himself better—it was the only way he would move up to where he belonged.

CHAPTER NINETEEN

Nora heard Floris moving upstairs, and she quickly cracked two eggs into the frying pan. She enjoyed the satisfying sizzle as they hit the hot margarine, cut two slices of rye bread, and put them in another pan. The bread was a few days old, but she knew how to make it last.

She wanted to make sure Floris would stay around long enough for breakfast. She heard him come in the evening prior and had been surprised to find him quietly tiptoeing into the bedroom. She shuffled around the kitchen, anxious for him to come down. She had found it surprisingly easy to settle into her spy role for the resistance.

It had been four months since Christiaan had asked her to join. Even though she'd been unsure about her ability to extract information from Floris at first, she'd been lucky: Floris had been promoted at work. He was now a sergeant, even though he preferred to continue calling himself a detective. The promotion meant he now had more people reporting to him as he led several teams. The new role gave him closer access to the higher ranks of the Sicherheitsdienst and Grüne Polizei and in turn made him more successful in hunting down Jews.

Even though Nora detested that part of his job, it made him an even more valuable source of information—he was now among the people planning the raids. With his promotion came more opportunities, both legal and illegal. His base salary increased, thanks in no small part to him taking a cut from his team's bounties, but he was also in charge of securing the houses they raided. His upstairs stash only continued to grow, an astonishing mix of cash and jewelry.

Floris was moving up in society, acquiring a certain standing within the party and police force. He no longer appeared to carry the chip on his shoulder, making him much easier to be around with.

She heard footsteps coming down the stairs, and Floris appeared in the kitchen a few seconds later. He wore regular clothes, which meant he was likely to be out on the streets today. Even though he could technically do all of his work from the office, he preferred to spend time with his teams in the city, joining raids and arresting those poor people.

"Something smells good in here," he said chirpily before taking a seat. *Good, he's not in a hurry.*

Nora scooped the bread and eggs onto a plate and set it before him. "I thought you might appreciate a hearty breakfast. You were home pretty late. How was the party?" she asked airily as she sat down across from him. She'd become an expert in hiding her true feelings.

He took a bite and spoke as he chewed. "It was great. There were many important people from the SD, and even some SS officers. It was interesting because they hardly ever come to Amsterdam, let alone attend our parties."

Nora sat up. It was never good to hear the SS appearing anywhere, especially in town. "Did they have a special reason to be there?"

"They sure did." Floris took a large swig of tea. "They were in the city to inspect how the transports were going and if there was a way to speed them up. It seems they're not sending enough Jews to the east. I think they were going back this morning, and they heard about the party."

"Did you speak to any of them?"

He shook his head. "No, they were mostly talking among themselves, but I stood nearby, so I picked up on some of the things they said."

"Anything interesting? I mean, it's closely linked to what you do?" She kept her tone casual. *Careful now, not too eager.*

She needn't have worried, as Floris smiled as he continued to chew and talk simultaneously. "They said they wanted to scale up the operations at the Schouwburg, wanting to get a quicker turnover."

Nora nodded. The Hollandsche Schouwburg used to be a Jewish theater, but was renamed and then turned into a collection point for the city's arrested Jews. Nora had heard stories of people waiting for days in the overcrowded building. The conditions were somewhat better than the Sicherheitsdienst's headquarters in a school on Euterpe Street, a place that gave her the shivers. People taken there to be interrogated were never to be heard from again. *That would be my fate if he ever found out what I am doing.*

"If they want to scale up the operations, I guess you'll be busier as well?" She needed to relate her questions to his work.

He cleaned his plate with the last piece of bread. "I suppose. It wouldn't surprise me if our quotas increase soon. Good thing I have plenty of informants." He shoved the bread in his mouth and smacked his lips. "I should get going." He wiped his mouth and got up.

"Wait, I got you some tea for your walk." She handed him a thermos. "I guess you'll be home late again? It sounds like you're going to be busy." She threw in the question offhandedly but held her breath. She needed to know about this, and she couldn't ask him about his informants directly.

"Yeah, don't wait up for me. We've got some operations planned today and the rest of the week."

He gave her a quick peck on the cheek and turned. Before closing the door, he turned back and said, "With a bit of luck, I'll be able to bring you home something nice. You never know what you might find, right?" He winked at her, and Nora forced a smile, holding it until she heard the latch click. She'd become good at playing the obedient wife. As soon as Floris turned the corner, she grabbed her coat and opened the door.

———

Christiaan was expecting her and opened the door within seconds. Even if someone suspected her—which she was sure nobody did— visiting her brother-in-law would arouse no suspicions. *Why wouldn't I see him?*

He closed the door and guided her to his small living room. She sat down on the sofa, and he looked at her with urgency. "And? How was the party? Did he want to talk?"

She nodded. "He was surprisingly fresh this morning. We were right. He wanted to impress some people last night. I think he hardly drank."

"And did he impress?"

"It seemed like the Germans weren't too interested in mingling with the NSB boys," Nora said, unable to suppress a grin. "But Floris wouldn't be Floris if he didn't listen in on what they were talking about."

Christiaan's face lit up. "My brother is always looking for oppor- tunities. It serves us well to have you spying on him. Come on, tell me, what did you find out?"

She told him about the SS' plans to increase the frequency of transport from Amsterdam. She was a little disappointed he didn't appear to be surprised. "You knew about this?"

He shook his head. "Yes and no. It adds up with what we've heard from our contacts around the Schouwburg. We knew people were taken to Westerbork from there, but recent news has been ..."

He looked troubled as he paused, appearing to search for words. "Disturbing, to say the least."

"What did you hear?" Nora was almost afraid to ask.

A shadow crossed his face. "You know how the SD, and even the Dutch police, are telling the Jewish people they're being relocated to work in Germany?"

"Sure." She felt dread build up in the pit of her stomach. *Something's not right.*

"We believe they're going to concentration camps in Poland. Reports from Westerbork suggest people there are being sent away in cattle cars. The doors are locked from the outside, and there's barbed wire wrapped around the cars."

Nora felt her throat constrict, and she swallowed hard. *This can't be true.* "Do they know where they're going? And what do you mean they're heading to concentration camps?"

"These camps are located in Poland, in places I've never heard of before. But one is called Auschwitz, and my contacts said they murder people upon arrival. To be honest, I find it all hard to believe."

"Murdered?" Nora was horrified. "How? Why?"

He shook his head. "Apparently, they have crematoriums in the camp, and my contact said they're always billowing smoke. Beyond that, I don't know. He said tens of thousands of people are taken into the camp, with only a few thousand coming out to work in the nearby mines and industry. The numbers don't add up. People are disappearing." Christiaan looked shaken, his voice trembling.

"Can you trust your contact?" Nora asked hesitantly, more in hope than anything else. *Christiaan is smart. He wouldn't just believe anything.* "This is thousands of kilometers away."

"I know. I had my doubts as well. Until I heard something that made so little sense that it has to be true."

"What?"

"You know how the Germans transport everyone to Westerbork? They tell everybody they're going to work in the east. But it doesn't matter if you're strong and healthy, or fragile; old or very, very young. Everybody's taken to Westerbork for reassignment to the east."

Nora nodded. "I thought they might send children and people unfit to work elsewhere?"

"That would make sense, but that's not what happens. Everybody is packed into the same cattle cars. From what I've heard, there is no real logic behind it. And what use are children in a work camp?"

"So you're convinced they're sending those people to get killed," Nora said, starting to believe it herself.

"Yes. Maybe not all of them, but I fear we'll find out more about it sooner rather than later." Christiaan was quiet for a moment, then cleared his throat. "Nora, I need to ask you something." He appeared to search for the right words, and she gave him a small, encouraging smile. "You've been doing a great job getting information to the resistance. Having you warn us about raids has saved tons of people in the past few months, but we're having trouble recruiting the right people to help with another important task."

Her ears perked up. "What kind of task?"

"Those people sent to Westerbork from the Schouwburg, many of them have children, some babies. Even the Germans realized the Schouwburg was no place to keep young children. It's too crowded, there is nowhere for them to sleep, and they become restless. So, the children are kept in the crèche across the street. When the parents are selected for transport, the children are then collected from the crèche to travel to Westerbork with them."

Nora's heart ached for the families. She could only imagine the horror of being arrested in the middle of the night, torn from their homes to be taken to a filthy collection point. Having their children ripped from their arms would bring anyone to despair. "What would you have me do? Help out in the crèche?" The thought of taking care of these children warmed her heart.

"Not exactly." Christiaan shook his head. "It's run by a Jewish lady, and the Germans insisted she could only have other Jewish women working for her." She was confused, and it must've shown, for Christiaan held up his hand before she could speak. "When we learned the people put on transport to Westerbork were sent on the long journey to Poland, we suspected something was off. Mind you, this was before we'd heard the reports of the concentration camps. But it was enough for the people in the crèche to start talking about saving the children."

"Save them?"

"Make sure they never make it to the train. We've started smuggling them away from the crèche. The security there is nothing like at the Schouwburg, and we've found a good way to bring them to safety somewhere else in the country."

Nora slowly nodded, feeling a mix of excitement and anxiety. "What would I do exactly?"

"I can't tell you the details. I can only bring you into contact with the people in charge, the people in the crèche. Would you be interested?"

Her work so far had been relatively risk-free. Smuggling children from under the SS' noses was quite a different matter. Her mind returned to the day of the strike and her meeting with the young woman and her daughter. If she had known what she knew now and had the chance to take that girl to safety back then, she wouldn't have hesitated one second. She wanted to accept, but needed to know one more thing. "Why me?"

"What do you mean?" Christiaan looked surprised.

"You said it was hard to recruit the right people. So why are you asking me? I've not done anything remarkable."

For the first time that afternoon, Christiaan smiled. "Nora, you're perfect for this because you're a young woman. If you are stopped with a child, people will assume it's your own. And we can't just trust anyone with these children. That's why we need you."

Even though she hadn't been blessed with children of her own, she could imagine how the people in the Schouwburg felt. She wasn't sure if she could do what they did: entrust their children to strangers, knowing they would probably never see them again. But then she remembered the alternative and shook her head—she wouldn't leave the fate of her children in the hands of the SS, either.

"Nora?" Christiaan's voice sounded distant, and she looked up. His eyes seemed pleading, hopeful even. A smile formed on her face, and she nodded—she couldn't let those children down. "Of course, I'll do it."

CHAPTER TWENTY

C hristiaan felt elated as he stepped onto Wilhelmina Street. Even though he had suspected Nora would help, there had always been a bit of doubt in his mind.

Nora had grown into her role, and after two months, she was the sole reason many people were still alive; her information on upcoming raids meant they could warn, and move, people.

Christiaan didn't ask about the situation at home, but he did notice her bruises had gone away. *Perhaps they've moved past this.* He certainly hoped so, but more importantly, Nora seemed happier since starting her work. He was sure she would be an even more significant asset in helping the children at the crèche.

He arrived at number 23, and his mind went back to the task at hand. He reached into his jacket and was relieved to find the thick stack of coupons there. Even though he was cautious, he did worry about losing them all the time.

Instead of taking the front door, he stepped to the side of the house, entering a narrow alleyway. From there, he entered the backyard and, staying close to the partition between the yards, headed for the back door and into the kitchen.

A flickering candle provided the only illumination in the small room, the curtains drawn as dusk was setting in fast. He found his contact Elsa sitting at the table. She hastily looked up as he entered, her eyes betraying a hint of anxiety that vanished as soon as she recognized him.

"Everything all right?" Christiaan asked. They didn't speak much, but Elsa lived alone, and they usually chatted for a few minutes. She would never say as much, but Christiaan suspected she enjoyed talking to him once a week.

"I think the neighbors found out."

Christiaan kept his face composed, but his heart beat a little faster. "Why do you think that?" he asked calmly.

"They were at the door the other day, asking about something I don't even remember, when there was a noise from the basement. I prayed they didn't hear it, but I could tell from their eyes that they had. I brushed it off, saying I was cleaning up and something probably fell from the racks, but they looked suspicious."

"When was this, exactly?"

She thought for a minute, then said, "Three days ago."

"And have they come back? Did they ask anything afterwards?"

Elsa shook her head. "No, but I can see them peeking inside when they pass by in the daytime. What if they tell the Blackshirts or the Germans?" Her voice trailed off at the end of the sentence, her hands shaking. She reached for her pack of tobacco on the table and started to roll a cigarette.

If they were snooping around, they might have even seen him enter just now. On the other hand, there was no reason to suspect they would report Elsa.

"How are the Abrahams doing? Did you tell them about this?"

"I told them to stay in the basement. Normally I'd let them out in the evening, with all the curtains drawn, but I don't trust it now. What if they're listening? These walls are pretty thin. I want them to leave before the SD get their hands on them, and I get sent to Camp Vught." There was fear in her eyes as she spoke.

"I'd like to go see them, check up on them if that's okay with you." It wasn't a question, but Christiaan knew Elsa would appreciate him asking.

"Of course, just make sure you keep your voice down." They walked to the hallway and she opened the basement door for him. She flicked a switch, and a faint light went on, guiding the way down. The steps creaked, and the musty smell of the damp basement entered his nostrils. It was a lot colder here, and he hoped the Abrahams had enough clothes to keep warm.

Elsa closed the door behind him, not following him down. He felt sorry for her. After their initial awkward meeting, he'd grown fond of the woman. She hadn't told him too many details, but he knew she was widowed, having lost her husband in the first war when he volunteered to help the British. They must've been pretty well-off if she could afford living in the relatively big house on her own.

He reached the bottom of the stairs and stepped onto the dusty floor, his eyes adjusting to the dim light below.

"Christiaan!" It was Lisa. Even though she spoke softly, he thought he detected excitement in her voice. She walked up to him and hugged him. He enjoyed the smell of her hair, but he could sense something wasn't right: her shoulders were tense.

Her parents sat at the simple table in the corner, and Christiaan greeted them. "I don't have much time," he said apologetically. "But I hear you've been down here for almost three days now? How are you holding up?"

"It's not that bad," Lisa's father, Antonius, answered. *He's always so positive.* "But we're worried about Elsa. She's so frayed, so nervous. Do you know what's going on?"

She hasn't told them why they're supposed to stay down here. For a moment, he considered keeping them in the dark, but then he caught Lisa's eyes, looking at him with affection. "Elsa is worried the neighbors may have heard something the other day."

To their credit, the Abrahams stayed calm. Lisa spoke up first. "We suspected as much, but thank you for telling us the truth."

"Do you think they did?" Antonius said calmly.

Christiaan scratched his chin. "I'm not entirely sure. From what she said, it's possible."

"If there's the possibility, we shouldn't take any risks, right? Should we get ready to move?" Antonius spoke with more authority now. Christiaan didn't blame him.

"Let me see what I can do. We'll need to see where we can move you to." He didn't mention the most obvious problem: it wasn't easy to find a new spot for the family. They were already struggling to find safe houses for the increased number of people looking to go into hiding.

Antonius nodded, and Christiaan turned to Lisa's mother. "How are you doing, Mary? Is Elsa giving you enough food?" He'd heard of hosts recently not distributing all the food to those in hiding.

"She's keeping us as well fed as she can, I think. I don't know what's going on out there, but I'm sure you're struggling yourself." Her eyes ran over him. "You look quite a bit leaner than a few weeks ago."

Christiaan was surprised, but Lisa agreed. "You're becoming bonier, Christiaan."

He didn't want to complain and simply nodded. "I better get going. I'll need to speak to someone about this. I'll be back soon." Antonius and Mary nodded at him, but Lisa followed him to the stairs. She put her hand on his arm.

"You'll make it work, right, Chris?" she said in a low voice. "I know my parents don't show it, especially my father, but they've been worried sick since Elsa told us we couldn't go back upstairs anymore."

Christiaan swallowed hard, looking into her dark brown eyes. He wanted to tell her everything would be fine, but he stopped. "I'll find you a new place. I'll keep you and your family safe, Lisa."

Her eyes glistened. "Thank you. Will I see you soon?"

"I'll be back before you know it. Hold on a little longer, and stay down here. It's the safest place to be for now."

She leaned and gave him a quick peck on the cheek. "Be careful," she whispered in his ear.

When he reached the top of the stairs, he looked back over his shoulder. Lisa hadn't moved, and even though the light was faint, he saw the sadness in her eyes before she caught herself and her lips curled into a faint smile. He returned her smile before switching off the light and opening the door into the hallway.

He found Elsa in the kitchen with another cigarette. "What will you do next?"

"You're right. It's too risky," he said, leaning on a chair. "Even if your neighbors don't suspect anything, we'll never know for sure."

Elsa's shoulders sagged, and Christiaan could feel her stress as she exhaled a large puff of smoke.

"I'm going to talk to my contacts tomorrow morning. It's too late for me to go there now. I'll be back soon." He walked to the door and grabbed the handle, turning to her. "Keep them safe, Elsa."

She took another drag and nodded but said nothing.

Christiaan stepped into the pitch-black yard. He felt safer than earlier, the night providing cover, as he exited the alley and stepped back onto Wilhelmina Street. He had another hour before curfew, and he made an effort to appear more relaxed than he felt. *At least I'm not carrying the food coupons anymore.*

As he walked through the quiet Amsterdam streets, he worried about the promise he made to Lisa. Even though he was confident leadership would do everything in their power to move the Abrahams, he also knew it wasn't up to him. He would do anything for Lisa, but that wasn't what had convinced him to make that promise. Elsa had worried him most of all. When hosts became nervous, they became unpredictable. It wouldn't be the first time a family was betrayed by their host. Christiaan didn't doubt Elsa's intentions, but he feared she might make a mistake. A slip of the tongue to the wrong person, an offhand remark while buying groceries. Or worse, losing her composure at a checkpoint and drawing too much attention to herself.

The Abrahams needed to move sooner rather than later. He neared his home and vowed to have Lisa and her parents out of that house no matter what. Stepping into the safety of his own hallway, he clenched his fists. *Even if it means taking them into my own home.*

CHAPTER TWENTY-ONE

Floris sat at his desk, thumbing through his unit's latest arrest reports. He loved his new job's power, with five squads reporting to him, but unfortunately, it also meant he needed to check their reports. When he started in his new role, he'd made sure the men knew how he wanted the reports: concise and to the point. They had listened, and the stack was usually manageable.

Today, he was disappointed to see they were lagging behind the targets set by the SD. The rumors had been confirmed, the Germans had upped the quotas a few days ago. His team used to include some of the best squads in the city, now they lagged behind at the worst possible time. He knew it was because of the growing resistance in the city. He'd initially been happy to see increased German police supporting them but then found it made his job harder, as the Dutch population seemed more willing to hide Jews in their homes.

There was a knock on the door, and he looked up to see Hans' familiar face. His former partner had grown with him and led one of the squads. It was hardly a surprise that Hans' squad was one of the best-performing ones. Floris had taught him well.

"You have a visitor," Hans announced. "It's Greta."

Floris sat up in his chair. This was a welcome surprise—she was exactly the person he needed now. "Send her in."

A petite woman in her early forties shuffled in. She fumbled with her hands, and Floris told her to close the door. "Have a seat," he said as he repositioned himself, leaning forward on his desk. As Greta sat down, he noticed her fingernails were bitten short. *Disgusting habit.* "Haven't seen you here for a while," Floris said, his tone casual. "Weren't you supposed to report in last week? Or did I miss you?" He knew he hadn't.

She cast her eyes downward, suddenly very interested in the small cracks lining the wood of Floris's desk. Then, without looking up, she said, "I'm sorry. I forgot all about last week. I just remembered last night, and I came down here right away."

She looked distraught, and he almost pitied her. "Forget about it. Just don't let it happen again." The relief on her face was palpable, and he continued. "So, tell me you have some good news. I could use some."

Her eyes shot up, and the worry was back. *Not a good sign.* "I ... I ... I don't have any new names."

Floris cursed and stood up. "Then why are you here?"

"I thought you'd be angry about last week, so I thought I should at least come in and explain what happened. I want you to know I'm still useful."

"What use are you if you don't give me any leads? I need addresses, Greta! This is the second time you've come in empty handed. Do I need to remind you what happens to people who are no longer useful?"

She turned pale. "I know. Please don't send me to Westerbork," she whispered.

Floris considered arresting her right there on the spot. It would be easy, and he'd add another number to his quota. But he hesitated —Greta had been one of his most valuable informants. As a nurse, people still came to her when something went wrong. Even people in hiding would reach out to her, believing they could trust her to take care of them. She certainly did take care of them, by passing their whereabouts on to Floris. The small, unassuming lady sitting opposite him was responsible for at least seventy—maybe a hundred—of his arrests. Sending her off now was too soon.

"All right, but you're stretching my patience. I expect you back here in two days, and it better not be empty handed. You're not playing me, are you, Greta?"

She shook her head furiously. "Of course not, no, no! It's just that I haven't had that many people reach out to me recently. But I'll ask around. I'll bring you more names."

Floris believed her. She was a shrewd woman, and she also knew he was the only reason she was still in Amsterdam. He nodded slowly, and in a soothing voice said, "All right, all right. Well, go on then, make sure you don't force me into a difficult decision." He dismissed her with a wave, and she stood up, quickly making her way to the door. As she turned the handle, Floris said, "Oh, and Greta. Don't even think about running or going into hiding. I'll find you, and when I do, you'll wish you'd been sent to Westerbork. I don't take betrayal lightly." He was pleased to see the fear in her eyes. "But I'm sure we won't have any issues. Now go." He turned his attention back to the paperwork on his desk as she left, softly closing the door.

Floris worked for about an hour, until there was another knock. Hans again. "Did you hear about the raid last night? The one on Herengracht?"

Floris nodded, feeling a pang of annoyance. It hadn't been one of his squads making the arrests. "Didn't they find two families hiding in the cellar?"

"They did, but the best news is that the people hosting them were also arrested. I just heard they're also being taken to Westerbork."

That surprised Floris. "That seems quite harsh. Weren't they regular Dutch people? Couldn't have been Jews."

"They found documents linking them to the Communist Party,"

Hans said with a grin. "Can you imagine that? Hiding Jews and part the CP."

"It's not that uncommon. We were probably lucky they kept evidence in their home. Was that what you came here for?"

"Well, I wondered if you were interested in inspecting the house? It's been barricaded off by the SD, but I don't think anyone from the Bureau has been there yet. Might be interesting to take a look?" Hans's eyes sparkled with greed.

"No one's been there yet?" Floris practically jumped out of his chair and grabbed his coat. "We better make our way over there, just to be sure everything's been documented correctly." Together, they hurried through the hallway and onto the street.

———

The Herengracht was a short fifteen-minute walk and located in one of the more upscale parts of the city. As they approached the house, Floris was surprised no one had decided to pay it a visit yet. It was one of the larger houses—a traditional canal house of four stories, with large windows and a distinctive neck gable—and Floris spotted the notice on the front door: "Entry prohibited, by order of the Sicherheitsdienst." He tried the door handle, which didn't budge. They walked around the house and found the back door locked as well. He looked to Hans, who'd already taken out his lockpick.

It took him less than a minute to force the lock, and they stepped into the back parlor. Everything looked neat and tidy; there was no evidence the people living here had been evicted last night. *They probably didn't have much time to react.* Floris knew the SD were efficient with their raids, overpowering the people inside, weapons drawn. That was usually enough for even the bravest of men to lift their hands and go willingly.

"Do you want to check upstairs?" Hans asked. "I'll look around here and the basement, although I doubt we'll find much there."

Floris nodded, already in the narrow hallway. Even though the house was spacious, the hallway was cramped, which was quite common for these houses. When they were built, the city charged only for the land. It resulted in the houses being built high and narrow. He looked at the open cellar door and considered going down—it was often interesting to see how those Jews in hiding lived. He tried the light switch, but nothing happened. He flicked it again, but all remained dark. Finally, he decided he didn't want to risk breaking his neck on the dark stairs and headed upstairs instead.

The second floor had four rooms, and he tried the first, which appeared to be the master bedroom. It was richly furnished, and the bed was immaculately made. Floris eyed a large cabinet in the corner and opened the door. It was filled with neat piles of clothes. He removed the first stack, and then another. To his disappointment, there was nothing there. Undeterred, Floris continued emptying the cabinet, including the drawers.

As he rummaged through the socks, he found a small wooden box in the back of the drawer. He smiled as he picked it up: it was remarkably heavy for its size. He tried opening it but found it locked. *That won't be a problem.* "Hans!" he shouted.

He heard footsteps on the stairs, and Hans entered the room a few seconds later. His eyes shot to the lockbox in Floris's hands. "Need me to open something?"

"I was considering just breaking it, but that might leave a mess, so why don't you give it a shot first?"

Hans already had his lockpick out and fumbled with the small lock. He kept his ear close, and Floris held his breath. Then, after a few minutes, there was a faint click, and Hans handed him the box.

Floris felt a tingle of excitement as he opened the little box. There was a piece of crumpled paper on top, which he quickly removed. What he saw next made his heart beat faster.

"Are those—" Hans cleared his throat. "Are those what I think they are?"

Floris carefully picked one of the shining objects from the box and held it to the light. "If I'm not mistaken, these are diamonds," he said as the gem reflected in the sunlight, spreading small beams of blue and red on Floris' hands. He placed it back into the box with the rest of the half dozen gems. He looked to Hans, who appeared mesmerized.

"How much do you think these are worth?" he asked.

Floris carefully closed the box. "I have no idea. But it must be hundreds, if not thousands of Reichsmarks. Much more than what we earn hunting Jews." He placed the small box in his jacket pocket. "Let's see if we can find some more stuff. We'll split these a little later."

They spent another half hour turning the house inside out. Other than some cash, the other rooms had little of value, but Floris wasn't too concerned. The diamonds—because he was sure that's what they were—were worth many times more than what they found in other houses.

He met Hans in the kitchen, where they placed their loot on the counter. Floris divided the banknotes and coins evenly. Even though he was Hans' superior now, he made sure whenever they found something, they always split it down the middle. It was the best way to keep Hans motivated and—more importantly—to make sure he didn't talk.

Floris then took out the small box, opened it, and put the diamonds on the table. As he looked at the little stones, he noted he'd miscounted earlier. There were seven gems.

"Why don't you take four, and I'll take three," Hans said, making the decision easy.

Floris slid three of the smaller diamonds to Hans, who eagerly scooped them up. Floris put his own gems in the inside pocket of his jacket. Then, he headed for the door. "Let's go back to the station. It's still early, maybe we can hit another address today."

In his rush to leave, Floris opened the front door and stepped into the street. Hans followed, and after he closed the door behind him, they turned to see two men in green uniforms heading in their direction, only a few meters away. *Shit.*

He had only a split second to make a decision, and he decided to play it cool. *Perhaps they won't look at the house.* He walked toward the men, nodding at them as they passed each other. He heard Hans mumble something in German, and he held his breath as he focused on the sound of the SD officers' boots behind him. As he controlled his urge to up his pace, the men paused, spoke to each other, and then said, "Halt, you two!"

Floris felt the tension in his shoulders increase as he slowly turned around, keeping his facial expression as neutral as possible. "Yes?" he asked sheepishly.

The Germans stood in front of the house, the tallest one pointing at the door. "Didn't you just come out of here?"

For a second, Floris considered denying it, but lying would only make things worse. He arched his back and nodded, slowly returning to the Germans. "Yes, we were. My colleague and I work for the Bureau, and we were just inspecting if everything was documented correctly. The Jews in this house were taken away last night, and we heard things were a bit rushed."

Hans stood next to him, nodding but not saying anything.

The Germans looked skeptical as they read the message plastered onto the door. "We heard nothing about this being done in a rush. In fact," he said as a grin appeared on his face, "I was part of this raid. Your people were here as well. Let's see some papers."

Floris cursed inwardly. *Just my luck. Stay calm.* He handed his papers to the tall German, who took his time going through them. Floris knew the man needed no more than a few seconds to verify he was indeed who he said he was. He wondered why he was making such a fuss—they were on the same side.

The German handed his papers back to him, then crossed his arms. "So, you and I both know yesterday's raid was executed perfectly. I'm sure you've read the reports, considering your position at the Bureau." Floris said nothing, and the man continued. "We documented everything, we took those people to the Schouwburg, and some of my colleagues sealed the house." He pointed at the piece of paper on the front door. "So my question is, What are you doing here the day after, when there's nothing left to do?"

Floris' mind raced as he considered his response. He'd never been caught before, and surely he could talk his way out of this. "I like to inspect the houses after arrests have been made, just to ensure everything is in order and we didn't miss anything."

The German's eyebrows shot up. "Missed anything? What, more people hiding?" His tone had turned, and Floris found the back of his neck burning. *Something's off.*

"We've often found documents after the initial arrests, evidence that allows us to find even more people in other locations. I like to be thorough." He hoped he sounded more convincing than he felt.

"And did you find anything interesting?"

"Unfortunately, no. Yesterday's squad did a great job."

"Hmm." The SD officer looked to his colleague, who shrugged, bored by the situation. Floris kept quiet, glancing at Hans. His face was a few shades paler than usual. The German turned back to Floris.

"Here's what I think is going on. I don't think you were looking for documents or evidence at all. Sure, it would be nice if you found something that would make it easier to explain why you were in here. But when you stepped out just now, I saw something on your face. On both your faces, actually. You were excited. I think you were in there to steal whatever you could." Floris opened his mouth, but the German raised his hand, cutting him off. "You know you're stealing from the Reich, right? And that's a crime." The man took out a notepad. "Let's have your papers again."

Floris looked at the German. His face was impassive, and for once, he was unsure what the man wanted. Then a thought struck him. *He wants the same as everyone else.* Not making a move for his papers, Floris took a step closer to the German.

"Say, what would it take to keep this between the four of us?" He reached into his back pocket and took out a stack of banknotes and nodded to Hans, who did the same. "How about we split these four ways? It wasn't a bad haul in there."

The German's expression didn't change, and they stood for a few seconds. The tall man looked at the crumpled notes and wrinkled his nose. "Name. Papers. Now!"

Floris reluctantly handed over his papers, as did Hans. He waited while the man took down his details, and turned to leave as the German handed back his papers, but the man stopped him. "I'll take that from you and place it into evidence." He pointed at the money in Floris and Hans' hands.

Floris' eyes went between the man's face and outstretched hand. He then realized the money was irrelevant. The German hadn't asked to search him, and he still had the most valuable items in his jacket. He feigned annoyance as he handed the notes to the SD man. Hans did the same and Floris couldn't resist saying, "How do I know you won't keep this yourself?"

"You don't," the man answered dryly before turning away. "You'll be hearing from us. We don't like corrupt police officers." He emphasized the last two words.

Floris and Hans stood in the middle of the street as the Germans walked off and turned the corner.

"Is this going to be a problem?" Hans said, his voice uneven.

Poor Hans. "Are you joking? Do you think anyone at the Bureau cares about a little bit of money? This happens every day. Besides, we're the best Jew hunters in the city." He slapped Hans on the back and took a few steps. "Come on, don't worry about it."

"I hope you're right," Hans said, a bit of color returning to his face.

"Hans, they took a little bit of money." He patted his chest. "Remember what we're carrying?" He laughed. "If they'd found those gems, we'd be in trouble. Instead, we're rich!"

As they returned to the Bureau, Floris had mixed feelings. Even though he didn't want Hans to know, he did worry about the SD men reporting them; it wouldn't look good. On the other hand, he knew he had plenty of credit with the station chief, and he wasn't too worried about the money they'd taken. He knew all his colleagues did the same, given a chance.

One of his squad leaders approached him as he walked toward his office. "Floris, one of your people was just in here. That Jewish lady."

"Greta?" Floris perked up, surprised.

He handed him a note. "That's the one. She told me to give you this. Said it was important."

As Floris read the note, he felt his heart beat faster, the corner of his mouth turning into a smile. Greta hadn't wasted time. He snapped his fingers. "Gather your squad. We've got some Jews to surprise."

CHAPTER TWENTY-TWO

Nora crossed onto the Plantage Middellaan, staying close to the side of the houses lining the slippery street. The sky was gray, the clouds threatening to release more sleet and snow. She wore her sturdy boots—hardly aesthetically pleasing but functional for this weather.

The Hollandsche Schouwburg building was only a hundred meters ahead, and her heart was in her throat. She pulled her coat a little tighter. She was allowed to be here, a Dutch Christian, midafternoon.

She scanned the street ahead, counting four SS soldiers guarding the entrance to the Schouwburg. The old theater still looked as imposing as always, its white-pillared facade contrasting sharply with the dark uniforms of the men standing guard. Nora had heard the stories of what happened inside the building. Floris had often escorted people there as they prepared to ship them off to Westerbork. He'd told her how the main hall had been changed from a majestic arena—where the Jewish community organized impressive plays and ballet shows only a year ago—to a depressing, overcrowded room with too little space for the hundreds, sometimes thousands of souls awaiting a fate unknown.

Nora shivered at the thought as she passed the SS soldiers. She could feel them leering at her but kept her gaze on the pavement ahead. Looking over her shoulder, to make sure the street was clear, she crossed quickly. She held her breath, waiting for one of the soldiers to call out, but it remained quiet. She glanced back and saw they now stood talking amongst themselves, one of them lighting a cigarette. *Keep going, Nora.*

It was impossible to miss the crèche. Even though the windows were blacked out, a trickle of light spilled through, as did the sound of high-pitched voices. Nora's heart surged as she thought of the children inside. She was surprised the front door was unguarded— surely the Germans would've thought to place someone here? She knocked, again expecting an SS soldier to appear.

Instead, the door was opened by a woman around Nora's age. She held a tiny baby in her arms, quickly looked Nora up and down, then opened the door wider. "Come in."

Nora stepped inside as the woman hastily closed the door. It was a lot warmer than she expected. A group of three boys bounded out from one of the open doorways farther down the hall to come running toward her. "Are you coming to visit us?" "Who are you?" "You are pretty!" They shouted simultaneously, their faces flushed, excitement in their voices.

"Boys, calm down! That is no way to treat a guest," the woman holding the baby said, her voice stern but her face friendly. The boys pulled faces and then turned around, running back from where they came. Nora looked at her and smiled. "You certainly have a way with them."

"They're sweethearts," she said, switching the baby to her other arm. "Well, most of them anyway. And you can imagine their excitement when someone other than the SS comes into the building. A woman coming in here is usually a good sign." There was a thin smile on her lips. "You must be here for Henriëtte. Follow me."

They walked down the long corridor, and Nora wasn't surprised to see all the doors open. Children of all ages filled the rooms; the babies were in a nursery lined with cribs, where young women spoke soothing words to the children. In other rooms, older children played on the ground or sat at little desks, quietly drawing but looking content.

"They all seem so happy to be here," Nora said as she and the young woman mounted the stairs at the end of the hallway.

"We try to look after them as well as we can," she said without looking back. "It's not easy for them. Most of these children were lifted from their beds by the SS or Gestapo in the middle of the night. When they arrived here, their parents were taken to the Schouwburg across the street, while they were brought to us. They were the lucky ones."

They reached the top of the stairs, the sound of the first floor ebbing away. The woman noticed Nora looking around. "Only the babies sleep downstairs. The other children have their beds up here. And we have a few offices here, which makes this a real calm place during the day." She knocked on the door closest to the stairs. There was a muffled response, and she opened it, holding it for Nora, her eyes inviting her in.

Nora entered a small office, and the door softly closed behind her.

"Welcome, please sit," said the woman who stood behind a narrow desk, waving her to the only other chair in the room. As Nora sat, she noticed the room, unlike the rest of the crèche, was brightly lit but without any windows—there was no need to blackout her workspace.

"I'm glad you came." The woman appeared to be in her late sixties, a simple black dress accentuating her gray hair and pale face. Her eyes shone brightly as she inspected Nora. "You never know if people will show up. You wouldn't be the first one to get cold feet." She sat down and clasped her hands, placing them on the neat desk in front of her. There wasn't a stray piece of paper on her desk.

Behind her stood a large filing cabinet. Everything looked incredibly organized.

"My name is Henriëtte Pimentel, and I've been running this crèche for over fifteen years," she said proudly. "I was here well before those boys in green took over, and I'll be here when they leave."

Nora smiled. She knew all about Mrs. Pimentel. Everybody in Amsterdam knew about the woman who ran the—now exclusively Jewish—crèche across from the Schouwburg. "I'm Nora, and I'm honored to meet you, Mrs. Pimentel."

"Oh, please, call me Henriëtte, like everybody else," she said, waving her hand. "There is no need for formalities here."

"All right, Henriëtte." Nora fumbled with her hands, not sure how to proceed.

"How much of what we do around here do you know?" the older woman asked, unclasping her hands, resting her palms upon the table. Nora felt her anxiety flow away and repeated what Christiaan had told her a few days ago. As she spoke, Henriëtte listened attentively, her eyes never leaving Nora's, occasionally nodding. When she finished, Henriëtte's eyes twinkled, but her face remained serious. She waited a few seconds before asking, "And you have no children of your own?"

Nora winced but swallowed hard as she shook her head. "My husband and I have tried for years, but I've come to accept it's probably never going to happen. That's why I want to help you and the children here. I don't know what it feels like to lose a child, but I certainly know how it feels to have no child."

Henriëtte looked at her for a moment, and Nora thought she saw compassion in her eyes. "I don't doubt that you want to help. Anyone who comes here does. But I'm not sure you realize how dangerous this work is. You saw the children on your way in, right?" She didn't wait for an answer. "The babies are the hardest to lose. Can you imagine what will happen if they're put on the transport trains to the east? Those journeys can take days, weeks sometimes." Henriëtte paused for a moment, the unspoken horror in the air. "The older children have a better chance of surviving, and their parents don't always want to leave them with us. It's not easy to convince the parents in the Schouwburg to leave without their children. Some still believe, or want to believe, they are going to work camps." She shook her head. "I've heard enough to know there are none."

Nora leaned forward and placed her hands on the desk. "So, what can I do?"

Henriëtte looked up, her eyes glistening a little. "You said you signed up for this because you want to save the children. Are you sure that's the only reason?"

Nora felt a flash of heat in the back of her neck and frowned. "What do you mean?"

"You said you've been trying to get pregnant for years but you've accepted it won't happen." Henriëtte's eyes were inquisitive but not unfriendly. She looked genuinely interested. "Does your husband feel the same way?"

Nora shifted in her seat. "It's something we've learned to live with," she said without conviction. Henriëtte's eyes stayed fixed on her, urging her on. "We both had trouble accepting it, him perhaps even more so than me, but we've moved past it." She opened her palms on the desk. "I'm here to help with whatever you need me to do. You're trying to save as many children from the trains as possible, and I want to do my bit."

Henriëtte looked at her for a few seconds, and an awkward silence hung in the air. "You've been with the resistance for a few months now, right?" she finally asked, continuing as Nora nodded. "Tell me why you decided to join back then. It wasn't about the children."

Nora thought for a moment. She joined because Christiaan had asked her, right? Then she saw Floris, and she knew Christiaan wasn't the real reason. She looked Henriëtte in the eye as she answered. "I joined because I could no longer look away from what was happening to our country." She told her about what she'd seen during the February Strike, and the older woman flinched at the mention of the boys on the bicycles struck down by German bullets. "When that happened, I looked for our own people. Our police. They were nowhere. That's when I knew the people we trusted to protect us were no longer there. I'm sure many of them aren't even on our side anymore. They're working with the Nazis, as part of the Sicherheitsdienst, or even the Gestapo." She cast her eyes downward, her voice down to a whisper. "I've seen it with my own eyes. That's when I decided I needed to do something, to fight back."

Henriëtte nodded. "I understand. You know, Nora, it takes a special person to do what you did. Most people choose the safe option, to stand back, keep their heads down, and hope everything will pass them by." She smiled as she stood up. "There's one thing I'm curious about."

"What's that?"

"Why didn't you tell me your husband is an NSB police officer?"

Nora's knees felt weak as she struggled for a response. She opened her mouth, but no words came. Henriëtte held up a hand, and spoke in a soothing tone. "Don't worry. I'm not offended. I just make it my business to know everything I can about the girls that work for me."

"So you knew, but you still invited me?" Nora asked, slowly recovering from the shock.

"Of course. I have to admit I was surprised to hear the wife of an NSB man was working with the resistance, but the people who recommended you only had good things to say."

"He's the reason I joined the resistance," Nora heard herself say.

Henriëtte smiled. "Of course he is. I suspected as much. I just wanted to hear it from you." She moved from her desk to the door. "Come, let me show you around. You need to know what you'll be doing in a few days."

Nora stood up, surprised. "A few days?"

"Of course, there is no time to lose." Henriëtte opened the door. "Don't worry. You'll be ready. You already are."

CHAPTER TWENTY-THREE

F our days later, Nora was back at the crèche. This was her third visit. After meeting Henriëtte, she returned the next day to meet some of the children. Talking to them had been both difficult and hopeful. None of them had been there for longer than two weeks, and the older ones spoke of the children that had left. Nora had been elated to hear some of them got out through the back, smuggled away from the trucks waiting outside the front door to take them to the eastbound death trains. But despite those successes, they couldn't save them all. It would be too suspicious. The women running the orphanage told Nora to never make any promises to the children and never get too attached.

When she left that day, she cried on the way home. She knew it would be impossible not to bond with the little ones running around, even if she was only there for a short time. Henriëtte told her that her visits from now on would be brief, just long enough to take the children away from the crèche.

Her hands were shaking as she passed the SS guard in front of the building. Henriëtte had told her to ignore him and only talk to him if he asked any questions. It would be better if he didn't remember her.

Much to her relief, the man was too preoccupied with a book, his eyes glued to the pages. *This is probably not the most exciting assignment for him.*

She entered the long hallway and made her way to the back. She nodded as she passed two other women escorting a group of children upstairs. It was almost seven in the evening, and they would be putting the children to bed.

Nora knocked and opened the door into a dimly lit room, where she found Henriëtte with a girl of about ten years old. The girl looked up, her big brown eyes betraying her anxiety.

"This is Nora." Henriëtte stroked the girl's long black hair. "She'll take you to the tram tonight. You can trust her, Steffie."

Nora knelt in front of the girl, smiling encouragingly as Steffie hesitantly met her eyes. "Are you ready to go on a trip?" She made an effort to sound confident, hoping the girl wouldn't pick up on her trepidation. To her relief, Steffie smiled.

"Good, then if we're all set. You have a long journey ahead of you," Henriëtte said, opening the door, the light from the hallway streaming in. Nora waited for Steffie to exit first, then followed them as Henriëtte purposefully led them down the hallway. Before long, they stood at the back door leading into the yard. A clock hung prominently above the door, and Henriëtte glanced at it before turning to Nora.

"You have seven minutes to get to the tram. Remember what I told you about crossing the road."

"Wait for another tram to arrive at the stop, then move away from the wall."

"You don't want anyone seeing you. There should be plenty of other trams passing by before yours." She turned to Steffie. "You be a good girl and listen to Nora. She's going to keep you safe. And remember what I told you about talking."

"No talking unless Nora tells me so," the girl said.

"Smart girl," Henriëtte said, stroking Steffie's head one last time before opening the door. "Now go! And good luck."

The cold December air activated all her senses as Nora stepped into the dark yard. The last time she was here had been during the day, but she remembered the layout and felt confident she would find her way. The door closed, and she turned to see Steffie standing closely behind her. She grasped the girl's hand and strode toward the dark outline of the back wall.

It only took seconds to reach the wall, which was around six feet high. She crouched down, feeling for the stool she knew was there. She felt a stab of panic when all she grasped was air but breathed a sigh of relief when she contacted the smooth wooden legs. Nora quickly put the stool upright and whispered to Steffie, "You will go first, I will give you a quick boost and then you'll climb over as quickly as you can. The ground on the other side is soft, so just drop down. You'll be fine." Steffie nodded quickly, and Nora sensed the girl was nervous. "I'll be right behind you. Just stay close to the wall."

Stepping onto the stool herself, she lifted Steffie—who was lighter than she expected—until she felt her grab onto the top, the weight easing off of her shoulders as she climbed over. She heard a soft thud on the other side, and Nora reached for the wall, quickly climbing over.

She found Steffie with her back to the wall, breathing heavily. "Well done," Nora said as she peered through the bushes. Even though winter meant most of the leaves had fallen off, the darkness of the evening meant even the bare bushes provided enough cover. Nevertheless, Nora felt anxious and restless as they waited.

The street was quiet, which was both a blessing and a curse. There was a clanging of a bell, a tram making its way around the corner, about 200 meters up the street. Nora heart's pounded in her throat, as she reached for Steffie's hand. It was clammy, just like her own. She bowed down and looked the girl in the eye. "Are you ready?" she whispered. Steffie nodded, determination in her eyes. What a brave girl.

The tram was almost at the stop, when two soldiers exited a building farther up the street. Nora's heart froze as the tram came to a creaking halt. The men chatted as they walked at a brisk pace, oblivious to their surroundings. They neared the tram as its doors opened. *Come on, just a bit closer.* Nora wished for the men to walk a bit faster, and then they disappeared from sight, the tram blocking their view. *Now!* In a flash, Nora got up, relieved to feel Steffie doing the same as they stumbled through the bushes. The small branches cut at her coat, but she didn't care. Within seconds, they were on the sidewalk and hurrying away, determined to put as much space between the bushes and them as possible.

The tram clanged its bell and pulled away from the stop. Nora held her breath—she needed to cross the street toward the stop in full sight of the soldiers. Even though there was no reason for them to be suspicious, she felt conspicuous just by being on the street, escorting a young child that wasn't hers.

As the tram cleared the stop and Nora crossed the street, the two soldiers came back into view. Nora's mouth felt dry as she made an effort to keep her pace steady and her stride confident. *There is no reason for them to stop me.*

She reached the tram stop in the middle of the street, watching the men in uniforms from the corner of her eye. They seemed as uninterested as earlier, and she relaxed a little. She glanced at Steffie, who looked back at her with big eyes. "Did we do okay?" she asked in a small voice.

Nora smiled and nodded. "You did really well, Steffie. Now we just need to wait for our tram. It should be here any minute now."

"Do you know where I'm going?" the girl asked.

"I'm sorry, I don't. They don't tell me everything, either. I just know where we're going now, and then there will be someone waiting for you."

The girl looked thoughtful, as if pondering her next question. Finally, she opened her mouth, but another voice interrupted.

"Good evening ladies; a bit late to be out, isn't it?" *A German voice.*

Nora froze as a jolt of panic shot through her body. Catching herself, she turned to look up into the face of a young man wearing the green uniform of the Sicherheitsdienst. The two lightning-strike-shaped *S*'s on his collar were enough to make her blood run cold. Yet, looking at his face, she didn't feel threatened. Instead of the stern faces she was used to, this man looked at her with an open expression—friendly, even.

"Where are you headed, young lady?" The tone of his voice was a little smoother now, his eyes twinkling.

"Home, officer," Nora said, pulling Steffie closer to her and stroking her hair. "Just waiting for the tram."

The man looked at Steffie, then back at Nora. "Not the best night to be out, right?" He held up his hand, catching raindrops Nora hadn't even noticed.

She nodded. "She was with her grandparents today, I came to pick her up." She pointed down the street. "They live a few streets over."

The man didn't follow her gesture, keeping his eyes on her instead. "Is she your daughter?"

Nora shook her head. "She's my niece. I'm looking after her this week. Her parents are traveling to Germany on business." She held her breath. She could still keep up the facade if he asked her for her papers, but he might have more questions. *What is keeping that tram?*

The man studied her face for a few seconds and then smiled. "Very well! I was surprised that a young woman like yourself would already have such a big daughter." He took a step toward Steffie and gently ruffled her hair. Nora had her hand on the girl's shoulder and felt her tense. Returning his attention to Nora, the smile still on his face, he said, "Would you mind if I asked you a bold question?"

"Of course," she said, faking enthusiasm. *Where is this going?*

"I would like to invite you to dinner sometime." He suddenly looked like the young man he was, despite the uniform. Nora could see a bit of insecurity in his eyes as his shoulders slouched in nervous anticipation.

"You know, I've never had such a proposition in the darkness of a tram stop before," she said, smiling back at him now. As she spoke the words, she heard a distinct screeching of metal and was relieved to see her tram turning the corner a few hundred meters away. "But you seem like a fine man, and I've always been impressed with a uniform."

The young German beamed back at her, his earlier insecurity vanishing with every word she spoke. "How about this Friday? I can come and pick you up."

Nora nodded, pointing at the tram pulling into the stop. "This is me. But Friday sounds great. Why don't you pick me up at five?" She gave him a fake address, which he hastily jotted down in the booklet usually used for citations.

The tram stopped, and as she moved toward the door, the German asked, "What is your name?"

She grabbed the railing by the door and put one foot on the steps, guiding Steffie up. "Juliette, and yours?"

Steffie disappeared inside the tram, and as the bell clanged, Nora hurried up the steps. Just as the doors closed, the young man said, "Max, and I'll see you this Friday, Juliette!"

Steffie had already taken her seat in the empty car, and Nora sat next to her. She was surprised there was no one else in the car but then realized it wasn't that common to be out on the streets now. Max had a point, she thought, as the rain ran down from the windows, casting a gloomy hue over the city outside.

Nora looked at Steffie, who stared out the window. She put her hand on her leg. "You're a very brave girl, Steffie. You didn't even flinch when that German touched you."

The girl shrugged. "You told me not to say anything. And he wasn't that bad, right? He's taking you to dinner."

For the first time that evening, Nora laughed out loud. "I'm not *really* going anywhere with him, Steffie! I even gave him a fake name and address. You heard that, right?"

The girl made a face. "I guess so. I mean, he seemed nice."

Nora patted Steffie's knee. "Nice enough for a German, yes. But I wouldn't go anywhere with him, don't you worry!"

They rode in silence for a few minutes as Nora counted the stops. They had quite a way to go, and Steffie appeared somewhat restless. "Are you nervous about where we're going?"

The girl nodded. "Maybe a little."

"That's okay. I often feel the same."

Steffie straightened her back and turned to Nora, looking surprised. "But you're not going anywhere. You're going home after."

"That's true, but I also don't know what will happen tomorrow. I may stay here, but I'll be thinking about you, knowing you're going to a safe place."

The girl thought about that for a while. "Do you know when I'll see my Papa and Mama again? The last time I saw them, they were on the stage."

Nora's heart ached, her throat felt dry, and when she opened her mouth, her words came out in a shaky, croaked voice. "I'm sorry, I don't. But I know that they will be thinking of you every second of every day." She cleared her throat. "And they will try to find you whenever they can." *That's not a lie.*

"I know what it means when you're on the stage," Steffie said. "It means you're taken to the train station. And from there, far away." There were tears in her eyes, but her voice was surprisingly even. "That's what the other kids said."

Nora clasped the little girl's face in her hands. "Don't listen to them. They don't know what they're talking about. I need you to promise me something, Steffie. And it's very important." The girl rubbed her eyes, then looked back at her. "When you get off this tram, you need to think only about yourself. You can't speak about your Papa and Mama anymore. You can't tell anyone you were in the crèche or that your Papa and Mama were in the Schouwburg. Do you understand?"

Steffie looked back at her, the frown and look in her eyes

betraying that she understood but needed some time to process Nora's words. "But I can't forget my Papa and Mama."

"And you don't have to. Of course, you should never forget your Papa and Mama, Steffie. But you need to keep them in the most important place in the world. Do you know where that is?" Nora put her hand on the girl's chest. "Right here, in your heart. And when you keep them there, they will always be with you, no matter what happens."

Steffie put her hand on Nora's and slowly nodded. Outside, the weather worsened as heavy raindrops pelted the windows. Inside, Nora held Steffie's hand as the girl rested her head against her chest, her rhythmic breathing soothing as the tram clattered along the tracks.

Nora closed her eyes and imagined they were somewhere else, someplace safe. Just for those precious minutes, she pretended she wouldn't have to hand Steffie to yet another stranger. She considered taking Steffie to her own home but immediately dismissed the thought. Floris was there, and to him, Steffie would be another bounty, another Jew to take off the streets. She clenched her free hand into a fist as she opened her eyes. Steffie had fallen asleep, her face serene, and Nora couldn't look away, her heart swelling as the girl tutted while readjusting her head. She thought about Steffie's future, all alone in the world. An orphan, in all but name. Nora knew what that felt like as a cold shiver ran down her spine. Nora suddenly felt angry: her parents had willingly abandoned her, leaving her in the orphanage all those years ago. Steffie's parents didn't have a choice. Nora wiped a tear from her cheek and shook her head— Steffie was not going to end up like her. The people in the north would take care of her. She would not need to be saved by a man like Floris.

They had been riding for fifteen minutes when Nora roused her. They were almost at their stop, and Steffie looked at her groggily. "Can't I stay with you? I don't want to leave you."

Nora's heart broke. She brushed the girl's hair from her eyes and said, "Where you're going is much safer than staying with me. But remember what I told you." She patted her chest. "You'll always have a place in my heart, Steffie."

Steffie smiled sadly, and Nora knew she understood. The tram slowed down, and they moved to the door.

Stepping down from the tram and into the rain, they found shelter at the tram stop. Another woman stood there, making no effort to board the tram. Then, as it pulled away, she spoke softly. "Are you ready to come with me, Steffie?"

Steffie looked back at Nora, who nodded. *Go.*

The woman took Steffie's hand, nodded at Nora, and walked into the rain, away from Nora, who followed them with her eyes until they turned into an alley. She felt a warm tear roll down her cheek as she stood alone. The dangers of being caught by the Germans weren't the most challenging part of her new job—it was letting go of sweet, gentle souls like Steffie.

CHAPTER TWENTY-FOUR

hristiaan descended the stairs to the basement, the musty air making him cough, announcing his arrival. Not that it mattered, for Lisa already stood waiting below. She threw her arms around him, making him lose his balance momentarily.

"Well, that's certainly a nice welcome," he said as he returned her embrace while finding his footing.

"I'm just glad to see you. It's been a while since you were last here." They walked to the table in the back, where her parents sat. "Any news on moving us?" Even in the dim light, he could see the anxiety in her eyes. "I think she's still pretty nervous."

Lisa was right. When Christiaan arrived earlier, Elsa had been waiting for him in the kitchen. He'd barely closed the door before she started going on about seeing Grüne Polizei patrolling the neighborhood more frequently. She was convinced they were preparing a raid, and it was only a matter of time until they broke down her front door. Christiaan sympathized with her but he needed to speak with the Abrahams first before making any decisions.

He sat at the table and cleared his throat—this wasn't going to be easy. "Lisa, have a seat, please," he said, gesturing to the stool beside him. "I did speak to the leadership, or at least, the people who make these decisions. It's not easy finding a new place, but it's even harder than I expected. That's why it took a bit longer." He paused, and the Abrahams looked back at him nervously. "We have so many people looking for a place to hide that some homes are now hiding several families in the same space you're in. There's hardly any privacy."

"We don't mind," Antonius interrupted, sitting slightly straighter. "We don't care about privacy or comfort. We just want to be safe."

Christiaan listened patiently before responding. "I know, but just moving you is risky, and that's what the people in charge said." He saw Lisa's face drop and quickly continued. "However, I made it very clear that keeping you here is even more dangerous. I believe Elsa, even though she might be imagining some things." If the Grüne Polizei were in the neighborhood to raid her home, they would've done so already, but he agreed suspicious neighbors were a problem. "And I convinced them you should be moved."

A nervous smile spread across Lisa's face. "That's great, Christiaan! Where are we going? And when?"

He shifted in his seat. "Well, that's the thing. You're not going to the same place. We need to split you up."

"Split up how?" Antonius asked.

"At first, they wanted to place the three of you at different addresses, staying with other families. I told them that should be the last resort. So you and Mary will stay together, and Lisa will go to an address on her own. I'm sorry."

There was a silence as Antonius looked resigned, Mary relieved and worried. Christiaan studied Lisa, who had an odd expression on her face—her eyes were unfocused, but the corners of her mouth were slightly raised, as if she were smiling, albeit faintly.

"What do you think?" Antonius asked no one in particular as his eyes went between Lisa and Mary.

It was his wife who spoke first. "I'm thankful for what you've done, Christiaan. I'm sure it wasn't easy. Unfortunately, I don't think we have much choice. We simply have to do this."

Lisa spoke up, her voice firm. "I agree. And it's important that Papa and Mama can stay together. I'll be fine wherever you take me, Christiaan." She looked at him with affection. "You'll still look after me, right?"

He nodded. "Yes, in fact, you're going to be staying with a good friend of mine." He turned to Lisa's parents. "I'm sorry. I can't tell you where she'll be for obvious reasons." They both nodded; they understood.

"So, when are we moving?" Antonius asked.

"You'll be leaving tomorrow. Lisa, you'll need to get your things packed. I'm taking you to the new place now." When he saw the shock on her face, he continued. "It's New Year's Day, and the streets are deserted. I didn't run into a single patrol or checkpoint on the way over. There's no safer time than now."

"Okay." Lisa stood up and walked to her bed, where she kept her things.

"Pack light, no more than a small backpack. We don't want to give anyone an excuse to stop us."

Mary moved to Lisa's corner and started helping her pack, leaving Christiaan with Antonius.

"Are you sure we'll be safe at the new addresses? Will Lisa be safe?"

"Lisa is going to be in the best place possible. She won't have to share the space with anyone. It won't be the most comfortable place, but she'll be safe. I've known the person she's staying with for many years, and I wouldn't want anyone else looking after her."

Antonius visibly relaxed as he listened. "That's all I wanted to know. I know we've never said this before, but we know we've been fortunate to have you as the person bringing us food coupons." He looked to Lisa and Mary, who were almost done packing. "And Lisa cares for you. I've seen how she responds when you come to visit, even if it's just for a few minutes. It's the highlight of her week, it lifts her mood and ours until well after you've left." Christiaan felt himself blush and was grateful for the bad lighting in the basement. Antonius wasn't done yet. "And from what I've seen, you feel the same way. I may not know you very well, but I see the way you look at her, the way you talk to her, and I know that's not how you talk to other girls. At least, I don't think so."

"I do care for Lisa, Mr. Abrahams," Christiaan said. "Just like I care for you and Mary."

Antonius' eyes narrowed, and he leaned a little closer. "You're not fooling anyone, Christiaan. Just take good care of my daughter. Keep her safe. That's all I'm asking."

"I think I've got everything I need." Lisa stood next to them, looking down. Mary stood next to her, her eyes a little swollen. *Poor woman.*

Christiaan decided not to make the farewell more painful and stood up. "I'll give you some time. I'll be upstairs."

As he mounted the stairs, he could hear the family crying. Their future had just become even more uncertain.

———

Ten minutes later, Christiaan and Lisa stepped onto Wilhelmina Street. Elsa had been surprised to see Lisa and her small bag come out of the basement at that hour—it was only three in the afternoon. Not to arouse any suspicion, Christiaan decided they would leave through the front door, but not before Elsa checked if the neighbors were watching.

Lisa took a deep breath. This was the first time in months she'd breathed fresh air.

"How does it feel?" he asked, gently nudging her down the street, wanting to put some distance between them and her old hiding place.

Lisa's eyes shot around, taking in the sights of the street. "A bit odd, to be honest. I can't remember the last time I've been outside, and Elsa's yard doesn't count." She peeked through some of the windows of the houses and shops. "Where are we going?"

Christiaan enjoyed watching her as they walked. There was a slight drizzle, and the street was deserted. He made a decision. "We still have a bit of time before it gets dark. Why don't we take a slight detour?"

"Are you sure?"

"Follow me."

It was only a few minutes until they reached their destination, and as soon as he saw Lisa's face as they entered Vondel Park, he knew their small detour was worth it. Only a handful of other couples were braving the cold, wet weather, and Christiaan and Lisa fit right in. They walked in silence as they passed the Melkhuis, a quaint restaurant that would be packed if it wasn't for the war. Now, it was deserted, apart from a scattering of people seeking shelter from the rain under the overhanging roof as they passed a flask between them.

"You see, people will find a way to enjoy life," Lisa said as she pointed at them. "It's the little things, right?"

Christiaan marveled at her optimism. "You've just spent the past five months in a basement."

"For all I know, those people are also helping us, giving some of their rations to people in hiding, stealing coupons, or even doing what you do," she said, lowering her voice as she finished her sentence. "I like to see the good in people. And you, Christiaan, have certainly given me plenty of opportunities to do just that." She took his arm and hooked it through hers. A warm glow radiated through Christiaan's body. He looked at her and had to admit Antonius may have a point. *Maybe I am only trying to fool myself.* For now, he enjoyed listening to Lisa as they walked through the park. Despite everything that had happened to her, she remained optimistic. He wasn't sure he could've done the same.

"So, where are we going next?" she asked as they made their way toward the park's eastern exit.

They stepped back onto the street, and Christiaan considered taking a tram. It was quite a trek to the new address, and dusk was setting in, the weak sun struggling to break through the clouds. Then again, he didn't mind having some extra time with Lisa, and it would only take them about an hour to get there. They would arrive well before the eight o'clock curfew, leaving him time to spare to get home.

"You're going to stay on the Zeedijk with a friend of mine."

Lisa looked surprised. "Really? Isn't that a bit of a rough area?"

"Rough?" Christiaan laughed. "I'm not sure that's a bad thing, considering your situation."

"No, I mean, there are a lot of bars, right? I'd expect there to be a lot of soldiers and police officers there. They'd be the only ones still able to afford places like that, right?"

"You're not completely wrong, although many of the bars are trying to accommodate normal Amsterdammers with jobs. For some people, it's still possible to go for a drink once in a while."

"Can you?" she asked somewhat mischievously.

He looked at her, pretending to be offended. "Me, a tram driver? Of course, I go there all the time!" They both smiled, and he continued. "But seriously, it's a great place to hide. You're literally under their noses, and the bar owner is a dear friend. She will make sure nothing happens to you."

"She?" Lisa seemed surprised. "Don't know many female barkeepers, let alone owners."

"You'll like her, I promise."

It took them a little under an hour to make it to the Zeedijk, where it was just as quiet as the rest of the city. Most of the bars were closed for the holidays, and they arrived at number 63 without a hitch.

"Cafe 't Mandje?" Lisa asked. "I've never heard of this place."

"In your words, this is probably the roughest place you'll find on this street. To be honest, the fact you don't know about it is somewhat of a relief," Christiaan said playfully. "Come, let me introduce you to Bet."

He opened the door to the familiar scent of stale beer and cigarette smoke. The bar was dimly lit, and a jukebox softly played Dutch music in the corner. Apart from the heavyset woman with blond hair behind the bar, the place was empty. She looked up as they approached, a cigarette dangling loosely from the corner of her mouth.

"Ahhh, master Brouwer! So glad to finally see you," she said, her gravelly voice suggested this wasn't her first cigarette. "I was getting a little worried. Didn't you say you'd be here around four? It's almost five thirty, you know!"

Christiaan held up his hands. "Do you want me to lock the front door?"

"And drive away all those customers? Don't you even think about it!" She reached under the bar and produced three small glasses and, in the same motion, grabbed a bottle of jenever from the shelf behind her. She proceeded to pour three generous shots. "Is this the girl you've been talking about?" She pushed two glasses across the bar and held the other in her hand.

"Bet, please meet Lisa. Lisa, this is the legendary Bet van Beeren, proprietor of Cafe 't Mandje, the *roughest* place on the Zeedijk." He handed Lisa a glass and held up his own.

Lisa took the glass and clinked it with Bet, who winked at her. "Welcome home, Lisa. I'm glad you're here, and I'll make sure you stay out of those Krauts' claws."

The jenever made its way down Christiaan's throat with a satisfying burn, and he looked to Lisa, who seemed to spin on her legs a little. She looked at him and smiled, then put the glass on the bar with a loud clunk.

"I should get back home," Christiaan said, putting his glass next to Lisa's. "Shall I take her to the basement, Bet?"

She nodded. "I've already prepared a bed for you, Lisa. I'm going to close up here, it's not like there's any business today, and then I'll come down and show you where you can find everything. When the bar's closed, you can come upstairs."

"I really appreciate you letting me stay here," Lisa said.

"Ah, don't mention it. It's nice to have a pretty face as a room-mate!" Bet said, grinning as she waved dismissively.

Christiaan took Lisa through the small storage room in the back, where he opened a hatch to the basement, climbing down the narrow ladder first. As he did, he flicked on the light, and Lisa handed him her bag and followed him down.

"She seems like a character," Lisa said as she put her feet on the sandy ground. "I think I like her already."

"I've known Bet for years. Behind that boisterous front is one of the sweetest, most caring people I know. There is no safer place for you. She's been an incredible asset to the resistance in more ways than one." He placed her bag on a small mattress in the corner, crouching to avoid the low ceiling. "It's not the most comfortable place to be, but I promise Bet will take good care of you."

Lisa sat down on the bed and patted the spot next to her. Christiaan sat as she said, "I can't thank you enough for what you've done for my family and me. And I loved going to the park today, even if it was dangerous." She put her hand on his leg. "Please take good care of my parents tomorrow. They're nervous, even if my father won't show it."

He put his hand on hers and nodded. "I'll take them to their next address safely. And if you want me to pass along any messages, just let me know."

"Thank you." They looked into each other's eyes, and Christiaan was wishing he could stay with her like this for a bit longer when they heard footsteps near the hatch. Lisa looked alarmed for a moment until they saw Bet's face peeking through.

"Okay, the bar's closed. Christiaan, it's time for you to leave through the back door. We don't want anyone getting suspicious."

Christiaan let go of Lisa's hand. "I'll be back in a few days to let you know how things went with your parents." He stood up, but Lisa grabbed his hand and stood.

"See you soon," she said, and she leaned forward to plant a lingering kiss on his cheek.

When he had climbed up the ladder, Bet was waiting for him. She gave him a knowing look as he walked past her. He opened the back door, stepped out into the darkness of a small alley, and headed for the main street. He smiled as he thought of Antonius's words earlier today. He was no longer fooling himself.

CHAPTER TWENTY-FIVE

Floris ascended the steps in front of the Bureau and reluctantly opened the door. He entered the hallway, which was mercifully deserted. He was in a foul mood and didn't want to speak to anybody. Quickly crossing the short distance to his office without running into anyone, Floris closed the door. Today had not been a good day—those pesky Jews were getting better at hiding. The resistance had grown significantly, and they were becoming more organized. They were somehow always one step ahead of him. It was the third time he raided an empty house this week. *It's getting embarrassing.*

He plopped down in his chair and took a moment to compose himself. *Have I lost my touch?* Some of the other squads at the Bureau had better luck, quickly reaching their targets. *Perhaps I need to find some more informants.*

He looked at the clock—only three in the afternoon. Certainly too early to call it a day and have a drink. *I could use one.*

There was a quick rap on his door before Hans opened it. "The chief is on his way. He doesn't look happy. Good luck," he said before he closed the door.

Great, just what I need. The Bureau chief hardly ever intervened with Floris' work. In fact, the man was relatively hands off, as long as things went well. When he came in for a chat, it was never good news. Floris shuffled some papers on his desk as he braced himself.

The knock was firm—the chief asserting his authority even through the closed door. Floris managed a stiff "Come in," but the frame of Rudolf Dahmen von Buchholz filled the doorway before he finished speaking.

Floris hurriedly stood up and saluted Dahmen von Buchholz. The chief half-heartedly returned the salute and told him to take a seat.

"How did today's raid go, Brouwer?" he asked as he pulled up a chair. "I didn't hear anyone come in." His tone was even, but Floris saw the trace of annoyance on Dahmen von Buchholz's face.

"No one in the house, sir," Floris started. "When we got there, we found abandoned spaces in the attic. Some cooking utensils and mattresses. We were definitely in the right place, but it looked like someone tipped them off."

"Tipped them off, eh? Who would do such a thing? Are you suggesting a leak at my Bureau?" He emphasized the last words, his voice strained.

Floris needed to choose his following words carefully. "I'm not saying it's one of our agents, but this isn't the first time."

"No, I believe it's the third time for you this week. Just you, though. The other squads have no such issues." He crossed his legs and stared at Floris, his eyes boring into him.

Floris shifted in his seat, racking his brain for a response. He had no explanation, no excuses, and Dahmen von Buchholz was not a man who took failure lightly.

"You know, Brouwer, I have to say I'm a bit surprised to see this happening to your squad. You've been one of our top performers, bringing in more Jews than some of the other squads combined. But recently, you've started lagging behind. Would you like to know what I think?" Floris simply nodded as the chief repositioned himself, leaning forward, wagging his finger at Floris. "I think you've lost your hunger. You're too comfortable."

Floris opened his mouth, but Dahmen von Buchholz cut him off. "Don't pretend to be offended. We both know you've never been too strict with the rules." He raised an eyebrow. "You know what I'm referring to, right? Did you think I didn't know about your trips to the empty houses? Or that you often had other people of your squad bring in the Jews? Think I didn't notice your shiny new clothes?" He sat back, his hands clasped on his stomach.

Floris hesitated. "I'm not sure what you're suggesting, sir. I've always been fair to my squad, splitting the bounties with them, as per the Bureau policy."

To his surprise, the chief started to laugh. "I'm not talking about the bounties, Brouwer. I'm talking about the extras you confiscate after taking those people from their houses. Don't deny it. I've known about it for a long time, and you're not the only one, trust me. And you know what, I don't have a problem with it as long as you perform and nobody knows about it. But here lies the problem." He reached into his jacket and produced a sheet of paper. He unfolded it and placed it on Floris' desk.

As Floris read the words, his heart sank. It was an official citation from the Sicherheitsdienst, reporting him for theft from the Reich. It was a serious accusation, and he cursed the men who'd reported him. *They didn't have a problem taking the money off me.* He controlled the anger building up and calmly put the paper down. "I remember running into these gentlemen a few weeks ago. I didn't think they'd go through this trouble for the few banknotes we found in the house."

"Well, they did, and let's just say my German superiors were less than impressed. A few days ago, I was summoned and had to explain why my men were running around pillaging Jewish houses," Dahmen von Buchholz said, his brow furrowed. "They wanted to arrest you, but I told them I'd handle it myself. I also told them you were one of our most valuable agents, which somewhat placated them. But damn it, Brouwer, you need to perform, or I'll look like a fool!" His face had turned a light shade of red.

Despite his boss' anger, Floris suddenly felt oddly calm. The chief had defended him when it would've been easier to throw him to the wolves. Perhaps things weren't as bleak as they seemed.

The chief stood, and Floris got to his feet as well. "I need results, Brouwer. If your squad doesn't improve its numbers, I might not be able to keep the Germans away from you." He spoke clearly, wagging his finger at Floris.

"Yes, sir. I'll make sure of it. I'll reach out to some of my informants."

The chief walked to the door, shaking his head. As he grabbed the handle, he turned back. "And don't give them another excuse to complain, you hear me? I won't be able to hold them off a second time." He didn't wait for a response and stepped out, slamming the door.

Floris slowly exhaled as he sank back into his chair. He put his hands behind his head and leaned back. *What am I going to do? I need results, today.* He was still stumped about how the Jews had known about those raids. Apart from his own squad, there weren't many people who knew the details. Not even his informants knew when he would strike, and surely they wouldn't be bold enough to sabotage their own tips? He shook his head. They knew what would happen if he found out.

He sat back up. The informants. It had been nearly two weeks since he spoke to Greta. She was getting on his nerves as she had gone quiet again. *She's holding out on me.*

He jumped from the chair and grabbed his coat. He opened the door and walked to the large common room, where he found Hans hovering at a colleague's desk.

"Hans, come with me. House call."

Floris knocked on the door. "Open up, Greta, we need to talk to you!" He tapped his foot while he waited. Hans peered in through a window.

"I'm not sure anybody's home. The lights are off," Hans said.

Floris banged on the door a little louder. "She's here. Where else would she be? She's hiding, and she knows she'd better come out and talk to me."

It took another few seconds until there were footsteps on the other side of the door. Floris heard someone fumble with the lock, and then Greta appeared in the doorway. She looked at him wide eyed, the fear evident. "How can I help you, detective?"

Floris smiled. *Smart woman.* He barged past her into the small hallway of the house. Hans followed him before Greta closed the door and turned to face them. "Greta, I'm going to be honest with you. You've not been a very good informant. When was the last time you provided a useful tip?" The small woman looked terrified as Floris took a step closer, towering over her. Her shallow, quick breathing confirmed his approach was working.

"I gave you that couple two weeks ago?" she said in a shaky voice.

"Two weeks ago! If all my informants provided me with leads that often, I wouldn't be arresting anyone," Floris said, throwing his hands in the air in half-feigned frustration. "If I didn't know any better, I'd think you're playing me for a fool."

"I ... I'm really not. I was going to ..." She paused for a moment as she tried to compose herself.

"Yes? You were going to what?" Floris noted, with delight, that her hands were shaking.

She took a deep breath. "I was going to tell you about this family. They live a few streets from here. I believe they're a small family, and you could handle them between the two of you. If you want, I could take you now?"

Floris backed away from her. *This is interesting. Maybe I don't have to burn Greta after all.* "How did you find out about them? And why didn't you tell me about this before?"

She looked exasperated. "I only heard this afternoon. I was going to come to your office first thing in the morning." She put her hand on the doorknob. "Would you like me to take you there now? It's only five minutes from here."

Floris looked at Hans, who shrugged. "How big is this family? Should we get backup?"

Greta looked unsure. "I'm told there's only three of them: two women and an older man." She eyed the batons strapped to their belts.

"Let's do it," Floris said, feeling an adrenaline rush. "I don't want to miss this chance." *Or allow anyone to warn them.* "Take us there, Greta." *If she's lying, we'll take her instead.*

It took them less than five minutes to get to the address, and Floris was surprised at the size of the house. Situated in the middle of a very nice neighborhood, the resistance had connections everywhere. Dusk was setting in, and Floris could see a faint light shining behind the blacked-out windows; people were inside. He rubbed his hands in anticipation. "Do you know the quickest way into the house?"

Greta shook her head. "I've never been here before."

"What do you mean? I thought you got your tips making house calls." Floris cocked his head. "Are you sure about this?"

Her eyes darted nervously between the house and him. "The person who told me works for the people living next door. She overheard them talk about lots of comings and goings. They also said the woman living here seemed on edge, not talking to anyone and staying indoors most of the time."

Hans stood by the side of the house. "Floris, I think we can get in through the back. We could surprise them?" He pointed at a narrow alley running alongside the house.

"Come with us," Floris said to Greta, who looked uncomfortable. "You're going to wait outside. And be quiet."

They stalked through the alley—Floris' heart was beating fast. It had been a long time since he executed a raid himself. And he couldn't remember the last time he'd done one without preparation or a larger squad. But if Greta was right, and there were only three people there, he had no doubt he could handle them. The people in hiding were often weak. He put his hand on his baton. *Perhaps I'll take him out anyway, just to make sure there are no problems.* He grinned —that would definitely keep those women calm. He suddenly felt very alive; the thought of bringing in arrests hours after getting chastised by the chief was exhilarating. *If you want something done you have to do it yourself.*

They reached a rickety wooden door, and Floris put a finger to his lips before whispering, "Hans, as soon as I open this, we run for the house. If the door's locked, knock it down or break a window. I don't care, but I want to get in there quickly. They can't get away." Hans nodded, and Floris turned to Greta. "You follow us but stay out of sight. You're not going anywhere until I tell you to. You're not lying, right? Last chance."

Greta shook her head resolutely. "They're here."

"Very well. Hans?"

"Ready."

Floris pushed the wooden door, which gave way. *Good.* "Go!"

They stormed through a muddy patch of grass, heading straight for the large door at the back of the house. They reached it within seconds, and Floris saw a flickering light through a gap in the curtains. A candle. He reached for the door handle, and as he pushed it down, the door opened with a loud creak.

He pushed the curtains aside and reached for his baton as he squinted in the semidarkness of the candlelit room. At the kitchen table sat a woman smoking a cigarette. She looked at Floris with weary eyes, almost as if she'd expected him, and slowly took a large drag from her cigarette.

"Take me to them," Floris said.

CHAPTER TWENTY-SIX

I t was dark by the time Christiaan arrived at Elsa's house, and a drizzle of rain came down. This was his last stop of the evening, and he was looking forward to sharing the good news. Even though he was especially happy about taking Lisa's parents to the new address tomorrow morning, he knew Elsa would be the most relieved. When he left with Lisa the day prior, Elsa's anxiety had been tangible: she asked him why the parents couldn't go with him as well. It had taken all of his patience not to snap at her—she meant well, but the pressure was consuming her.

As he approached the house, he fingered the last of the food coupons in his jacket and had to admit he was feeling the pressure himself. He had started with a handful of houses, but he now found himself delivering the precious pieces of paper to more and more addresses each week. While he was proud of what he did—saving lives—the Germans and the Dutch police were intensifying their hunt for both Jews in hiding and the people helping them. As their organization grew, the number of arrests grew every week. Christiaan knew this came with the territory. More people working underground meant more people running their mouths to the wrong person or secret police infiltrating the organization.

He opened the gate to the yard and thought about Floris. He hadn't spoken to him in over a month, and he wasn't sure if he could control himself were he to run into him. His brother was probably preparing another raid or barging into a building of unsuspecting people at this very moment. At least recruiting Nora had paid off. Her information meant they saved dozens of people, and as far as they knew, Floris was none the wiser to the informant sleeping next to him.

Christiaan approached the back of the house, and immediately sensed something was wrong. The back door was open, but the kitchen was completely dark. He froze in place, the hairs on his neck standing up. Elsa would be in the kitchen, cooking dinner or reading one of her many worn books by candlelight, as she waited for him.

He looked up to the dark windows of the adjacent houses and considered turning back. The yard was shrouded in darkness, surely no one had seen him yet. He dismissed the thought almost as quickly —he needed to check on Elsa and the Abrahams.

A feeling of dread built in the pit of his stomach as he moved closer to the house. The open door creaked softly as the wind swung it back and forth. Christiaan cautiously stepped inside, closing the door and drawing the curtains. He strained his ears. Only the distant ticking of the clock in the living room disturbed the eerie quiet. He considered calling out for Elsa but shuffled to the hallway in silence instead, careful to avoid the loose floorboards.

There his fears were confirmed. The door to the basement was wide open, the light of the single bulb at the bottom faintly spilling out. *The Abrahams would never leave the door open, nor would Elsa.* Controlling the urge to rush to the door, his steps remained calculated but a little quicker, and as he reached the open door, he stopped and listened for any sounds downstairs. He held his breath, straining—and hoping—to hear something, but he knew it was in vain.

After counting to ten, he breathed out and stepped onto the stairs. As he slowly descended, a thought struck, and his foot froze in midair. *What if this is a trap, and they are waiting for me? It's too quiet.* He listened again, a little harder this time, trying to make out the slightest sound of someone breathing, shifting their feet. There was nothing. There was no one there. *I'm imagining things.*

He reached the bottom of the stairs and felt a mix of sadness and relief as he observed the scene. The space was empty; the table where Lisa's parents usually sat patiently waiting for him, a mess. There were two half-eaten plates, a fork, and a knife on the sandy ground next to a chair on its side. The Abrahams had been interrupted during dinner. Christiaan swallowed hard as he walked toward the table, turning a knocked-over water glass upright, the water still dripping onto the sandy basement floor. He walked to the sleeping area and saw a neatly packed bag next to one of the mattresses. *They were waiting for me. They were ready to go.* He shook his head and felt his eyes sting. *I was too late.* Whoever took them hadn't even allowed them to take their clothes.

Christiaan sat on the mattress and opened the bag. He found two sets of clothes for both Antonius and Mary. They had packed light like he told them to. He then felt something hard and pulled a small pendant and chain from the bag. It was heavier than it looked, and he held it between his fingers. As he did, he felt an engraving on the back. He held it up to the faint light, the gold glittering as he did. It read, "Mary & Antonius—2 July 1921." He clicked the small clasp on the pendant's side, revealing a black-and-white photo of a young, beautiful couple smiling for the photo in a park. On the other side, the same couple, a few years older, holding a tiny baby, beaming with pride. *Lisa.*

Christiaan suddenly felt like an intruder and closed the pendant, sliding it into his jacket. He got up and decided he needed to leave. Nora had told him Floris often came back after an arrest to do what he called securing the location. In reality, she said, he came to loot the place. Christiaan suspected his colleagues probably did the same.

He quickly went through the three drawers of the small cabinet next to the bed. He found nothing but some old clothes, and he hoped the Abrahams had hidden their other valuables somewhere else.

He mounted the stairs, taking the steps two at a time, before flicking the light off. When he reached the top, he was relieved to hear all was quiet upstairs. He made his way to the back door and peeked through a slit in the curtains. The moon now illuminated the empty yard. He took a deep breath and opened the door, half expecting a battalion of police officers to spring from the darkness. As none appeared, he hurried into the alley. As he ran from the house, there was only one place he could go.

CHAPTER TWENTY-SEVEN

L isa had her head down as Christiaan sat with his arm around her. She was shaking softly, and as he thought of something comforting to say, words failed him. So instead, he gently stroked her shoulder. After leaving Elsa's house, he headed straight for the bar, and they now sat in the basement, the low hum of music and talking people seeping in through the floor above them.

After a few minutes of silence, Lisa turned to him and cleared her throat. "What do you think happened?"

Christiaan turned to her, looking into her bloodred, swollen eyes. On his way over, he thought about how he would approach this. Entering 't Mandje, Christiaan decided to tell Lisa the truth but wasn't sure if he could bear to tell her what he thought—no, what he knew—happened to Antonius and Mary.

"From everything I saw in the house, they must've been surprised by the police, or maybe even the SD," he started reluctantly. "They knew exactly where to go: the house was in order, they didn't search. Someone told them where they were. I was too late, Lisa. I'm so sorry." He gripped her shoulder tightly as he tried to channel his guilt, this feeling of powerlessness.

She surprised him by responding evenly. "It's not your fault, Chris. We knew Elsa was getting nervous." He felt her swallow as she paused. "You were going to move them tomorrow, right?"

A day too late.

"There's no use in blaming yourself." Lisa read his mind. "You tried your best." She took and squeezed his hand. "Do you think they've taken them to the Schouwburg?"

Christiaan nodded. There was no doubt the Abrahams were taken there, or perhaps to the headquarters of the Sicherheitsdienst on Euterpe Street. He prayed it wasn't the latter, as this meant the Germans considered them interesting enough to interrogate.

He also feared for Elsa. Hiding Jews was a serious crime—she would most likely be at the SD's headquarters, an interrogation stop before being transferred to Camp Vught in the south of the country. How long would she last under the brutal SS interrogation methods before giving them enough information to lead them to him? His blood ran cold.

"What are we going to do?" Lisa said.

Christiaan wanted to tell her he could help her parents. That somehow, he could track them and liberate them from wherever they were being held. But he couldn't promise her that. His group focused on keeping people hidden. Once they were discovered and arrested, there was nothing they could do. The SS-run operation from the Schouwburg via Camp Westerbork on to the east was too well organized, too secure for them to sabotage. He shook his head. "I'll do everything to keep you safe. I can try to find out where your parents are, but I can't promise anything." In reality, even finding out where they were or where they would be taken would be difficult. As soon as the Abrahams were put on transport to transit camps Westerbork or Amersfoort, the German administration took over, and people disappeared from the Dutch records.

Lisa nodded silently, tightening her grip on his hand. Christiaan's heart ached for her, and he pulled her closer. She rested her

186

head on his shoulder as they sat in the semidarkness, listening to the people moving about above them.

Christiaan reached for his pocket. "You should see this." Lisa sat up as he pulled out the pendant, and Lisa let out a small shriek as she took it from him.

"Where did you find this?" she asked shakily, holding the piece of jewelry to the light filtering through the floor.

"Your parents had a bag packed, and I found this inside."

A tear rolled down Lisa's cheek, but she smiled as she opened the locket. She stared at the photos, her breathing irregular. After a minute, she closed it and turned to Christiaan with a grateful look. "You can't imagine how much this means to me. Thank you." She leaned forward and gently kissed him.

Christiaan pulled her closer and returned the kiss. For a moment, he forgot about all his worries as he savored the moment, the warmth of Lisa's lips radiating through his body. He would do anything he could to keep her safe. *Anything.*

Their moment was interrupted as boots stomped on the floor above them, followed by harsh commands in German. Lisa pulled away from him, fear in her eyes. His heart pounded in his throat as the comforting sounds of the bar's jukebox and clinking glasses were replaced by the shuffle of feet and panicked voices. Christiaan put a finger to his lips as he signaled for Lisa to follow him to the corner furthest from the ladder. The hatch to the basement was hidden from sight, but the Germans might be acting on another tip. He felt the blood drain from his face as he considered the possibility of the soldiers coming down. *We're trapped.*

They hid behind a stack of old barrels in the corner, and Christiaan looked up at the ceiling. Light filtered through a crack and he could see the shadows of people moving about haphazardly. The soldiers told everybody to stay where they were, but the people in the bar weren't listening.

Suddenly, the lights went out, and Christiaan and Lisa—along with the people upstairs—were shrouded in complete darkness.

Christiaan then heard the back door to the bar open as some people managed to escape.

"Turn on the lights now!" The command was unmistakable. "Nobody move!" There was the click of a gun cocking, and Christiaan held his breath.

He then heard the unmistakable sound of Bet's voice directly above them. "*Licht kaput! Licht kaput! Nicht schietzen!*" She spoke in broken German, but the message was clear: the lights are broken, don't shoot.

Christiaan knew Bet was near the stairs leading away from them. He heard boots stomping overhead, a German voice saying, "Get the lights back on, woman. We need to inspect your cafe."

"*Oben, oben*—upstairs, upstairs," Bet responded, the steps creaking as she made her way up. The German followed her, and Christiaan overheard them talking.

"Hurry up, woman, we don't have all evening," the German said.

For a minute, nothing happened, and then the lights went back on. The people in the main room were told to line up against the bar, and from what Christiaan could make out, they were being patted down.

Bet was still on the stairs, out of sight from the patrons, and Christiaan was startled by the words coming out of her mouth. "*Heil Hitler!* Glory to the Reich. I will help you find what you're looking for, but there's nothing up here. Let's not get the people over there suspicious. *Heil Hitler!*" She spoke in perfect German, and the surprise in the German soldier's voice was evident.

"I didn't know you were a supporter of the party." Even though Christiaan couldn't see him, he could hear the softer tone in the man's voice. He looked to Lisa, who appeared confused. "Say, is there anything we could help you with?"

"Sure. Schnapps!" Bet said dryly, and the German soldier laughed as he walked away.

"No problem, we'll take care of that!"

It took another fifteen minutes for the soldiers to finish

inspecting everybody's papers, and Christiaan focused on controlling his breathing to be as quiet as possible. Then, the door closed,
and everything upstairs went quiet. Christiaan heard the lock fall
into place, and the creaking of the hatch on the other side of the
basement.

"You can come out now," Bet said. "They're all gone."

Christiaan and Lisa slowly crawled from their hiding place to
find Bet climbing down the rickety ladder. When she reached the
basement floor, she flicked the light switch. She was holding a bottle
of jenever, no glasses.

"What did you do?" Lisa asked incredulously. "Did you know
those men?"

Bet smiled and shook her head. "Sometimes, you just have to
play dumb and go along with it. Looks like they bought it this time."
She handed the bottle to Christiaan. "You could use a shot."

Christiaan took the bottle and, without thinking, took a swig. He
handed it to Lisa, who did the same before passing it back to Bet.
Christiaan felt his pulse return to somewhat normal, but Lisa's face
suggested she was far from okay.

"That was much too close," she said, her face pale as a ghost's,
blinking hard as she turned to Bet. "You got rid of them this time, but
what if they return?"

Bet said nothing, looking at Christiaan instead. They had been
lucky, and there was no guarantee the next raid wouldn't be quite as
slapdash. But what was he going to do? He'd only just moved her
here. He couldn't imagine he'd be able to find her another spot.

"I don't feel safe in Amsterdam," Lisa said, almost deciding
for him.

Christiaan looked at Lisa, stood in the dim light, her pleading
eyes causing his chest to pound. He slowly nodded. "You're right. I
thought you would be safe with Bet." He turned to the barkeep
holding the bottle. "And if it wasn't for your quick thinking, she
might have been in the back of a truck now, but we can't risk it
again."

Bet nodded. "Not all those SD boys are this easy. I think you're safe for another night, at least. They raid the places around here, but never two nights in a row." She handed the bottle to Lisa, who took another sip, twisting her mouth as the strong liquor burned her throat.

"We need to find a way to get you out of here. Let me reach out to some people. They might have options," Christiaan said. He'd heard about people making their way to the north, or even down south, into Belgium. *I'll worry about the logistics later. First, I need Lisa to remain calm.* To his relief, Lisa sat down on a crate, still holding the bottle. She looked a little more relaxed, the alcohol was working.

Christiaan knelt and took her hand and looked into her eyes— there was a sparkle of hope. "Stay put, Lisa. Give me a bit of time. I'll be back as soon as I can. Bet will look after you until then."

"All right," she said, the look on her face changing into something more determined as she clenched her jaw. "I know you'll find a way. You always have." She leaned forward and kissed Christiaan's forehead.

He got up and turned to Bet. She simply nodded, and he knew he could count on her. "I'll be back before you know it." He headed for the hatch, grabbed the ladder, and looked back one more time. Lisa and Bet's eyes were on him, and he made an effort to give them the most encouraging, confident smile that he could. Then, he climbed up. He would make this work, no matter what.

———

Floris took another drag from his cigarette as he stood on the corner, watching a group of green uniforms load up two young men. He was off, but when he heard about a large raid carried out by the SD that evening, he knew he had to be there. So far, it had been underwhelming, and he was ready to leave after this cigarette. It looked like most of the Grüne Polizei were getting ready to pack up, and most other patrons were leaving the Zeedijk as well.

Raids could be exciting, like the one he witnessed last week. They'd acted on a tip and found a whole weapons cache in one of the houses in the Jordaan district. Even his impromptu raid last night had been exciting. It was better than nothing despite only finding two of the expected three Jews in the basement. He was especially pleased the woman hiding them hadn't put up a fight, and he'd handed her over to the Sicherheitsdienst as well. They weren't always lucky enough to catch the hosts red-handed. He'd made sure the men processing her at the SD knew he had brought her in. He could use all the goodwill he could get. The chief's warning was still ringing in his ears.

He took a last drag and flicked the cigarette onto the ground. One of the nearby trucks fired up its engines, with some German policemen running to jump on board as it started moving. Floris was about to leave when the door to one of the bars opened. The figure hurriedly leaving looked familiar. Floris stopped in his tracks and did a double take. *What is he doing here?* He counted the seconds until he expected Christiaan to pass and, as he kept his face averted, heard the distinctive quick pace of his brother as he walked by.

When he was certain Christiaan hadn't noticed him he looked up and saw his brother halfway down the Zeedijk. Floris was stumped and turned back to 't Mandje.

Floris had his eye on the bar for a while now, and he'd even visited it a few months ago. The owner was an odd woman, and she'd been reluctant to cooperate. When he told her he could come back with some of his German friends, she'd shown him the upstairs area and the supply room in the back. He'd been disappointed not to find anything—or anyone—there. Despite that, he still had the feeling something was going on in that peculiar bar.

As the last of the Grüne Polizei piled into their trucks, he wondered if he was wrong. He'd seen them go into 't Mandje, but leave without taking anyone. He shook his head; it still didn't explain Christiaan's presence.

He looked down the street and saw Christiaan turn the corner.

He took a few steps, ready to pursue him, then changed his mind—what was he going to ask? And what would Christiaan say? They hadn't spoken for months now, since Christiaan had made it clear he considered him a traitor. Interrogating him on the street while he was obviously in a hurry to get away from here would only make him suspicious.

Christiaan has no business here. Floris lit another cigarette and strolled to 't Mandje. The lights were off, and the place looked like any other bar in this area. Floris put his ear to the door but heard nothing. He shrugged. *It doesn't matter.* If the Grüne Polizei hadn't found anything, perhaps it wasn't worth his time.

As he walked from the bar, doubt continued to gnaw in the back of his mind. He couldn't shake the odd feeling about his brother. *Something's not right.*

As he turned onto Geldersekade—the dark canal looming up ahead, the water gently splashing against the sides—he couldn't let this go. What was his brother up to? He certainly wasn't going to ask him—he'd find out with good old-fashioned police work.

CHAPTER TWENTY-EIGHT

The next morning, Nora sat in a small room at the crèche. It was still early, the sounds of hustle and bustle could be heard in the hallway. She smiled, and enjoyed listening to the children, excited to get to breakfast but probably even more thrilled to play after.

When she arrived, she'd asked Mina, one of the women looking after the babies and now a good friend, if she could let her know when the mailman arrived. Mina had looked at her with interest but had said she'd better wait in the room in the back, and she would send Koos over as soon as he arrived.

Nora knew Koos would normally deliver the mail early in the morning, often personally handing it to Henriëtte. Because she didn't know how long it would take for him to get here, Nora had brought a book, but she was struggling to focus on the pages. Instead, her mind kept drifting to the evening prior.

She had been more than a little surprised to find Christiaan at her door—he hadn't been around to their house for a long time, and if Floris had been at home, things could've become unpleasant. When she invited him in, he declined. He appeared rushed and had asked if she knew any way to get Lisa out of the city. When she asked him why, he told her about what had happened to her parents, and the raid at the bar. Even though she'd heard about raids becoming more frequent, her heart still ached for Lisa, and she imagined how the girl must be feeling—the horror of knowing you're all alone in the world wasn't alien to her, either. She told Christiaan she'd reach out to the people helping smuggle the children from the crèche. If anyone knew how to get someone out of the city, it would be them. They agreed she would check first thing in the morning and report back to him after. Floris had come home only minutes after Christiaan had left, and he seemed in a pensive mood, not talking, silently brooding at the kitchen table. Nora hadn't been able to get much from him, and he'd gone to bed early.

She turned another page in her book. The murmurs in the hallway had died down, the children were probably having their breakfasts now. She smiled. Mealtime was perhaps the only quiet time in the crèche. She'd read only a few paragraphs when she was startled by a soft knock on the door. It opened, and a man in his midthirties stepped inside, carrying a large bag.

"Koos, I'm so glad you're here." Nora stood up and waved him to a chair. "Would you like some ersatz or tea?"

He put his bag on a table and sat down, shaking his head. "I've got quite a few places to be, so I don't have much time, thank you," he said in a thick Amsterdam accent. Nora had only met him twice before, when they passed each other in the hallway. Their interactions had always been brief, but now that they were in the same room, she noticed Koos, despite his rough exterior, had soft, intelligent eyes that looked at her with interest. "Henriëtte said you wanted to see me?" His tone was neutral, with only the slightest hint of curiosity.

No dallying around then, very good. "I was hoping you could help me with a situation similar to what we do in the crèche." Koos leaned forward in his chair, and Nora continued. "I have a friend who urgently needs to get out of Amsterdam, and I was hoping you might know of a way to do that, considering your connections." She spoke cautiously, deliberately maintaining eye contact, trying to read Koos' thoughts.

He had no trouble holding her gaze and remained quiet for a few seconds. Then, to her surprise, he nodded. "Is your friend in trouble with the police?"

"She's Jewish, and the SD are on her trail. We're hiding her, but we fear they may find her sooner rather than later."

Koos rubbed his beard. "I don't think getting her out of the city will fix your problem."

"What do you mean? Aren't we taking the children into the countryside as well?"

"We are, but it's much easier to hide a child in the north, or perhaps explain that they're family and staying there because their parents can no longer look after them, for whatever reason. I'm assuming your friend is about your age?" When Nora nodded, he continued. "She would raise suspicion in these small communities. We can't take her north."

Nora let out a deep sigh as her lungs deflated. She had been certain Koos would be able to help her when she came up with the plan the evening prior. "But there is another option. Your friend is not the only person who needs to disappear from Amsterdam."

"What can we do?" Nora felt a sparkle of hope.

Koos looked thoughtful. "It's not an easy option. Not that the north would be easy, but the logistics of smuggling an adult out of the city are more complicated." He looked at her. "We'd need to get her out of the country."

Nora gasped. "Is that even possible? Aren't the borders closed?" She couldn't imagine Lisa crossing into, well, where would she go?

"The borders are open, as long as you have the correct papers. But this is where it gets tricky. It takes time to get the papers in order." He paused before adding, "But even more importantly, it takes money to get to Switzerland."

Neutral Switzerland. Of course. "But how would you get there?" It would take going through Belgium and France, both occupied countries.

Koos shook his head. "I don't know exactly. The only thing I know is that there are people in Amsterdam, even, who can make this happen. They have connections to get into Belgium, and then different people will guide whoever crosses the border to the next stop. I don't know how the network operates or what the route looks like. I just know many people have made their way down south."

"Then we must get her to Switzerland," Nora said with determination.

Koos held up his hands. "Not so fast. It takes time to prepare. She's not the only person who wants to flee the country. We'll need to prepare documents for her and contact the people on the route. And most importantly, we need to get money for her to travel. She'll need to take trains and pay some of the people helping her along the way."

A slight panic gripped Nora as she stood up. "There's no time to wait. Every day she spends in Amsterdam, the chances of her getting caught increase. There has to be another way." Koos remained seated, his eyes following her as she paced the room. She thought of Christiaan. She promised him she'd take care of this. He was counting on her. Lisa's life was in her hands.

"There might be another way, but it's more dangerous," Koos finally said, interrupting her thoughts.

She abruptly turned to him. "What is it?"

———

Christiaan sat across from Nora at his kitchen table, his hands wrapped around a steaming mug of tea. He slowly nodded. "We can make that work. We don't have another option. I know the SD will be back at the bar any day now. Or the Dutch police. It's only a matter of time until they find the hatch leading into the basement."

The pain on his face was clear as he spoke, and Nora slid her hand across the table, gently patting him. "I think it's the best option for Lisa. From what he told me, crossing into Belgium is the hardest part of the journey, as she'll have to contact people on the other side herself. No one will be expecting her. From there, they can start planning her journey down."

"I understand," Christiaan said, taking a sip of his tea. "Did he say anything about border patrols?"

Nora shook her head. "Nothing too detailed, no. He said more people had recently crossed successfully. I think it's our best chance, Chris."

"So that leaves the matter of paying for the journey, right?"

"Yes, Koos said most refugees are sponsored by the Dutch government in London somehow. They're mostly students looking to get to England and join the British army. He told me some of these men have come back to fight the Germans. He called them *Engeland-vaarders*. They've done the same for Jewish refugees, but it takes time to plan this."

"Time we don't have. But I'm not sure Lisa could afford the journey. And I'm not exactly rich."

"I may have a solution to that," Nora said. On her way to Christiaan's, she'd considered the option Koos had outlined. It required money—and lots of it—to make it work. Koos had assumed that would make the undertaking impossible, but Nora had surprised him. "I know where Floris keeps his ill-earned loot. And I can't think of a better way to use it than to send Lisa to safety, can you?"

Christiaan looked confused. "Wait, you mean Floris's bounties from arresting Jews?"

"That, and a whole lot more." She told Christiaan about Floris' looting of the Jewish houses, and as she did, she could see the conflicting emotions on his face. They went from anger and disgust —she knew how he felt—to hopefulness and finally to elation. "The best thing about it is that he owns all kinds of currencies, making it easier to travel through these different countries without attracting too much attention. Lisa wouldn't even have to exchange money anywhere. She'll have enough to cover her to Geneva, even if she needs to take detours," Nora concluded, speaking quickly. She felt hopeful, her head buzzing with excitement. *We are going to make this work.*

Christiaan didn't immediately respond. She could see he was mulling it over, his brow furrowed as he looked at her. She wanted to shake him, to make him see how brilliant her plan was, but she controlled herself. Instead, she stood up and filled a glass with water while she waited.

"What if Floris finds out? Don't you think he would suspect you?" Christiaan asked. "Maybe there's another way."

Nora could no longer control herself. "Let me worry about Floris," she said, her voice rising. "The most important thing is getting Lisa out of the country. There is so much money there that he probably wouldn't even miss it right away. It could take weeks, months even, before he'd find out. He's been stealing so much, and he can't spend most of it anyway."

Christiaan shuffled in his chair, admiration on his face. "You would risk this for a girl you've never met?"

"Are you serious?" Nora felt the blood rush to her head as she spoke. "I've been spying on my husband for over six months now. I've smuggled children onto trams while chatting up SS officers. I'm sorry, but I think I can handle Floris." She sat back down, feeling flushed as she looked at her brother-in-law. She put her hands on the table and spoke in a softer tone. "I don't know Lisa. I've never met her. But I can tell that you care about her. And that's all that matters to me."

Christiaan was silent. He hadn't interrupted her once. For the first time that morning, he had a sparkle in his eye. She pushed on. "I've already told Koos I'll get the money. This is not your decision anymore. I'm taking the money, and we're saving Lisa."

Slowly, Christiaan nodded. "Tell me what we need to do."

CHAPTER TWENTY-NINE

That evening, Floris stood a few houses from the tram depot on the Amsteldijk. He loitered in a doorway, somewhat hidden from sight as he kept his eyes on the trams entering the depot, their dimmed lights giving off just enough illumination to make out what was directly in front of the vehicle. As soon as he saw tram 8 appear, he lowered his cap and peered to make out the driver's face. It was Christiaan, and he was relieved to see his brother was too focused on guiding his tram through the narrow gates of the depot to pay attention to the man down the street.

Floris dropped his cigarette and crunched it with the toe of his shoe as he waited for Christiaan to come out again. After ten minutes passed, Floris worried his brother might have used a different exit. All of a sudden, Christiaan strolled through the gates.

Floris pulled up his collar and followed his brother, keeping a safe distance. The weather was mercifully decent, and there were still plenty of people on their way home, making it easier for Floris to blend in with the sidewalk traffic. He followed Christiaan for a good twenty minutes, and it soon became clear he was headed for the

Zeedijk. Floris rubbed his hands in anticipation, hoping his brother would go back to the bar. He was looking forward to catching him red-handed with whatever he was doing.

They entered the Zeedijk, where the foot traffic decreased. Confident he knew where his brother was going, Floris dropped back a little. He wanted to make sure Christiaan entered the bar before catching up with him.

As Christiaan entered 't Mandje, Floris upped his pace, his mind racing. Even though he was confident his brother hadn't spotted him, he also felt a little apprehensive about entering the bar. The last time he'd been there he kicked up quite a fuss, and the patrons had sided with the female owner. He wasn't sure what would happen if things turned sour between him and his brother—was Christiaan one of the regulars? This wasn't Christiaan's normal scene. He reached the door and stopped. *But what if this is Christiaan's scene? How well do I really know my brother?* He thought about it for a moment, then chuckled and dismissed the thought. He was an experienced police officer, he could read people. *I know something fishy when I see it. I can trust my intuition.* He opened the door. The warm air, along with the smell of sweat and stale beer, hit his face as he entered. He was surprised to find the place almost empty: only three tables were occupied, with another two men sitting at the unmanned bar.

There was no sign of Christiaan as he quickly scanned the room. Confused, Floris took another step, making sure he hadn't missed a table around the corner. There were none, and as the people at the table nearest to the door turned around, he suddenly felt very conspicuous.

"Close the door!" a man with a surprisingly high voice yelled from another table. "You're bringing in a draft!"

Floris stood holding the door handle when there was movement at the bar. A woman entered from the back, carrying a tray of glasses, and said something that made the men sitting at the bar laugh.

Floris recognized her immediately: it was Bet van Beeren, the owner he'd crossed last time. He turned and left hastily, the door closing with a thud as he stepped back into the cold.

He stood for a moment as he collected his thoughts. He was certain Christiaan had gone in, he'd seen it with his own eyes. There had been perhaps thirty seconds between them entering. So where had he gone? And that woman had been away from the bar at the same time. Something didn't add up.

"Do you mind?" A voice shook him from his thoughts. A young man stood a few yards from him, an impatient look on his face. "I'd like to go inside." Floris stepped aside as the man entered. Floris walked farther down the street.

He racked his brain about what his brother was involved in until a thought struck. He stopped in the middle of the street, shocked at his own reasoning. *Christiaan is helping the resistance.* He shook his head. The thought of his little brother—the righteous tram driver who loved to help people—being involved with those people seemed too absurd to be true. But as Floris walked on, it suddenly didn't seem too much of a stretch. Christiaan had made no secret of his repulsion for what Floris did. In fact, he'd been outspoken in calling him a traitor. That still stung Floris, but he looked at that remark in a whole new light now.

As he left the Zeedijk, something else hit him: after their big fight, his brother had cut all ties with him. He knew he still sometimes spoke to Nora—even though they thought he didn't know— but he avoided Floris. Could there be more to this than he initially thought? Could it be that his brother was involved with the wrong people and wanted to make sure his allegiances were never questioned? That he wanted to make sure he would never accidentally share information with him?

As Floris walked home, his mind continued forming all sorts of connections. By the time he reached his front door, he was convinced his brother was consorting with the wrong people. As he turned the key to unlock the door, the only thing he wasn't sure about was how deep in his brother was. There would only be one way to find out. Instead of going inside, he stepped back into the street, softly closing the door.

CHAPTER THIRTY

C hristiaan looked at Lisa in the faint light in the basement. They sat on small stools that Bet had brought down from the bar. The low murmurs of the people above them reminded Christiaan he needed to keep his voice down.

"So, what do you think of the plan?"

Lisa looked up, and despite the tired eyes—lined with dark rings —her voice was surprisingly even. "I don't want to sound ungrateful, but I never thought about leaving the country. I guess I'm a little overwhelmed."

Christiaan didn't blame her. He would've been anxious, too, were he asked to trek halfway through Europe on his own, through occupied countries at that. And he wasn't even Jewish. Instead, he looked at her with compassion and steadied his voice. "Once you enter Belgium, you'll reach out to the resistance groups there, and they will help you along. After that, you probably won't even have to travel on your own."

She nodded, halfhearted. "What do you think? Do you think it's the best option?"

"Yes," he answered without hesitation. After Nora had laid out the plan, he'd gone over it several times in his head on the way to Lisa. It wasn't perfect, but the only alternative—wait and join another group of students or refugees looking to make it to England via Geneva—would take too long and carried no firm guarantees. Floris' money was the key to their plan; it allowed Lisa to leave on the next train from Amsterdam. She wouldn't have to depend on the generosity of the Dutch government to fund her escape south. "It's your best chance to get out of the country as soon as possible."

"How soon?" She sounded more confident. *Good.*

He paused before answering. "Tomorrow."

Lisa's eyes went wide for a second, but she quickly recovered. "I'll be ready." She crossed her legs. "Don't think me ungrateful, Chris. You and Nora are doing more than anyone has ever done for me. It's just that …" She stopped and looked away. Christiaan moved his stool closer, taking her hand.

"It's all right. You don't have to thank me. Just get out of here safely."

She turned back to him, her eyes glistening as she moved a strand of hair from her face. "I'm scared. I've never been farther than an hour from Amsterdam, and now you're telling me I'm going to Switzerland? I don't even speak French. How am I going to make my way across France?"

"You're not the first person to take this route. There will be people helping you along the way. Trust me, they will look after you. They will show you where to go, which train to take, and whom to speak to." He squeezed her hand, and as their eyes met, he saw her panic make way for calm. "You can do this, Lisa."

"I wish I didn't have to do this on my own," she whispered as she moved her feet on the sandy floor. "Here, at least I know I have you and Bet. When I leave, I'll have no one." She returned her gaze to Christiaan. "Why don't you come with me?"

He met her gaze. Lisa looked vulnerable, a little scared even. He opened his mouth but thought better of it. "I can't abandon the resistance," he said as he stood up, averting his eyes. "People depend on me."

Lisa was quiet as he paced to the other side of the basement. He turned to find her looking at him. Through the semidarkness, he could sense she was a little calmer than a minute ago.

"I understand," she said softly. "I can't ask this of you."

He felt a stab of pain in his heart, and he rushed back to her. "There is nothing I'd rather do than come with you," he said as he knelt in front of her. Lisa's eyes glistened, and he swallowed hard. "But I can't leave everything behind. It's been harder to find good people, and the police are ramping up their efforts." His voice sounded shaky.

"I know, it was a selfish thought, after everything you've done for my family and me. Those other people need you as much." She wiped her eyes with the back of her sleeve. "No, they need you more, even."

He rose and held her face in his hands. "I don't want to lose you, but my fight is here as long as the resistance needs me."

Lisa leaned forward and put her arms around his neck. "I know, and I will wait for you in Geneva." Her touch was warm, and his neck tingled. He leaned in, and he closed his eyes as their lips met. For a blissful minute, Christiaan forgot all his worries.

When they broke their embrace, Christiaan checked his watch. He would need to hurry to make it home in time for curfew.

"Will you be here tomorrow?"

He nodded. "Of course." They walked to the hatch and kissed again. *I don't want to leave.*

"Be careful. I want to see you tomorrow," she said.

———

Fifteen minutes later, he turned onto his street, where all was quiet. Christiaan was anxious to get home—he was exhausted.

He approached his house and reached for his keys. As he did, he noted the front door to his building wasn't closed properly and froze —a beam of light danced behind his darkened windows. It disappeared as quickly as it came. *There's someone inside.*

He looked up and down the street—there was no one else. He doubted anyone had seen him, as the rest of the street was shrouded in darkness; not even the moon was out on this cloudy evening. Christiaan considered storming in and surprising whoever was inside, but he realized there could be more than one intruder. In fact, that was the most likely scenario. It wouldn't be the first time that one of the houses in his neighborhood was robbed. It had become more common since the arrests started. Christiaan used to have plenty of Jewish neighbors himself, and when it became known that they were no longer there, the looters would appear. *Have they mistaken my house for abandoned?*

Whatever it was, he decided he wasn't going to chance getting into a fight with multiple burglars. He crossed the street to a dark passageway between two rows of houses—the burglars wouldn't see him there.

He leaned against a wall and kept his eyes on his house. There was an occasional flash of light behind the windows. Whoever was in there was pretty confident they weren't going to be disturbed.

In the silence of the night, he suddenly heard the familiar creaking of the stairs of his building. *Good thing they left the front door open.* He leaned forward, focusing on his house, some 25 meters away. His eyes had adjusted to the darkness, and he could soon make out two figures cautiously exiting his home. They were whispering. He was surprised to see them stand outside his house, making no effort to move away from the scene of their crime. They did not appear worried about being seen. One of them even lit a cigarette, and Christiaan thought he saw something familiar in the way the man expertly timed striking his match. Christiaan frowned—this was very odd. He then noticed they carried no bags, their hands were empty.

They continued their quiet conversation for another minute

before they went their ways. *Shit. Which one should I follow? They haven't stolen anything? If they weren't interested in taking anything, why were they there?*

As his eyes went between the two, Christiaan felt his mouth go dry. That gait. He felt the back of his neck burn and wiped his sweaty palms on his trousers. He did a double take, hoping the night's events and fatigue were playing tricks on his mind. As he did, the man across the street stopped and turned in his direction. Even though Christiaan knew he couldn't see him in the dark alley, he could clearly see the contours of the man's face, and his heart sunk. It was Floris.

PART IV

AMSTERDAM,

4 JANUARY 1943

CHAPTER THIRTY-ONE

Nora was up early the following day. She had a restless night, tossing and turning as Floris snored next to her. After Christiaan had left yesterday, she'd spent the remainder of the morning pacing around the house. She'd gone upstairs to check on Floris's loot and was surprised at how it had grown. Apart from the cash, Floris had taken an interest in jewelry—rings, earrings, and plenty of pendants encrusted with gems, all neatly stacked in the large crate in the attic. She felt sad as she imagined what had happened to the previous owners and placed everything back the way she found it, careful not to raise any suspicion. As she returned downstairs, her sadness made way for anger; if this was the result of Floris stealing from the people he sent to the east, she could only imagine how much was stolen by the Dutch police and the Sicherheitsdienst in the rest of the country. She balled her fists. *Nazi scum.* It made her even more determined to take the money for Lisa. *It's the least I can do.*

When she realized Christiaan had feelings for Lisa, Nora decided the farther she was from Amsterdam, the safer she would be.

Confident Lisa would be ready to leave today, she'd left the house for the crèche the day prior. She'd found Henriëtte and asked her to relay her message to Koos in the morning, as they'd agreed. Henriëtte didn't ask any questions, but Nora could see the approval and pride in the woman's eyes—she didn't need to tell her what was going on. If there was one person in the city who knew what she was going through, it was Henriëtte. When Nora left, the older woman had only warned her to be very careful.

"You're up early." Nora turned and found Floris standing in the doorway, fully dressed in his police uniform. *That's odd. He hardly wears the uniform.* Floris preferred to wear his civilian clothing, making him less conspicuous on raids. *Perhaps he doesn't have any planned today*, she thought with relief.

"I was having trouble sleeping, so I decided I might as well start the day early," she said, putting on an airy, cheerful tone. "Would you like some ersatz? I was just about to make some." She took the kettle from the stove and scooped some ersatz powder into a pot. Floris sat down and picked up a book from the kitchen table.

"Where did you get this?" he asked as he studied the cover. It was another bundle of assorted poetry by her favorite poet, Gerrit Achterberg.

"Oh, I borrowed it from a friend," she said as she added water to the pot. Christiaan had brought it, but she avoided talking about him with Floris.

"I don't like him," Floris said as he put the book down. "I hope they keep him in the madhouse for a bit longer. There's talk about letting him out later this year. After what he did to that poor woman and her daughter, I can't believe you still want to read his work."

Nora ignored him as she poured the coffee. She was well aware of the mental issues Achterberg struggled with, but his poetry helped him to recover from those demons. Locking him up in a mental hospital wasn't the solution, but she didn't want to get into an argument with Floris this morning. There were more important things to pry from him.

"So, you're looking fancy today," she said, changing the subject. "Do you have something important planned?"

Floris blew on the steaming ersatz before taking a sip. He smacked his lips and smiled. "Not really, but we may have some bigwigs from the SD coming in today. The chief asked us to wear our uniforms in the office."

"No raids today?" she asked offhandedly.

He shook his head. "None that I need to be a part of, anyway. I'll probably be home early. I need to take care of some other business." He suddenly looked uncomfortable as he spoke the last words, and Nora's ears pricked up. *Something's bothering him, but he's not telling me.*

"Should I count on dinner?"

He nodded. "It shouldn't take too long." He drained the last of his drink and stood up, taking the jacket from a chair. He kissed her cheek on his way out and took a minute to find his shoes before closing the door behind him.

Nora sat at the table in silence. She hadn't seen him act like this for weeks, months even. She wasn't sure how much to believe his story about having to wear the uniform. This was the first time he mentioned such a protocol. He was being far too nice to her.

Nora stood up and placed the mugs in the kitchen sink and leaned on the counter for a minute. She looked at the clock. Almost eight. There was plenty of time before she'd meet Christiaan and Lisa, but she felt restless. Something was gnawing in the back of her mind, something was off.

Putting her worries aside, she decided she could no longer sit at home. She needed to get out of the house. She grabbed her purse, took the stairs two steps at a time, and stepped into her bedroom, where she took the key Floris hid under a vase. Seconds later, she stood in the attic beside Floris' crate. She turned the key and opened it, staring at the pile of neatly stacked bank notes. There was new and old currency from Europe, but most were guilders, the Dutch currency. She hesitated for a moment, then grabbed plenty of guilders and Belgian and French francs. Koos had given her a rough estimate of what Lisa would need to get to Geneva, but Nora took extra. *Better be safe than sorry.*

The money easily fitted in the purse, so she stuffed even more notes into the little bag. She looked at the loot still in the crate and questioned whether Floris would even notice the missing notes; there was so much left. She stacked the notes as best she could, and decided it would have to do. She would worry about him later. She needed to get to Lisa now.

As she descended from the attic, her heart pounded in her chest. She replaced the key under the vase and rushed down the stairs. There, she looked at her reflection in the window and forced a smile. *You can do this, Nora.* She turned to the front door and headed out. She was early, but it didn't matter. For the first time in weeks, the sun was out, and she decided she would spend some time outside before meeting up with Lisa and Christiaan. *This is going to work.*

———

At the Bureau, Floris sat in his office with Hans across from him. Their faces were severe as Floris leaned back in his chair, rubbing his neck.

"Are you sure you want to do this? It's quite the accusation," Hans said, breaking the silence. "What if you're wrong?"

Floris didn't immediately answer but stood and stared out of the window. Outside, the clear blue sky did little to lift his spirits. When he went to bed the previous night, he'd felt a heavy weight on his shoulders, and he'd hoped a good night's sleep would lessen that somewhat. Instead, when he left Nora an hour ago, the weight had only increased. *Yes, what if I'm wrong? But I'm not, am I? I saw him there with my own eyes. He's involved with the wrong people.*

"We didn't find anything in his home," Hans continued.

"But what is he doing hanging out at 't Mandje?" Floris turned around. "You and I both know that is a place where a lot of shady stuff happens, even if we've never been able to catch that barkeep herself."

"Bet, you mean," Hans said, nodding. "Plenty of people have seen her moving in resistance circles."

"Yeah, but we've never been able to catch her in the act," Floris said, frustration spilling into his voice. "But if my brother is consorting with her, that makes him suspicious. And I don't care that we didn't find anything in his house. I want to bring him in, even if it's just for questioning. There's a reason he's been avoiding me, and I want to know what's going on."

Hans stood up and slowly paced the room.

"Think about it for a moment." Hans stopped pacing, his face scrunched up as he spoke. "If you bring Christiaan in, everybody will know about it. It's quite a story: a Bureau man arresting his brother? That can only mean one thing, right?" Floris nodded. He'd considered how it would reflect on him. "If you're right, you're the man who brings in a resistance fighter, your brother even. It would reflect extremely well on you," Hans continued. "But if you can't prove your brother is guilty, you'll look like a fool. Worse even, people will wonder if they can still trust you. The Bureau man whose brother is an alleged member of the resistance? I don't need to tell you how that would look."

Floris was silent for a moment. Hans was right, as usual. "It would be the end of my career."

"At best. Everything you'd do from there on would be questioned, people would suspect if you somehow leaked information to your brother."

"You're right. I need to be certain. But there is only one way to know for sure."

Hans sunk into the chair opposite. He looked pensive, his eyes alert. "There is. But he's never going to tell you outright, you know that. And do you think arresting him will suddenly make him talk?" Hans shook his head. "He'll never tell you."

Even though he and his brother hadn't talked for months, and the discord between them only simmered on day after day, he was still his brother. But if Christiaan was part of the resistance, he was a true enemy. He would have no qualms about arresting him. He looked to Hans, who looked back in silence.

"I'm not going to arrest him. You're right. And there's only one way to be sure. I need to have him observed at all times."

Hans nodded. "I think that's a great idea. Would you like me to assemble a team?"

"No. I'd like to keep this under wraps for now. I'll do it myself." Floris stood, and Hans did the same. "Can you keep an eye on things here? Some paperwork needs to be processed today, but other than that, there shouldn't be much going on."

"Of course, Flo, I'll take care of it."

"Perfect." He grabbed his coat and left his office, quickly stopping in the bathroom. As he washed his hands, he looked in the mirror and was reminded he was wearing his full uniform. That wouldn't do. He decided to head home and change before setting out on his mission.

CHAPTER THIRTY-TWO

On the other side of the city, Christiaan hastily stuffed some clothes into a backpack. He played it safe and packed mostly gray and black sweaters, along with two pairs of brown trousers. Functional and certainly not flashy. He wouldn't want to attract any attention. He checked his bag and decided it would have to do. A stab of pain shot through his head as he closed the bag. He winced and rubbed his forehead, slowly breathing in and out as the pain subsided. He'd hardly slept that night, and that, combined with the stress of the day before, was starting to take its toll on him.

When Floris had disappeared out of sight the night before, Christiaan had waited for a good five minutes before coming out of his hiding place. He wasn't sure if he had set a trap, and as he cautiously walked back to his house, he'd half expected his brother, along with a host of his colleagues, to appear from nowhere. It hadn't happened, and when Christiaan opened the door to his home, all was quiet. Inside, his brother and whoever was with him had left no trace of their visit. Christiaan had taken that as a good sign. If they had wanted to intimidate him, they would've ransacked the place.

He'd heard of other people in the resistance coming home to find their homes a mess.

Despite that, he worried. It was clear Floris had been looking for something, and probably hadn't found it. He also didn't want Christiaan to know he'd been there. *So what does he want?* Christiaan had racked his brain as he spent most of the evening staring out the window into the dark street. When all remained quiet, he managed to get a couple of hours of sleep between midnight and two, when he awoke to the sound of an engine. Alarmed, he peeked through the curtains, but he was relieved to see the truck barrel past his house and out of sight. It had shaken him enough to make further sleep impossible, and he spent the rest of the night waiting for sunrise.

Christiaan took one last look outside his window and felt reassured to see plenty of people walking the streets, enjoying the rare winter sun as it reflected on the cobblestones. Taking a deep breath, he slung the backpack across his shoulder and stepped into the hallway, where he ran into his neighbor, who nodded at him before disappearing into his own apartment. Christiaan descended the stairs and opened the door, the bright sunlight momentarily blinding him.

He kept a brisk pace and scanned the people around him. He saw more people smiling than he'd seen in the past few weeks, the sun lifting his fellow Amsterdammers' spirits. Despite this, he was on high alert, glancing over his shoulder to check if some faces might look a little too familiar. He stepped off the main thoroughfares several times, cutting through narrow alleys and waiting to see if anyone followed him. When he was sure he had no tail, he crossed the Bantammer Bridge and stepped onto the Zeedijk. It was early, and most bars were still closed. Cafe 't Mandje was, too, and he made for the back door, as agreed with Bet.

He knocked twice, and the door swung open almost instantly. He stepped inside, and Bet quickly closed it. "You're nice and early," she said.

"Is Lisa okay? How was your night?"

"Everything's fine. Lisa and I stayed down here together last night. I made sure she ate well and cooked her a big breakfast today, and we double-checked to see if she has everything she needs for the trip." Bet looked serious. "But you should know she's very nervous. She's worried she won't know where to go, or will be unable to find the people who will help her. You should talk to her, Chris." Her eyes went to his bag. "What did you bring?"

Christiaan put it down, and that's when Lisa's head poked out of the open hatch. "Chris! You're here!" A big smile—a mix of joy and relief—spread across her face as she climbed up and hugged him. "I'm so glad you're here. I hardly slept."

He was about to tell her about Floris' visit to his home when there was another sharp rap. Bet signaled for Christiaan and Lisa to hide behind a stack of boxes before opening the door. It was Nora, and Christiaan introduced her to Bet and Lisa.

"You can't imagine how grateful I am to you," Lisa said as she hugged Nora. "Chris told me everything about you."

Nora frowned. "Everything? Really?"

Lisa held up her hands. "Sorry, I didn't mean it like that. If it weren't for your connections, I don't know what I'd do."

"Don't worry, Lisa, I know what you meant." She smiled and handed her purse to Lisa. "This is for your journey. According to my contact, this should be more than enough to get you to Geneva. And if you ever run into trouble across the way, I've added plenty of francs." She turned to Christiaan. "How are you doing? You look a bit pale."

Christiaan sighed, and the three women turned to him with different states of worry. "When I got home last night, Floris was there." Lisa let out a soft shriek. Christiaan held up his hands. "He didn't see me." He told them what had happened.

"So he knows something is up," Nora said. "I mean, why else would he be following you and breaking into your home? This is bad, Chris. You know what he's like. He'll arrest you if he even suspects you're part of the resistance."

Christiaan nodded. "I know, but I'm not sure he's convinced yet." Nora gave him a questioning look. "If he was certain, he would've already arrested me or taken me in. But he hasn't. I think he was at my home last night to see if he could find anything. He wasn't alone, either. If I hadn't spotted their flashlights, I would've walked straight in."

"I'm sure it was his friend Hans, those two are thick as thieves these days." Nora looked thoughtful. "But I think you're right. He wouldn't hesitate to arrest you, but I'm sure he's considering his reputation. Arresting your brother? I think even his colleagues at the Bureau would be shocked."

It was quiet for a moment until Lisa said, "So, what are you going to do, Chris? If you're correct, and your brother is after you, you can't continue doing what you're doing. I mean, if he's following you now, you can't meet the other people of the resistance, and distribute the food coupons, can you?"

"No, I can't," he said. "If we're right, I'll be seeing plenty more of him and his colleagues very soon. I doubt he will let this go. That's why I've decided I need to leave the city." He looked at Lisa, her face registering surprise, before the meaning of his words sunk in.

"You're coming with me!" Her eyes sparkled as her face lit up.

"I am. When I saw Floris, even before what Nora just said, I knew it was no longer safe for me here. If we can escape the country together, and get to Switzerland, perhaps there's another way to help, I don't know."

Lisa threw her arms around him, squeezing him tight. Nora looked on and smiled, although he saw a hint of sadness in her eyes. Bet stood silently, and Christiaan read approval in her eyes.

"It's a good thing I've packed plenty of money for you both," Nora said.

There was another knock on the door, and they looked at each other. "Are we expecting someone else?" Bet asked, alarm evident in her voice.

"That should be my contact," Nora said, holding up her hands. "He'll explain how to get to Belgium."

Koos entered, and they made quick introductions. He appeared surprised to hear Christiaan was also joining but didn't ask any further questions. He knew it wasn't his business, and Christiaan appreciated the man's discreetness—the mark of a good resistance agent.

"You joining her is a good thing. A traveling couple will draw less attention than a woman alone." Koos ran his eyes over Lisa and Christiaan. "Let's address the most important thing first. You're leaving in a bit of a rush, which means I couldn't arrange papers." He turned to Nora, who looked on evenly.

"I brought a lot of money," she said, nodding at the purse in Lisa's hands. She handed it to Koos, who inspected its contents, paying particular attention to the Belgian francs.

"Very good. These francs are going to be your ticket into France. It will be relatively easy crossing into Belgium without papers, but you'll be traveling a large portion of your journey through France, taking trains. From what I've heard, you're almost sure to be checked at least once, probably more often." He handed the purse back to Lisa, who nodded without saying anything.

"So, how do we get the papers we need?" Christiaan asked as he took Lisa's hand. It felt cold and clammy, and he squeezed it reassuringly.

"Well, once you get to Belgium, you will reach out to our contacts there. Normally, they would know you're coming, and they would be waiting for you at the border. But because you're leaving on such short notice, you'll need to seek them out yourselves," Koos said.

"So these people would be able to supply us with papers?"

"Yes, they have connections with people working in the municipal offices. It may take a while, but they will make it happen."

"And how do we know we can trust them?"

Koos rolled his eyes. "From this moment on, you have no choice but to trust the circle of people you meet. They're all connected, and each only knows the next person on the route. We've smuggled hundreds of people out of the country with the help of the Belgians on the other side. They're just as committed as the resistance on this side of the border. Trust me." He emphasized the last words almost challengingly.

Christiaan held up his hands. "Sorry, I didn't mean to offend. I know we're all on the same side here."

"None taken," Koos said in a soothing tone. "I realize you're taking a big risk. I would be nervous, too, if I were in your place."

They were silent for a moment until Lisa spoke up. "How long will the journey take?"

Koos shook his head. "It depends on how quickly the people in Belgium and France are able to get your papers. Once you can start taking trains, it shouldn't take you too long to cross the Swiss border. I've heard of people getting to Geneva in less than a week. For you, I imagine it might take a little longer, but things can move quickly once you have your papers. The trains are still operating in France."

Lisa turned to Christiaan. "What do you think? Are you ready to go?"

"Of course," Christiaan said, surprised. He expected he might need to convince her to go. Instead, there was determination on her face, even though he could still feel her hand shaking a little. *She knows there is no other option.* "How do we get into Belgium?" he asked Koos.

"You're going to take a train south to Breda, which leaves in about an hour. When you get there, you'll transfer to another train to Bergen op Zoom, where you'll take a bus to the village of Putte, which is right on the border. You'll then go by foot to find a small bridge east of town. There, you can cross into Belgium. There are no border patrols there because the people in the village go back and forth all the time. You'll be fine. From there, you can take a tram to Antwerp, and meet up with the people from the *Joods Verdedig-ingscomité*—the Jewish Defense Committee, or JVC. They can help you get your papers." He handed Christiaan a scrap of paper. "Memorize this address. When you get there, you're looking for Mr. Goossens."

Christiaan studied the paper and then handed it back to Koos. "Goossens, JVC, Antwerp. Got it." He turned to Lisa. "Are you ready to go?"

She nodded and took a deep breath as she closed her eyes. He could feel her tense, and when she opened her eyes, she looked calm and determined. She turned to Bet. "Thank you so much for letting me stay here, and for what you did the other night. If it wasn't for your quick thinking, I wouldn't be standing here today."

Bet looked uncomfortable, and for the first time since Christiaan met her, she seemed at a loss for words. She pulled Lisa close. Christiaan caught Bet's eyes twinkling a little as she let Lisa go. She caught him looking and gave a quick shake of the head. Christiaan smiled and winked.

Koos appeared to sense he was the odd man out and wished them well before leaving. Bet disappeared back into the front of the house, leaving only Nora. Looking at his sister-in-law, Christiaan could see she struggled to control her emotions. His throat felt dry, and he swallowed hard before speaking. "Are you going to be all right here?"

She frowned, pretending to be offended. "Me? Of course, I'm going to be fine. I'll handle Floris, don't worry."

"What about the money? This is too much. He's bound to find out sooner or later."

"I have an idea on how to explain that. He has no reason to suspect me. Just go, Chris. Get yourselves to safety. This war won't last forever." They were all trying to convince each other that things would work out fine, but nobody knew for sure. Despite Nora's brave words, he worried about her. If Floris did find out about what she'd done, there was no doubt he would take out his rage on her. He looked at Nora. She was still beautiful, but the past months had taken their toll. The stress of her work had added a few lines to her face, but her eyes were the same: bright, with kindness emanating from them.

"Okay, sis, we need to get moving. I promise I'll see you soon," he said as he stepped closer to Nora and held her tight. With her mouth close to his ear, he could hear that her breath was shaky, and he closed his eyes to keep his composure. *Be strong, Chris.*

When they broke their embrace, Nora looked at Lisa. "Be safe, and look after him," she said, her voice breaking.

Lisa threw her arms around Nora. "I'll never forget what you did for me," she whispered, loud enough for Christiaan to overhear. "I'll repay you in the future, somehow. I don't know how yet, but I will."

Nora broke their embrace. "Just get to Geneva. That's all I want."

Christiaan took a step to the door, and Lisa slung her small bag around her shoulder. He opened the door, and daylight streamed into the stuffy room. Lisa stepped out, and Christiaan looked back one more time. Nora remained where she was, leaning against a stack of boxes. Christiaan opened his mouth, but Nora held up a finger. *Go.* Without another word, he stepped into the alley and took Lisa's hand. Behind them, the door shut with a loud clang. He didn't look back as they turned onto the Zeedijk and made for the train station.

CHAPTER THIRTY-THREE

Nora remained in the storage room alone, her eyes fixed on the door. She felt torn; relieved that Christiaan and Lisa were on their way to safety, but worried about what was ahead. There were so many unknowns to their journey, and even though she knew she'd done everything she could, she still wondered if, maybe, there was more she could've done for them.

"It's hard, isn't it?" She turned to find Bet in the doorway, her arms crossed, but her face compassionate. "I can see you deeply care for him."

"Chris is like a brother. He's always been there for me." She could already feel the void in her heart. He would no longer come around to deliver books or for a quick chat.

"I know what it feels like." Bet moved some crates to conceal the hatch to the basement again. "Lisa wasn't the first person to come through here. Last year, a young couple stayed with me for almost two months. When they left, I felt like I'd lost family."

Nora nodded, helping Bet stack some more crates. The hatch was hardly visible anymore, and she was impressed. "Do you know what happened to them?"

Bet shook her head. "I haven't heard from them, but I'd like to believe they made it."

"I should be heading out myself. Take care, Bet."

Bet doffed an invisible cap. "And you. Look after yourself; they will take care of each other."

———

Nora reached the front door and entered, quickly climbing the stairs. As she stepped into her own home, all was quiet, and she breathed a sigh of relief. She would need to find an explanation for the missing money. She ran upstairs and entered her bedroom. *It's too neat.*

Her eyes focused on the vase on the cupboard. She swiped it, and it hit the floor to shatter into dozens of pieces. She picked up the key to Floris' crate and pocketed it before opening the drawers of their dresser, tossing clothes haphazardly onto the floor. Their neat little bedroom was now an acceptably burglarized mess, she noted with satisfaction.

She sprinted down the stairs and did the same in the kitchen and living room, sprawling the contents of the drawers across the kitchen floor. She then ran up to the attic and opened the crate. As soon as she stared at the riches in the box, she realized she'd made a mistake—she'd left too many valuables to make this a believable robbery. Her eyes scanned the contents and she picked up a large pendant containing a ruby and considered taking it. Then she heard the loud creaking of the steps in the hallway and froze. Floris. He always stomped up the stairs in a particular way. She dropped the pendant back into the box and hurried downstairs, leaving the key in the lock.

She reached the upstairs hallway just as she heard him open the front door. She carefully closed the door to the attic and slipped into the bedroom, where she knelt near the dresser and waited.

Nora heard him enter the kitchen, a pause in his footsteps. She held her breath as he cursed and moments later heard him sprint up the stairs. She took a deep breath and steeled herself as she stood up and hurried to the doorway.

"Floris! I'm so glad you're home!" she said as she put up a worried face, the panic in her voice only partly faked as she braced herself for his reaction. *Is he going to buy it?*

"What the hell happened here?" he said as he brushed past her. His cheeks were bright red as he scanned the room, his eyes instantly focusing on the shattered remains of the vase. The anger on his face made way for shock, and he turned to her. "Tell me, what happened?"

"I ... I don't know! I got home a few minutes ago, and the whole house was a mess. I only just got up here," she said, now shaking, partly because she was terrified of his reaction once he went to the attic.

"What do you mean, you just got here?" He pushed past her, heading directly for the door to the attic. He put his hand on the handle and turned back to her. "Where did you go? You didn't tell me you had plans."

"I went out to the market. I was away for maybe half an hour," she said.

He shook his head. "I can't believe this." He opened the door and rushed up the stairs.

"Can I help you?" Nora said, cautiously putting her foot on one of the steps.

Floris reached the top and looked back at her. His eyes shot fire as he hissed, "No, stay down there, I need to check on something. Why don't you see if anything's been stolen downstairs?" He disappeared, and Nora stepped away from the stairs. She had no intention of going downstairs as she listened to Floris' movements. She heard him go straight for the crate, its hinges creaking as he opened it. He seemed to pause, then rummage through the contents, cursing as he did. She went downstairs so as not to arouse any unnecessary suspicion.

When she reached the kitchen, she started to pick up utensils from the floor. Floris would be downstairs soon. Would most of the jewelry still being there make him suspicious? That was a big mistake on her part, but she hadn't thought that far ahead this morning. She'd been so focused on getting enough cash for Lisa that she hadn't considered taking anything else.

She had replaced almost all the cutlery when Floris came back down. He appeared to have calmed a bit, and the color of his face had returned to normal. His eyes, however, betrayed the barely concealed anger brewing underneath the surface. He held the key to the lock as he headed for the small hallway. She noticed he'd changed into regular clothes.

"Are you leaving?" Nora asked, feigning surprise. "Shouldn't we check to see what's missing?"

"We can do that later. I have something more important to do first," he said as he put on his boots.

Nora's chest tightened as she looked at her husband's back. His calm, calculated way of speaking worried her. She'd hoped he would respond to the burglary with a little more emotion, clouding his judgment. Instead, he went straight into his police officer mode, taking charge and heading out to do whatever he needed to do. *Has my plan backfired? Has this only made him more suspicious?* A knot formed in her stomach, and she said, "Where are you going? I don't feel safe staying here on my own." It was a stretch, but she had to try something.

He finished lacing up his boots and turned to her. "None of your business. I'll send some officers this way. Besides, those thieves aren't coming back anytime soon. They already took everything they were looking for, I'm sure."

Nora suppressed a frown as she thought of the crate's contents. "If you say so. But please hurry back."

"I'll be back as soon as I can," he said curtly before heading out without another look at her. The door slammed shut, and Nora soon heard him rush down the stairs. She walked to the window and saw him disappear around the corner. Her heart was pounding, she could feel it in her throat. She knew exactly where he was going, and she prayed he'd find no clues there.

———

As he raced through the streets, Floris had trouble controlling the anger bubbling up inside. He wasn't sure what he was more annoyed about, that Nora had left the house to allow this to happen or that he hadn't secured his loot better. The vase was probably too obvious a hiding place. *I should've held on to the key myself.*

It also angered him that whoever had robbed him had known precisely where to look. If Nora had been away for only half an hour, they must've been waiting for her to leave. It didn't add up, and it all seemed a little too easy. Whoever robbed him knew about his loot and knew exactly where to look. The only people that knew about his side venture were his colleagues, and he was sure none of them would be bold enough to rob his home.

He tried to take his mind off the robbery as he arrived at Christiaan's. He could still make something of this day, and he was sure his brother would provide him with the answers he needed. On his way from the Bureau, he'd thought about how he'd handle this. If he came straight out and accused Christiaan of being part of the resistance, he would simply deny being involved. Instead of talking to him as a police officer, he was going to come by as his brother and pretend he was there to patch things up. He needed to regain his brother's trust before he could try and make him trip up.

He smiled as he rang the doorbell: it was a brilliant plan. And there was still a chance that Christiaan had some perfectly sensible explanation for his trips to Cafe 't Mandje. He reminded himself to be patient.

After ten seconds, he took a step back and looked up. The closed curtains made it hard to make out if anyone was home, and he rang the doorbell again. As he did, the door opened. The man holding a garbage bag looked at him with an odd expression. "Can I help you?" he said, making it clear he wanted to do anything but.

Floris forced a polite smile. "I'm just trying to reach my brother, Christiaan. He lives at number 3. Have you seen him?"

The man stepped outside, purposefully closing the door. "Your brother, huh? You don't look much alike." He placed the garbage bag to the side of the building.

"Yeah, we get that a lot," Floris said, gritting his teeth. "I can't get ahold of him, so I'm a little worried. We haven't heard from him in days."

The man fumbled in his pockets before finding his keys. "Perhaps he doesn't want to get in touch with you." He raised an eyebrow before turning away and unlocking the door. As he opened the door, Floris pushed in after him.

"Hey, what do you think you're doing? Get out!" the man said, shoving Floris.

Floris was much stronger, and he forced the man into the hallway, kicking the front door shut. He reached into his pocket, pulled out his Bureau identification, and thrust it in the man's face. *Good thing I brought this with me.* "Listen, you're going to tell me when you last saw my brother, or you can come to the station with me, and we'll have a nice little chat there." The man's earlier bravado disappeared, his eyes wide as he quickly nodded.

"I last saw him this morning. He was in a rush."

"What time?"

The man thought for a moment. "Late morning. I was just coming back from the park. Probably around eleven, I think."

"Did you talk to him?"

"No, he looked keen to leave. We hardly ever talk, though, so I didn't think anything of it."

Floris was disappointed. Not only had he missed his brother, but there appeared to be little interesting going on. "Anything else? He was in a rush?"

"Yes, he practically ran down the stairs and looked very tired, like he hadn't slept or something." Floris was losing interest. *This man is useless.* "Oh, and there was one more thing. He was carrying a back-pack, which looked quite full. That made me think he might be going somewhere."

"Going somewhere?" Floris's eyes shot back to the man.

"I don't know; it just seemed like a big bag to carry," the man said matter-of-factly. "But that's all I saw. He was out of the door in a few seconds."

Floris nodded. "Okay, thank you. You've been very helpful. When my brother returns, would you mind letting me know? We're quite worried about him." Christiaan wasn't going to return, but he handed the man a piece of paper with his name and the Bureau's address anyway. "And reach out to me before telling him I stopped by." He looked at the man sternly, the unspoken threat clear as the man swallowed.

Floris left him in the hallway. He considered going to the Bureau but decided he needed some time to collect his thoughts. It was almost five, and the sun was already behind the buildings. He decided to make for the Nieuwmarkt. It would take him through the former Jewish neighborhood, and he could use some quiet time.

As he strolled past the rows of impressive canal houses in the city center, his mind went back and forth between his brother and the robbery. He wondered if the neighbor was right. Had Christiaan really left? And why? Did he find out about Floris's interest in him? Did the resistance tell him to leave? He thought about the past few days. He was sure Christiaan hadn't spotted him; he'd been meticulous.

His mind went back to the robbery, and suddenly something Hans had said earlier drifted back into his consciousness. *What if Christiaan had known about the raids somehow?* He suddenly felt nauseous as the pieces started to fall into place. What if the leak was closer to him than he'd ever imagined, and he hadn't even realized it?

He could now see clearly: the failed raids, Christiaan disappearing the morning after he'd searched his house, and his own home robbed only hours later. Christiaan wasn't the person he needed to worry about. *How could I have been so blind?*

He sat down on a bench and closed his eyes as he tried to control the urge to throw up. He let out several quick puffs, and the nausea passed. He balled his fists as he channeled the anger of this betrayal, clenching his jaw. He sucked in a deep breath of the cold evening air, and his anger slowly faded. He opened his eyes and looked at the city —and the situation—from a new perspective.

If she was indeed responsible for his failed raids these past few months, she was more valuable than he thought. He wasn't going to let her get away with this. Instead, he was going to make sure there was no way for her to deny her involvement. And when he caught her, he was going to bring down the whole operation.

CHAPTER THIRTY-FOUR

C hristiaan looked out of the window as their train slowed down. The city outside was unfamiliar to him—he'd never been to Brussels before—but the architecture was similar to Amsterdam's, perhaps a little more grandiose, or pompous, even. He looked to Lisa opposite him, who was practically gawking at the scenery. It was certainly very different from Antwerp, the city they'd left two hours ago.

They'd left Amsterdam less than two days ago and somehow had made it to Brussels. The journey in the Netherlands had been surprisingly uneventful, as they weren't checked on any of the trains. There was a small scare when it appeared they had missed their bus to the border village of Putte but had been relieved to find it was only running late. They were about to turn away when the bus approached. The driver hadn't asked any questions, and he'd even wished them well when he dropped them before turning his empty bus around at the final stop.

In Putte, Christiaan was sure someone would ask them what they were doing there. From the looks of it, he would have been surprised if 200 people inhabited the village. But as they set out on foot—following Koos' instructions—people didn't give them as much as a second glance. Christiaan had been suspicious at first but then realized these people were probably used to strangers passing through. When they found the bridge Koos had mentioned, they simply walked into Belgium. No border guards as far as the eye could see, a small sign welcoming them instead.

They'd made their way to Antwerp on another bus—the tram wasn't running—where the only person paying them any attention was the driver as they paid their fare. He had been entirely unconcerned by their Dutch accents as he handed them their tickets. The ride had taken a good hour and a half, and Christiaan had held his breath every time the bus slowed down to stop. He was sure the German police would climb aboard to check their nonexistent papers, and that would be it. But nothing had happened as they made it to Antwerp in the early evening, where they found Mr. Goossens. The man had been more than a little surprised to find two exhausted Dutch travelers on his doorstep but had quickly invited them into his home.

They'd told their host about their intentions of making it to Switzerland over a simple dinner of watery broth and stale bread— the best meal Christiaan had in years. To their relief, Mr. Goossens said he would take care of their Belgian papers. It would probably take him a day or two, but they were welcome to stay in his basement for the night, as long as they kept out of sight.

"What are you thinking about?" Lisa asked in a low voice. Even though they had their own compartment, they hadn't spoken much, and when they did, they made sure to keep their voices to a whisper.

Christiaan shook his head. "I was just thinking of Mr. Goossens. I still can't believe he managed to arrange those papers within a day."

"I think it helped that we had quite a bit of money. That usually moves things along," Lisa said, as she turned her gaze back to the city rolling by outside.

"I don't know. He seemed genuinely happy to help us, even allowing us to stay in his home," Christiaan said.

"I'm not saying he wasn't. But it was probably easier to convince whoever had to forge those papers to put us on top of the pile."

The buildings made way for the platform as they pulled into the Brussels-North station. Christiaan reached for his backpack, and they exited their compartment as the train came to a stop. Stepping onto the platform, Christiaan took a deep breath of the cold air. It smelled different from Amsterdam, like a foreign place. He looked to Lisa, who watched the other passengers disembarking. A smaller crowd shuffled about impatiently as they waited to board. "Come on, let's go. We still need to get to the other station," Christiaan said, gently nudging her toward the exit on the far side of the platform.

Exiting the station, they stepped onto a large square buzzing with activity. They stopped until they were pushed aside by a man hurrying inside. He growled something at them in French without breaking stride. They walked onto the square, marveling at the grandeur of the buildings surrounding it. To their left, the Palace Hôtel stood proudly, where a lady wearing a fur coat accompanied a man in a German army uniform. Directly in front of the hotel, trams stopped side by side, allowing passengers to board before departing in various directions.

As they waited at the tram stop, Christiaan studied the people around them. For most Belgians, unlike the woman entering the swanky hotel, the German occupation was just as unkind to them as it was for the Dutch. An older couple next to them sported torn jackets, the woman wearing a skirt and stockings with holes. The man's trousers were patched together like a jigsaw puzzle.

Their tram approached, and they boarded the already packed car. Christiaan looked for a conductor but found none. He'd chance it; they wouldn't be on the tram for long anyway.

They stood in silence as the tram navigated its way along broad avenues. Christiaan saw numerous signs of the German occupation, with plenty of buildings flying the Nazi flag. He glanced at Lisa and saw her look the other way—somehow, Amsterdam didn't have such a clear Nazi presence. Perhaps it had something to do with Brussels's wider avenues and taller buildings providing a more impressive stage for their propaganda.

After fifteen minutes, they arrived at Brussels-Midi, the south station, and nearly all passengers spilled out; the *Brusselaren* rushing to make their connections.

"How long do we have until the train leaves?" Lisa asked as the tram pulled away, and they made their way through the small park in front of the station.

"About half an hour," Christiaan said, looking up at the station. It was an impressive building, built in neoclassical fashion with imposing columns supporting sculptures silently observing the commuters passing through its arched entrance. He admired Amsterdam's Central Station, but had to admit this station was no doubt more majestic.

"I still feel a bit odd wearing these clothes," Lisa said as she locked her arm through Christiaan's.

He nodded, enjoying her touch as he searched for a free bench. Even though it was chilly, a weak sun struggled to make its way through the clouds as passengers waited in the little park. "Me too, but what Mr. Goossens said makes a lot of sense. Besides, I feel more confident wearing this." He patted the smart tweed jacket their host in Antwerp had given him. Lisa also wore a relatively new coat, and they looked every bit the wealthy travelers they pretended to be. When they left Antwerp, Mr. Goossens told them they would need a good alibi if they were stopped. He suggested they pretend to be a couple traveling to France for business, preferably supporting the German war effort—which would explain why they didn't speak French. Christiaan and Lisa had bought and traded some of their own clothes to fit the lie.

They sat down on an empty bench, and Lisa put her hand on his lap. "Are you scared about crossing another border?" she asked, her voice a little uneven.

"I haven't thought about it," he said, surprised. "I guess I was so focused on getting into Belgium that I didn't think that far ahead. Are you?"

She shook her head. "I observed the people on the train today, and I realized that, even though life on the streets is very different these days, the trains are the same as they were. I expected German police to check our tickets and papers, but apart from that ticket inspector, it felt like there was no war going on."

"You're right, it did seem pretty normal. I hope it's the same going to France. Our papers look and feel quite real, and as long as we don't give them any reason to suspect otherwise, I think we'll be fine."

"Have you thought about what we'll do once we get to Geneva?" Lisa said.

Another tram stopped, and Christiaan observed the passengers disembarking and rushing into the station. "I don't know anything about Geneva. All I care about is getting there safely."

While he wanted to reach Geneva with Lisa, to get her to safety, he felt a strong sense of guilt about leaving Nora behind. He'd awoken the previous night and had found it hard to get back to sleep. Would Floris connect the dots between his disappearance and the stolen money?

"Are you all right?" Lisa looked at him with affection and he forced a smile.

"Just thinking about Geneva." He stretched his legs before standing up. "Come on, let's go inside. Don't want to miss our train."

They entered the station hall, busy with commuters hurrying to their trains. They joined the stream of people, and as they approached the platform, Christiaan felt Lisa squeeze his hand. He looked at her, her face lined with fear. He followed her gaze and his heart skipped a beat. Four uniformed German soldiers blocked the stairs to the platform. A small line had formed, and around half a dozen people stood patiently waiting their turn as the soldiers checked tickets and papers.

"What are we going to do?" Lisa said, slowing down as they

neared the queue. As she did, one of the soldiers waved one of the commuters through and looked up. His eyes lingered on Lisa, and Christiaan made a quick decision. "We're going to get in line. If we turn away now, it will only look suspicious." He tried to sound confident, but he felt his neck burning up, his throat getting dry. He squeezed Lisa's hand a little tighter as they joined the queue.

Christiaan eyed the German soldiers, who appeared to have plenty of time as they questioned the passengers. His hands shook a little as he took out their tickets and papers, rubbing them between his fingers as they waited. Then, the last person ahead of them cleared the checkpoint, and the youngest of the soldiers gestured for them to move forward.

With his heart in his throat, Christiaan greeted the man with his best German, handing over the tickets and papers without being asked.

The German soldier nodded and first checked their tickets, giving them a cursory glance before moving on to their identity papers. Christiaan held his breath as the man looked up to check his photo. He was sure he would have questions, but instead, he flicked over to Lisa's papers.

He seemed more interested in her as he asked, "So, what is the purpose of your visit to France, Mrs. Wouters?"

Christiaan glanced over at Lisa, whose face had turned pale. *Oh no.* He could see her struggle to keep her composure as the young German shifted on his feet. Then, finally, she said, "We ... we're going to Paris for a family matter."

"Really? What kind?" the German asked, and Christiaan wasn't sure if he was genuinely interested or just trying to extend his time speaking with Lisa.

She didn't respond, and her eyes shot to Christiaan instead.

"I'm sorry, you'll have to excuse my wife. She's quite distraught. We're heading to Paris for the funeral of her favorite uncle. He passed away a few days ago, quite unexpectedly."

The German soldier looked a little annoyed at the interruption, but when Lisa sniffled, his face softened. "I'm sorry to hear that." He handed back their documents and turned to Lisa. "Go ahead; your train is leaving in a few minutes. And my condolences." He tipped his helmet and stepped out of the way.

As they climbed the stairs, the smell of burning coal hit their nostrils. Lisa gave him a look, but they remained silent until they entered their compartment, which was mercifully empty. Lisa sank into her seat with a loud sigh. Christiaan sat across from her and looked outside as the last people hurried toward the train.

"I'm sorry, I panicked," Lisa said, embarrassed. "I completely forgot our cover story."

"It's fine; it worked. It was probably a better story anyway, considering how pale you looked. He bought it."

———

If Brussels was a little different from Amsterdam, Paris was another world. Stepping out of the Gare de Nord station in the early evening, the constant rows of four- to five-story buildings across the street overwhelmed Christiaan. He'd heard of Paris and had seen photos of the city in better times, but as they made their way into the city, he gawked at his surroundings.

The wide avenues were near deserted. The only motorized vehicles on the road were marked with German army symbols. Even though Christiaan had expected Paris to be different from what he'd seen in his books, this was quite a shock.

"Do you remember where we're going?" Lisa asked. The farther they went from the train station, the more the foot traffic thinned. Mr. Goossens had made a reservation for them in a small hotel a few blocks from the station and had provided Christiaan with detailed instructions on getting there.

He looked at the street names, feeling flushed when he couldn't decipher if they were going in the right direction. "Hang on. I think we need to go left here." They walked on until the next intersection, and he breathed a sigh of relief when he found the street he was looking for. They walked for another five minutes without running into anyone else.

"It seems awfully quiet here," Lisa said as she pulled her scarf a little tighter. She shivered, and Christiaan upped his pace.

"I think we're almost there. The hotel should be on the next street. He pointed at an intersection ahead.

"Can you believe they didn't ask for our papers on the way over?" Lisa rubbed her hands as she spoke. "Did you see those people getting escorted off the train when we arrived?"

A group of SS soldiers had gathered on the platform, and for a moment, Christiaan thought they were waiting for Lisa and him. He prepared for the worst and had even considered fleeing. Then he controlled himself and realized that was only going to make things worse. When the doors opened, he was surprised to find no uniforms waiting at their door. Glancing back, he'd seen the German soldiers waiting near the second-class car as a group of miserable-looking people was escorted down the steps. That's when he realized Mr. Goossens had probably saved their lives with a small but crucial bit of advice: he'd told them to opt for first-class tickets on the trains between Antwerp and Paris, and preferably on later segments.

"If he hadn't told us, I probably would've opted for the cheapest tickets, and who knows if someone would have gotten suspicious on the train," he said to Lisa, who nodded. "I'd never think to book these tickets in first-class, but it does make sense. Any self-respecting businessman would be traveling in comfort."

They reached the intersection, and Christiaan spotted their hotel just down the street. The four-story building blended in with the surroundings in the dreary street as its signboard dangled loosely above the main entrance. It was the perfect hiding spot. Christiaan couldn't imagine any Germans deigning to stay here. Encouraged, he upped his pace—he was keen to get inside, as the curfew would be in effect in less than an hour.

The front door was locked, but there was a faint light inside.

Christiaan knocked and waited. Nothing happened, and he knocked again. *Surely they are still expecting us?* He strained his ears to make out the sound of distant footsteps inside, and after a few more anxious seconds, a figure appeared from around the corner.

The man hurriedly opened the door. "*Entrez, entrez*—Come in, come in," he said as he gesticulated impatiently, his eyes scanning the street as they stepped inside. The first thing Christiaan noticed was the comfortable warmth in the hallway soothing his cold bones.

Their host said something in rapid French. Christiaan held up his hands and said, "Sorry, *nous ne parlons pas français*— we don't really speak French." Mr. Goossens had taught him a few important phrases before they left, and Christiaan had made sure he remembered this particular one.

"Name?" the man asked in German, now standing behind a desk. This Christiaan understood, providing him with their new Belgian names. Next, the clerk searched for their names. "You're in room five."

Christiaan took their key and paused, digging for the words he needed to say next. "*Avez-vous ...*" He closed his eyes as he tried to visualize the sentence. "*Avez-vous reçu du courrier pour nous?*—Did you receive any mail for us?"

The man looked at him blankly, and Christiaan felt a wave of panic. *Does he not understand me? Did I not remember this correctly?* Before Christiaan repeated the sentence, the man turned around and double-checked the pigeonhole marked with the number five. He shook his head and shuffled some papers on his desk, speaking in rapid French.

"It's not here, is it?" Lisa asked.

"I'm afraid not. Let's just go up to the room," he said before turning to the man at the desk. "*Merci, monsieur.*"

The man at the desk nodded. "*Bon nuit, madame, monsieur*— Good night."

They climbed the stairs to the second floor, where they found a simple, cramped room with a double bed. The air was stuffy, as if the room hadn't been aired in a while. Christiaan wanted to open the window but they needed to talk first.

"Wasn't our French contact supposed to reach out to us? I thought Mr. Goossens said he would leave a note?" Lisa asked. She dropped her bag on the bed. There was a hint of panic in her voice, and Christiaan had to control himself not to go along with it.

"Maybe something happened, and they got delayed. It was all pretty last minute. Let's try to stay calm." Despite his best efforts, he heard the strain in his voice and hoped Lisa didn't pick up on it.

She lay down on the bed, putting her hands under the pillow as she rested her head. "Is there any way we can get in touch with them?"

Christiaan thought before answering. Mr. Goossens had been very clear: his connections would reach out to them. But he hadn't told them what to do if they didn't. "Let's sit tight and try to get some sleep. I'm sure they'll be in touch soon enough," he said, mostly trying to convince himself.

Lisa sat up and looked at him. "If you say so."

He sat on the bed and took her hand. "Look at us. Two nights ago, we were still in Amsterdam, and now we're in Paris. No one knows us here. However you look at this, we're safer than we were in Amsterdam."

"I'm worried something went wrong, and Mr. Goossens' message didn't come through. What will we do then?"

"Let's try not to worry about that too much tonight," he said. "I'll go down to the reception tomorrow morning. I'm sure they just ran into some delays. I trust Mr. Goossens. He got us to Paris, right?" Lisa looked skeptical as she stifled a yawn. Christiaan stretched out onto the bed, and Lisa moved closer to him. She wrapped her arms around him and put her head on his chest. Before long, he felt her body relax, and as he listened to her slow and regular breathing, he closed his eyes, drifting to sleep almost instantly.

CHAPTER THIRTY-FIVE

Floris rubbed his hands as he considered lighting up a cigarette. The wind tugged at his jacket as he stood in an alley near his own home. If he ran into any neighbors, he'd simply pretend he was on his way home and head out into the street. Not that he worried too much about that happening; the street was quiet this morning.

He decided against the cigarette. If anyone did walk by, it would draw attention to him. He shifted on his feet and kept his eyes on his front door. It was the second day he'd stood out here, and he had high hopes for today. This morning at breakfast, he'd made up a story about a number of large raids planned for later this week. He'd mentioned it almost casually, but Nora responded as he had hoped. She appeared shocked, but now that he looked for it, there had been a sparkle of excitement in her eyes. He'd set the trap, and now he waited somewhat impatiently for her to make her move.

After he came back from Christiaan's—now three nights ago— he'd made sure to act normal to Nora. She had already cleaned up most of the house, and he'd offered to tidy up the attic. When he got there, he was relieved to find his inventory list, which he kept hidden under a loose floorboard, untouched. As he went through it, he quickly found it was only cash that had disappeared. It all made sense: if Christiaan needed to flee, he would have little use for jewelry. Few people would be able to buy it, and he suspected he probably needed money and lots of it. He was now sure Christiaan and Nora had worked together. Even though it still infuriated him, his chance to make this right would come soon enough.

The door to his home opened, and he was pleased to see his wife step out. She looked up and down the street, almost as if expecting someone, before closing the door and heading toward the bridge farther up the street.

Floris grinned as he pulled up his scarf and adjusted his wool hat, nearly obscuring his entire face. Even if Nora looked back, he was confident she wouldn't recognize him. He kept a safe distance and stayed close to the houses lining the canal.

He briefly lost her as she turned at the next intersection, but he knew the street she stepped into didn't have side streets until much farther. So he sped up a little and saw her about 200 meters ahead of him. She walked quickly, the way one did when they had a clear goal, and it lifted Floris's spirits. *Perhaps she'll take me to her contact today!*

He followed her for a good twenty minutes as they headed north. When they reached Waterloo Square, she headed into the former Jewish quarter. She crossed another couple of bridges and then reached the Nieuwmarkt. Floris was a little disappointed; it looked like Nora was simply going to the market. Was this a waste of time?

It was still early, and the crowded market made it easier for Floris to blend in. Nora stood talking to one of the vendors, and she smiled as he said something—it was clear they knew each other. Floris snuck a little closer, keeping an eye on her hands when she reached into her pockets. He was disappointed to see her pull out a food coupon before moving on.

She seemed to have all the time in the world as she navigated the market, stopping to chat at a few more stalls. Floris tapped his foot, there wasn't anything odd about her behavior.

Nora reached the end of the line of market stalls, and Floris moved to the side, pretending to be interested in something at one of the stalls while keeping an eye on her. He needed to be careful—she could turn around and come back the way she came. As he followed her movements, he was surprised to see a woman approach her. Nora greeted her like an old friend, and Floris's interest was piqued. The interaction took less than twenty seconds, but Floris noticed Nora handing a piece of paper—a note?—to the other woman, who nodded and then walked in Floris' direction. When she passed him, he noticed she looked worried. He turned to see Nora leaving the market, walking at a much slower pace than before. She looked relaxed.

He needed to decide who to follow. The woman was obviously involved. Was she Nora's contact, and was she about to pass on the message about the planned raids? Floris made a quick decision and turned around, following the woman, who went against the stream of people. He barged into an elderly lady and mumbled a quick apology. Bystanders gave him disapproving looks which he ignored and he kept his eyes on the young woman as she left the market.

He felt excited as they headed south and back through the Jewish quarter. Even though the streets were quiet here, Floris didn't have to worry about the woman spotting him—she hadn't looked back once. They reached the busy Waterloo Square. She headed straight for an oncoming tram, and Floris sped up, expecting her to jump on board. She didn't, instead crossing the bridge to the Botanical Gardens. Floris was wondering where they were going—it couldn't be much farther, or she would've taken a tram, he thought.

She then slowed her pace as the Hollandsche Schouwburg came into view. Floris looked at the SS soldiers standing guard outside the grand building, looking as bored as ever. On a typical day, he would stop to have a chat and get the latest news from Germany, but today he was relieved to see no familiar faces. He didn't want to be recognized.

The woman crossed the street and—to Floris' surprise—entered the Jewish crèche. She disappeared inside and Floris stood looking at the closed door from the other side of the street. He was confused. What was she doing in that place filled with children? Did she work there, and was his hunch wrong? He shook his head: he'd seen Nora pass the note, the woman was definitely involved.

Should he wait for the woman to come out again? Perhaps she was just stopping by before moving on? That didn't make sense, either—she had been in a rush to get here. The crèche had to be connected to whatever was going on. *But what can I do now?* For a second, he considered knocking on the door. *What is that going to do, other than make them become suspicious? And what am I going to say?* He shook his head, he needed to remain patient. If something were going on at the crèche, he would find out about it.

CHAPTER THIRTY-SIX

Christiaan woke up in a dark room and didn't recognize his surroundings. They were still in the Paris hotel room. He sat up in bed and heard Lisa's soft breathing next to him. He climbed out of bed, careful not to wake Lisa, and checked the clock on the small dresser in the corner. It was seven in the morning. He sighed as he peeked through a gap in the curtains. It was raining, and the street was deserted. This area of Paris wasn't quite what he'd expected, but he couldn't care less at this point. This had been their second night here, and they'd spent the day prior anxiously waiting for news. When they hadn't heard anything by the early evening, he'd gone downstairs to find something to eat. The man at the front desk said the restaurant had been closed for two years, but he could fetch them something simple. He came to their room with a small tray, profusely apologizing for the lack of hospitality from what Christiaan could make out with his limited French. Christiaan and Lisa had dined on hard bread and indeterminate pieces of cheese and sausage. It had been delicious.

As he stepped into the bathroom, his stomach was already grumbling. He ignored his hunger and looked at the tired face in the mirror. The previous day had taken its toll on them both. With nothing to do but pace their hotel room, occasionally peeking out of the window, their minds started to conjure scenarios about what had gone wrong. At one point, they thought they heard someone approach in the hallway, and Christiaan's mind had gone between hope and trepidation in mere seconds. When the footsteps passed, and they heard a door farther down the hall open, Christiaan had felt both relief and disappointment.

He washed his face, the cold water jolting him back into the present. The stubble forming on his cheeks and neck reminded him he needed a shave, but he had no idea when he'd have that opportunity. He patted his face dry and stepped back into the room, where Lisa sat in bed.

"Morning," she said, rubbing her eyes. "How long have you been awake?"

"Just woke up," Christiaan said as he sat down next to her. "How did you sleep?"

"The one good thing about this hotel is that it's nice and quiet. I guess there aren't too many guests." She swung her legs out of bed and opened the curtains. Faint morning light streamed into the room as the sun rose behind the rain clouds. She stretched as she looked outside. "Not sure that dinner last night will last me through today." She turned back to him. "You look worried."

He took a deep breath. "I am. I think food is the least of our problems. Whomever Mr. Goossens contacted isn't coming."

She looked at him thoughtfully as she leaned against the wooden windowsill. "You think they got cold feet?"

"I don't know, maybe. Or something went wrong, and they don't even know we're here. Or someone got to them." He'd thought about it for most of the night, tossing and turning as his mind came up with all kinds of nightmares. "And we need to consider the possibility that if they got caught, they might talk. If they frequently use this hotel to hide people, we could be in trouble."

Lisa walked over and sat on the opposite side of the bed. She spoke calmly. "Chris, I understand what you're saying. And you might well be right. But you shouldn't assume the worst right away. Do you remember when my parents and I stayed in the basement with Elsa?" She grimaced slightly.

"Of course."

"I never told you this, but when you let us know Elsa was getting nervous, we considered leaving that very night. We were terrified she might do something reckless like turn us in. We'd heard stories of hosts trying to save their skin by giving up the people they were hiding."

Christiaan closed his eyes and nodded. "I worried about that, too. But—"

"But there was nothing we could do about it at that point," Lisa interrupted, her voice rising an octave as she leaned forward. "And in the end, it was my mother who convinced us we should stay put. She told us we needed to trust the people outside. Where were we going to go in the middle of the night?" Her voice trailed off a little, and she wiped a tear from her cheek. "We trusted you, Chris. My mother said you would do everything you could for us, but we needed to be patient. She was right. You are the reason I'm still alive, why I'm in Paris."

Christiaan struggled to swallow the lump in his throat. He shuffled toward Lisa. She put her hands on his shoulder and looked him in the eye. "And just like I had faith in you, you now need to have a little more faith in the people in Paris."

He looked at the woman across from him. Behind her brave words, her bottom lip was quivering, as she fought more tears. He pulled her closer and whispered, "You're right. We'll wait a little longer."

———

They spent the rest of the morning in the hotel room, only interrupted when the man from the front desk brought them some bread. This time there was no cheese or meat, only a smattering of margarine, but it didn't matter to Christiaan and Lisa. They wolfed it down all the same.

It was almost noon when there was a sharp knock on the door. Lisa turned from the small desk where she'd spent the past hour doodling and writing, and Christiaan held his finger to his mouth. She nodded and turned toward the door, not getting out of her chair. Christiaan stood from the bed and sneaked toward the door in his socks.

His heart was in his mouth as he put his ear on the door— holding his breath—straining to make out a sound on the other side. If it was the police or the Gestapo, he expected to hear several people breathing or talking. To his relief, he only heard a single person shuffling on their feet. He held up one finger to Lisa, who nodded and gestured for him to open the door.

Christiaan pushed down the handle and opened it, half expecting whoever was on the other side to rush in. He was surprised to find a man half his size, twice his age. The man wore round spectacles, and his green eyes looked at Christiaan inquisitively. "Can I come in?" he asked in heavily accented Dutch. He didn't wait for an answer as he brushed past Christiaan, quickly closing the door. He nodded to Lisa as he went straight for the window and appeared to check the street. Lisa stood and moved next to Christiaan. The hotel room was suddenly rather cramped. Even though the man was small of stature, he presented a strong aura, naturally taking charge of the situation.

"I'm glad you're still here," he said, apparently satisfied with whatever he'd spotted—or hadn't—out in the street. "To be honest, I was worried you might not have been." There was tension in his voice.

"We thought you forgot about us," Christiaan said.

"No, no, no, absolutely not." The man shook his head and

wagged his finger. "We've never abandoned anyone. I'm afraid what happened was much worse than that. The evening you arrived, the Gestapo raided the houses of some important people in our organization. We're certain someone ratted us out, but well, you never really know." He looked at them and Christiaan nodded.

"We've experienced plenty of raids in Amsterdam as well. Even though our network is strong, it was always possible someone said a little too much, or other times it's bad luck."

The man nodded. "Alas, then you know. Even though we have no proof, I'm sure someone talked. I'm not saying they did so on purpose. The Gestapo have many ways to get people to talk." He was quiet for a moment as the words hung in the air. Then he waved his hand in front of him. "So when these houses were raided, we needed to stay out of sight for a while. For all we knew, the Germans were waiting us out. I feared they might have heard about this hotel. I'm so relieved you're still here." He paused and squinted as he took off and polished his glasses. "I fear we don't have a lot of time. Do you have all your things packed and ready to go?" The man scanned the room, his eyes focusing on their small bags on both sides of the bed.

"We can leave right now," Christiaan said. He couldn't wait to go, especially with the threat of the Gestapo learning about their hiding place. He could picture the arrested men and women being interrogated as they spoke. There was no time to lose.

"Very well." The man reached into his coat and produced two small sheets of paper. "These are tickets for the two o'clock train to Annecy."

"Annecy?" Lisa spoke for the first time, surprise in her voice. "Aren't we taking the train to Geneva?"

"That would be the best way, normally. But I'm afraid that's not an option now." He seemed uneasy as he turned and looked out of the window. Christiaan glanced over at Lisa, who raised an eyebrow. After a few seconds, the man turned back to them. "You're right, it would be quickest to take the direct train."

"Is it not running anymore?" Lisa asked, impatience in her voice. "Our contact in Antwerp recommended that route."

He shook his head. "It's still running, but it's dangerous. You can imagine there are more people, not just Jews, keen to get to Switzerland. The Germans require young French men to report for duty in the German factories."

"Just like at home," Christiaan mumbled, almost to himself.

"Exactly. And like everywhere in Europe, you can imagine our young men aren't too keen. You know, with the British bombers paying more and more visits to exactly those factories. Now, the German patrols obviously take a special interest in the trains running across the border. You can't cross without the correct papers."

"I thought your organization would secure those?" Christiaan said, worried about the sudden change of plans.

A look of sympathy crossed the man's face as he leaned against the desk. "That's the other complication. After this week's raids, we've lost our contact in the municipal office. He would've provided you with papers clearing you for travel into Switzerland on official business."

"He's the only one who could get us those?" Lisa asked, her voice now trembling.

The man nodded. "Do you have any papers at all? You must have something, coming in from Belgium?" He looked hopeful.

Christiaan handed him their Belgian papers, and the man took his time inspecting them. As he did, the air in the room felt heavier, and Christiaan found it harder to breathe. He longed to open the window, but he knew they couldn't risk being overheard. After a minute, the man handed back the papers.

"Will it work?" Christiaan asked.

"It will have to," the man said without conviction. "What's your story, again?" As Christiaan told him, the man listened without interrupting. "It's good enough, and will probably fool most casual ticket inspectors on the way to Annecy."

"What if we run into German patrols?"

"It's very rare for the Germans to check the local trains, especially the ones going to smaller places." There was more confidence in his voice now. "Just be careful on the way there. You'll need to worry more about curious people overhearing you speak in a foreign language. Try to talk as little as possible."

Christiaan and Lisa looked at each other. He could sense her anxiety, and his own confidence in their journey was fading as well. Everything about getting to Paris had been so easy; perhaps he'd underestimated the dangers ahead. "What do you think?"

Lisa's eyes went from Christiaan to the man in the corner. "You're saying there won't be too many Germans on this route. What about the French police?"

"You'll travel to Annecy via Lyon. There's a good chance you'll be asked for your papers when boarding the train in Lyon, or somewhere between there and Annecy. It is close to the border, after all. When they do, I've found the best thing is to bluff your way through." Lisa looked doubtful, but he held her gaze as he continued. "Your cover story is good. Your papers allow you to travel through France, but not into Switzerland, which will reduce suspicion. And remember that the rules change so frequently that most police officers have trouble keeping up."

Christiaan thought about the man's logic and remembered the cursory manner in which the German soldiers in Brussels had checked their papers. And that was for an international train. He looked at Lisa, who still seemed unconvinced, and then at the man at the desk. He looked back with an odd expression—there was sympathy but a trace of arrogance as well, as if he was challenging Christiaan to come up with a better solution. He tried to visualize the journey ahead. "What happens when we get to Annecy?"

The man folded his hands in his lap and smiled. "You'll meet your contact near the train station. She runs a small shop, and you'll be safe there. Once you're there, Switzerland is only a few kilometers away. We have people there who can take you across safely, and without being seen by the border guards. Trust me. We've done this many times before."

Christiaan looked at Lisa. For the first time that morning, he saw her cautiously nodding her head. He took her hand and said, "So, we'll do it, then?"

He saw a sparkle of confidence returning to her eyes as she spoke, her voice clear and steady. "I don't think we have much of a choice."

CHAPTER THIRTY-SEVEN

Nora had a spring in her step as she neared the crèche. She couldn't help but be excited about the evening ahead. She opened the front door, hearing the children running in the hallway well before seeing them. Her heart swelled, as it did every time she walked in. There was something about the innocence of the little ones that made her momentarily forget everything else that was going on.

It had been hard not to worry about Christiaan and Lisa—they had been away for four days, and she wondered how far south they were now. She hoped they should be somewhere in France. Paris, hopefully. She pushed the thought of them getting caught far from her mind; it simply wasn't an option, and she trusted the resistance in Belgium and France to take good care of them, as good as the care she gave the children in the crèche. Besides, with the money at their disposal, they should be able to get anything they needed.

"Nora, in here!" A face peeked out of a doorway at the back of the hall, and she hurried to the room. She closed the door, the faint light providing just enough illumination to make out a tiny baby in a crib in the corner. Beside it stood Henriëtte Pimentel and the young woman who'd called out her name—Nora hadn't met her before. She bowed to take a closer look; the boy was sleeping.

"How old is he?" she whispered.

"Only four months," Henriëtte responded. "His parents are scheduled for tomorrow's transport, so we need to move him out. Little Samuel is on the list as well." She sighed deeply. "Can you believe they would put this child on a cattle train to the east?"

Nora's heart hurt. "There's no way he would survive."

"I can't recall us smuggling out many babies younger than him." Henriëtte looked at her inquisitively. "Are you up for it?"

"Of course. I'll be very careful." She almost felt offended, but she knew the older woman meant well. If she was completely honest, she was a little nervous about carrying such a tiny baby out of the crèche. Samuel cooed, and her heart ached for his parents. She couldn't imagine the pain they'd gone through, having to hand their child over to strangers. *It's for the best.*

"Very well then." Henriëtte opened the door. "Leonie here will help you get him wrapped up, and then you leave immediately. After that, you can take your usual route. They'll be waiting for you at the end of the line. Good luck, Nora." She stepped out, leaving the door slightly open.

Leonie lifted Samuel from the crib, expertly wrapping him in thick blankets. The child didn't stir, softly purring in his sleep. Nora looked on, hoping she could keep him this calm throughout the journey. Leonie handed her a small bag. "There's a pacifier in there, in case you need it, and some warm milk. If he starts crying, he's probably hungry, so the milk should soothe him." She gave Nora a sympathetic look as she pulled a wool hat over Samuel's head. "Ready?"

Nora nodded, taking the child and instinctively pulling him to her chest. Samuel smelled of fresh baby powder, and Nora held on to him while Leonie attached a strap around her shoulder and waist to keep Samuel safely secured.

"Is it tight enough? Are you comfortable?" Leonie asked.

Nora adjusted Samuel a little and nodded. "We're good. Can you sling that bag over my shoulder?"

They stepped out of the room and into the brightly lit hallway. As they turned toward the back door, Nora realized she wouldn't be able to climb over the wall with Samuel strapped to her chest like that.

"Don't worry, I'm coming with you. I'll lift him over the wall," Leonie said, softly patting Nora's shoulder.

Behind them, the sound of the playing children intensified as the front door opened. Nora smiled as she reached for the back door handle—the children loved visitors. Their shrieks made her turn around, curious to see what excited them so much. As she did, the smile vanished from her face, her blood turning to ice. Standing at the other end of the hallway was Floris. He ignored the children, his eyes focused on her as the door closed behind him.

He began to cross the short distance to where Nora stood, still holding the door handle. She felt Leonie's eyes on her and turned to the younger woman. Leonie looked as if she'd seen a ghost. "Are you okay, Nora? Who is that man?"

"He's my husband," Nora said softly, wrapping her arms around little Samuel. "Give me a minute, please."

Leonie stepped away as Floris reached them. He looked at her curiously before his eyes focused on the baby strapped to her chest. "What's going on?" he asked, but it wasn't a question.

Nora's mind raced as she struggled to come up with the proper response. Her mind went blank, and she knew she needed to buy some time. What was he doing here? Did he follow her? Did he know what was going on, or was he here on a hunch? "Come, let's talk in here." She pulled Floris into the room she'd vacated a minute ago.

"What are you doing with a baby strapped to your chest?" he asked as she closed the door. He sounded oddly calm, almost as if he was interrogating a suspect. Then she realized that was *exactly* what he was doing. When she didn't answer, he continued. "Going somewhere?"

Nora considered her options. There was little sense in denying what he had just seen. But what else did he know? He hadn't accidentally come to the crèche today.

"And what if I did take him somewhere? Do you know where he would go if I didn't?" It felt as if she were listening to someone else talking as she spoke. "Do you know how old this baby is? Four months, Floris. His name is Samuel."

Floris was quiet before a grin spread over his face. "I knew it," he said softly but with a righteous air. "You're not denying it? You were going to steal this baby?"

Nora felt her cheeks flush. "Steal? I wouldn't quite use that word. His parents want us to save him. This little boy is actually on the transport list for Westerbork tomorrow." She clenched her jaw as she repeated the destination. "How would he survive the journey beyond Westerbork?"

Floris shrugged. "That's not up to us, Nora. You can try telling yourself that you're not stealing the child, but you are. The children in this crèche belong to families who have been arrested. They're just transiting through here before their journey to the work camps in the east."

"Work camps," Nora said in disgust. "You believe they're work camps? I think we all know what happens to those people. They disappear, Floris. We never hear back from them, ever again." She looked at him challengingly, no longer able to contain her anger. "But sure, let's pretend they're taken to work camps, just for argument's sake. "What use do they have for a baby in a work camp?"

To her frustration, he remained icily composed, seemingly untouched by her fury. "I'm not having this conversation with you. It's not up to you or me to decide what happens. Besides, a baby should be with his parents."

"His parents will be dead in a week. And so will he if he's put on a transport."

"Enough!" Floris held up his hand. "These people have clouded your judgment."

Nora wanted to lash out but bit her tongue. Nothing good would come from arguing with him. She looked down at Samuel, his head resting against her chest, oblivious to what was going on. She envied the little boy. If only she could be so blissfully unaware of the evil surrounding her. She looked back up at Floris and caught him looking at the boy. There was something in the way he looked at him —compassion, maybe?

The moment passed as his cold eyes met hers.

"So, now that you know, what are you going to do?" She clasped her hands together to stop them from shaking. Floris' eyes never left hers, and she could see he was considering his options—calculating how to go about this.

———

Floris looked at the woman he'd called his wife for years. The first time they'd met, he'd been intoxicated by her. What had happened to them—how could she betray him like this, working with the resistance to sabotage his work. He shook his head. There was only one way to handle this.

"You leave me no choice, Nora," he said solemnly. "I'm going to have to take you in—you and your friends. This isn't the first time you're doing this, is it?"

Nora looked away. "I did what I thought was right. Did you see the children in the hallway when you came in? They were excited to see you, a visitor, a new person coming into their lives. They don't deserve to die, Floris, nor do their parents."

"It doesn't matter whether you think you're doing the right thing. You're breaking the law, Nora." He sighed, feeling his frustration mount. *Why doesn't she understand?* "How long did you think you would keep this a secret? If I hadn't found out, someone else would have."

"So you're going to choose your job over your family," she said softly. "Are you going to turn in your wife? After everything we've been through?"

"It's not just about you—"

"You're right. It's not," she interrupted. "It's about all the people in this crèche, the children we'd save from certain death. Could you live with yourself, knowing you caused their deaths? Take another look into that hallway."

Floris didn't answer but looked at Nora. He saw the passion in her eyes, something he hadn't seen for years. He wondered where he'd lost her—how he could've been so blind to what was happening to his wife, under his roof. Then he looked at the child again, and an unfamiliar feeling washed over him. Even though Nora was breaking the law—no, worse, she was active in the resistance—the baby strapped to her chest had done nothing wrong.

He suddenly wasn't so certain anymore. If he arrested Nora and the people working in the crèche, he would score a huge win with his superiors. The Germans at the Sicherheitsdienst would surely hear about it, and he would likely be promoted.

On the other hand, it would mean death for the child. And Nora. There would be no mercy. But if he let her go, he would be an accomplice to the resistance. Someone would make the connection. He'd spoken to Hans about the crèche.

He looked at his wife as she stroked the baby's head. She hadn't denied her intentions with the child—and that was enough to take her in—but there was one other thing he needed to know. "Did you take the money?"

As soon as Nora looked up, he knew. She didn't even need to answer, but when she did, it came as no surprise. "I did what I had to do to save Christiaan from you."

Even though Nora confirmed his suspicions, Floris felt nothing but emptiness inside. He experienced none of the usual rush he felt upon completing a successful raid or arresting resistance fighters. Instead, he leaned against the wall and closed his eyes.

"You were going to arrest your brother, right? Well, at least he got away from you. You won't be able to catch him where he is now. He's far, far away from us," Nora said, her voice cracking.

He opened his eyes. Nora's face was wet with tears. He felt torn. He was impressed by her strength—something he'd never seen before—but the anger of the betrayal was stronger. "I can't look the other way," he said as he massaged his throbbing temples. "You betrayed your country."

She took a step forward, startling him. Her face was only inches away from his. "There is only one traitor here, and it's you. You're just too blind to see it." Her eyes shot fire. "But I understand, Floris. You need to take me in. It's what you do. You arrest innocent people and hand them off to the Germans to do their dirty work. You pretend to buy into their ideas, their beliefs, but you only care about one thing: yourself. You'll climb over a thousand corpses to make it to the top."

Floris was quiet as the words hit him like buckshot. He wanted to say something, but Nora continued.

"And you know what? In a way, it's a relief that you've found out about the money, Chris, and what's happening here in the crèche. Because now I no longer have to pretend to be your wife. To live with the stares of the people in our neighborhood. They hate us, Floris. They hate you." She paused for a moment, letting the words sink in. "But at least I don't have to care anymore. It will be over soon." She stepped back and lowered her head, her hands stroking the tiny baby's hair inches from her chin.

Floris opened his mouth but stopped. He had no energy left. He knew what he needed to do, and he wanted to get it over with. Without waiting for Nora to answer, he stepped toward the door.

"Wait, there's one more thing," Nora said in a softer tone, stopping him midstep. He met her eyes and thought he saw a flash of the love they used to have. "I know nothing I'll say or promise can save my life. But can you at least let me save Samuel?" She leaned forward, revealing the sleeping infant's face. "Look at him, Floris. He's done nothing wrong; he doesn't even know what's going on. Let me take him out of the crèche and onto the tram. When he's safe, I'll come to the station with you and admit to everything I've done."

Floris looked at her incredulously. *Is she mad? Does she really think she's in any position to negotiate?* He was about to tell her that in no uncertain terms when he caught a glimpse of the baby opening his eyes. They were bright blue and they looked straight at him. Little Samuel let out a contented sigh as Nora ran her fingers through his fuzzy crop of hair. Floris couldn't help but reach out to the boy and gently stroked his cheek. Samuel cooed and closed his eyes as he drifted back to sleep.

"He could've been ours," Nora whispered. "In another life, we could've been holding him together. It's not too late. We could take him with us."

Her words snapped Floris back to reality, and he recoiled from her. "Don't start that. It's not going to work; we're way past that." He reached for the door handle. "It's time to go."

The light streaming in from the hallway blinded her, and it took a few seconds for her eyes to adjust. When they did, Floris stood in the hallway, gesturing for her to follow him. Her heart sank. *At least I tried.* Samuel burrowed his face into her chest, and she stroked the back of his neck, pulling him in a little tighter.

The children were still racing around between the various rooms, unaware of the danger the man in the hallway posed. Nora stood for a moment, taking in the sounds and sights of the laughing children, and decided it had all been worth it. She thought back to the night she smuggled Steffie away and smiled. She was confident the girl was somewhere safe in the north of the country by now. And it wouldn't stop with her: there were so many people —good people—willing to fight the good cause. They would continue to take in orphaned children, hide Jewish families and other people fleeing from the Germans. And one day, this war would be over, and they would build a better country. *Evil will not prevail.*

She looked at Floris and suddenly pitied him. He would take her in, but she wouldn't give her Gestapo interrogators anything useful. *They'll have to kill me before I talk.* Nonetheless, she shivered at the thought of being taken to the Gestapo. She'd heard the stories.

Nora took a deep breath and stepped out of the room, turning toward the front door, when she felt Floris's hand on her arm. She recoiled a little and looked up. His eyes were ... soft? "This way," he said, turning her in the direction of the back door. *What is he doing?*

As she was led by him, Leonie stood near the stairs, and Nora forced a smile. "It's okay, he's coming with me," she said to the girl, who looked terrified.

"Where are we going?" she asked Floris, speaking softly. He didn't answer, instead opening the door and stepping into the dark yard. He quickly closed the door, and they were shrouded in almost complete darkness.

Floris put his hand on her shoulder. "How do you exit?"

"What do you mean?"

"Is there a gate somewhere? How do you take the child out of here if it's not the front door? I saw you getting ready to leave just now. You obviously don't go through the front door with the SS soldiers right across the street."

Nora was still confused. *What does he want me to do?* "You want me to give up our escape route?"

"Come off it, Nora." There was frustration in his voice. "This is the last time you'll smuggle a child out of here. After that, I'm taking this place down."

Her throat went dry. "You're going to let Samuel live?"

She was met with silence as she tried to make out his features in the dark. His breath was audible, and for a moment she thought she'd misheard him. Then, she saw a flash of his teeth.

"Everything's been prepared for the boy to be picked up along the route, right?"

"Yes, of course," she said cautiously. *What does he want?*

"I know you think I'm a monster, Nora, but I'm not. I'm doing what I think is right, you're doing whatever you think is right." He spoke calmly. "I don't agree with what you've done, especially the part where you informed the resistance about my raids." He went silent, and Nora bit her lip. "But you're right about one thing. That boy wouldn't survive the journey beyond Westerbork. It's too cold, and I've seen how those people are shipped off."

Nora could hardly believe her ears. "So, what are you going to do?"

"I'm coming with you on the tram, and we're going to take that boy to whomever you're meeting," he said with finality. Nora's hopes rose. *Maybe there is some good in him, after all.* "And then you and I are going back to the Bureau, and you're going to tell me everything about your organization."

Nora let out the breath she didn't know she was holding and felt a tear roll down her cheek. She was grateful for the darkness as she choked back the other tears. "Okay, Floris. I can live with that. You win." She reached for his arm, grabbed his elbow, and guided him toward the wall.

———

"We'll have to climb over here," Nora said as she placed his hand on the cold surface. "It's a bit hard to make out, but it's less than two meters high." He heard a tram pass by on the other side, feeling slight vibrations as the wheels hit the nearby tracks.

"And then what?"

"We cross to the stop on the other side of the street and catch the tram going north from there."

Floris was impressed. *How have they been able to keep this a secret for so long? And how many children have they smuggled away like this?* He wanted to ask, but he knew this wasn't the time or the place. He'd have plenty of time to ask Nora all about that once they were back at the Bureau. And not just Nora, of course. He glanced at the building behind them. There were so many accomplices. *The information I'm going to get from this raid.*

"Are you ready?" Nora's voice sounded far away, but it was enough to shake him from his thoughts.

He nodded, then realized she couldn't see him. "Yes. How do we do this?"

"Well, I can't climb over with Samuel in my hands, so why don't I go first, and then you pass him once I'm on the other side?"

He was about to protest—she could make a run for it—but then quickly dismissed the thought. She wasn't going to abandon the child. "Very well, sounds fair."

He heard her unwrap the sling and then felt her step closer to him. Her arms touched his as she searched for him. He held out his arms, tapping her lightly on her elbows. "You can hand him over now." He thought he sensed a slight hesitation but then felt the warmth of the tiny human as she carefully placed him in Floris's arms. He marveled at how light the boy was—he weighed next to nothing.

"There's a stool where I'm standing. Use that when I'm on the other side. I'll hold out my hands and take Samuel from you."

Floris found the stool with his feet and heard Nora climb up, panting a little as she swung her legs over the wall, then heard a soft thud as she landed on the other side.

He stepped onto the stool and stood motionless for a few seconds, listening to little Samuel in his arms. He leaned in closer and felt the boy's gentle breathing. *He has no idea what's going on.*

"Floris, I'm ready," came the muted call from the other side.

He shook his head, and as he prepared to lift little Samuel, the boy started to cry. His wails pierced the silent evening sky, and Floris almost dropped him, catching himself just in time.

"Quick, hand him over before someone hears." Nora's words were urgent, louder, and Floris pushed himself against the wall as he stretched his arms, lifting Samuel over the wall. The boy struggled a little, and Floris pushed himself into the wall. His arms ached, but the weight was lifted as Nora took him on the other side. Seconds later, the crying stopped as Nora whispered soothing words.

"I'm coming your way," he said softly, but there was no response. *Did she run, after all?* He reached for the top of the wall, wrapped his fingers around the edges and pulled himself up. As his head cleared the wall, he saw Nora. It was a little lighter on the other side—the clouds in front of the pale moon had cleared—and he could make out her face. She was rocking Samuel, shushing and whispering as she did. She looked up at him with a curious expression—calm and serene, as if whatever happened next didn't matter now that she had the boy in her arms. She stroked Samuel's hair and smiled at Floris. It reminded him of when they first met: he hadn't seen that smile in years. "Thank you, Floris." Her smile disappeared as she took a step back from the wall. "And I'm sorry."

His brain struggled to comprehend what happened next as he felt an intense pressure pulling on both of his legs. He tightened his grip—his nails digging into the softer top of the wall—and struggled for a few seconds until he could no longer hold on. He crashed to the muddy ground and opened his mouth to scream. As he did, a strong pair of hands wrapped around his neck, instantly cutting his breath as his scream transformed into a gurgling sound at the back of his throat.

He clawed at the hands, but it was no use. His assailant was on top of him, now digging his knees into his chest. The man held him in a death grip, and when his vision started to blur, Floris knew this was the end. He looked up at the sky as the moon disappeared behind the clouds again. It wouldn't take much longer now, and he relaxed, his head spinning as his heart struggled to provide enough oxygen to his brain. Finally, he was floating, no longer feeling the pressure of the man's hands. Stars danced before his eyes before everything went black.

CHAPTER THIRTY-EIGHT

C hristiaan heard Mademoiselle Meunier shuffle through the small shop underneath. The low heels of her boots made a clacking noise every time she moved around, and even though it had been annoying at first, Christiaan had come to find the sound reassuring—calming, even. It meant the woman hiding them was still there, and her steps meant everything was under control. There was someone else in the store, speaking in a low voice: a man.

Christiaan sat at the small table in the remarkably well-furnished second-story apartment. Lisa sat near the window, and even though the curtains were drawn, she sneaked a peek into the street below every once in a while.

"It's nice and sunny outside, but there's not a lot of people out," she said with a sigh. "I wish we could get some air."

"Don't worry, there will be plenty of chances to get fresh air soon," he said as he got up and moved to the window. "Switzerland is only ten kilometers away, let's be patient."

"When do you think we'll get to go?"

"Mademoiselle Meunier said getting in touch with the people on the other side of the border might take a few days. I'm sure she's just as keen for us to leave."

Lisa shrugged. "I'm getting a little anxious about being in one place for a longer time."

"Our French friends seem to know what they're doing. We've made it here from Paris, after all." He put his hands on her shoulders and gently massaged her.

The train ride from Paris to Lyon was straightforward enough, but when they transferred to the platform for their southbound train, Christiaan was dismayed by the swarm of people. He worried they might not be able to get on board as people jostled as soon as the doors opened. Lisa had held on to him as he nearly fought his way onto the overcrowded train.

As they searched for a seat, it became clear they would be standing the entire journey. It had been uncomfortable, but it had proved to be a blessing in disguise. When the ticket inspector passed by, he seemed rushed and was only interested in their tickets, not bothering to ask for identification. Christiaan had had his cover story ready, with the man in the Paris hotel having taught him some new phrases to explain why they carried only Belgian identity papers.

The train had emptied along the route, and by the time they stepped onto the platform in Annecy, they had managed to sit for a good hour. Even though they were tired, the fresh mountain air gave them new energy and optimism. They could almost see the Swiss border now.

As they set out to find Au Mimosa—its shopkeeper supposedly sympathetic to their cause—Lisa had marveled at the simple architecture of the French mountain town. She loved the small square outside the station, lined with cafes that had seen better days. As they walked the streets, she pointed out the brightly painted houses, their window shutters closed, but Christiaan could imagine what the town must look like in summer, the small squares surely lined with tables filled with people enjoying the good weather. Finally, they'd found the store, just a few streets from the station, where they met Mademoiselle Meunier. Christiaan had been nervous about meeting her and explaining their arrival—the lady wasn't expecting them, after all—but as soon as he opened his mouth and uttered a few words of broken French, she switched to a mix of German and Dutch and had quickly escorted them upstairs. She didn't seem surprised to find them on her doorstep and explained they might need to stay hidden for a few days. When Lisa had asked if it was safe, she had smiled: they wouldn't find a safer place in France.

The kind woman brought them two meals a day and usually stayed to chat for a few minutes. By now, Christiaan knew she'd lived in Annecy her whole life and lived a few streets down with her elderly aunt, whom she took care of. Christiaan assumed her little store was a popular place in town from the activity downstairs.

"How many people do you think have passed through here before?" Lisa asked.

"Don't know, but we're definitely not the first."

"Mademoiselle Meunier seems very comfortable looking after us, and I haven't seen any Germans on the streets outside. It's almost sleepy here."

"They probably don't care about a small town. There will be French police around here, surely. I'm sure plenty of people attempt to cross the border in these parts."

They heard the door in the shop close, its little bell clanging. Mademoiselle Meunier moved from the entrance to the back of the store, and then they heard her mounting the stairs. There was a soft knock on their door, and Christiaan rushed to open it. Their host walked in, a smile on her face. Marie Meunier was in her sixties, her wrinkled face and weary eyes betraying a tough life. She exuded an air of confidence and calm, and Christiaan had found it easy to trust her.

"I have good news," she started in her mix of German and Dutch. "I made contact with Geneva, and they've taken care of your paperwork." She handed Christiaan an envelope. "This contains papers allowing you to travel within the Haute-Savoie region."

Lisa raised an eyebrow. "Why do we need those? We're leaving soon, right?"

"Yes, but before you do, you'll need to take the bus to the border. There are *gendarmes*..." She struggled to find the right word.

"Police?" Christiaan said.

She nodded. "Police, exactly. There are police around the border, checking papers. If you're found without papers, you'll be arrested, and when they discover you don't speak any French, they'll hand you over to the Germans. These papers are important, trust me."

"How did you get them?" Christiaan said, trying to decipher the words.

She smiled. "We have our connections here at the municipal office. Don't worry, they're legitimate. Your biggest challenge will be getting across the border. We don't have any papers that allow you to do that."

Christiaan wasn't surprised. He hadn't expected to cross the border freely, but Lisa looked worried. "How *do* we get to Switzerland, then?"

"The border is quite long," Mademoiselle Meunier started as she sat down. "And while there are lots of patrols, they can't be everywhere all the time. You're going to sneak past them."

Lisa still looked concerned, the frown on her face deepening. "But how? Where do we go? And when we get to Switzerland, how do we know where to go?"

Mademoiselle Meunier held up her hand. "Calm down, dear. You won't be doing this alone. We have people who know every single blade of grass and stone around the border. They will take you. You will be in good hands."

Christiaan put his arm around Lisa. "It will be fine. These people know what they're doing," he said softly. She nodded, and he turned to Mademoiselle Meunier. "When do we leave?"

"Right now," the woman answered as she pulled out a small map. "Let me show you where to go."

———

An hour later, they were the only passengers on a small bus pulling out of Annecy. The driver had grumbled something at them when Christiaan indicated their destination but then proceeded to completely ignore them as he focused on the road. Christiaan suspected he was used to foreigners on his route north.

"Did you ask him to drop us off just outside Collonges?" Lisa asked as she looked out the window at the vast fields stretching ahead of them as they left Annecy behind. In the distance, they could see the snowy mountains of Switzerland.

"I did, and I think he understood me. Either way, I'll keep my eyes on the road ahead. Mademoiselle Meunier said once the road splits at Mouvis, we should exit at the next bus stop."

Lisa kept her gaze out the window, and they rode in silence for a few minutes. Christiaan did the same. He had been fascinated by the mountains on the train from Lyon, but the Swiss mountains were something else—they embodied safety. He couldn't wait to cross the border, and he felt excitement in his stomach. Mademoiselle Meunier had said they might cross as early as tonight, depending on the people at the seminary. He hadn't been surprised to hear people of faith would help refugees escape the Nazi regime—they, too, were persecuted for not subscribing to Hitler's doctrine. Christiaan had seen his fair share of priests hauled off in Amsterdam, and he didn't doubt the same was happening here in France.

Lisa was tapping her foot next to him, and he put his hand on her leg. "Are you all right? You seem nervous."

"Aren't you? We're so close now."

"Hey, we're going to make it. You heard what Mademoiselle Meunier said. They're going to take us across. Maybe even tonight!"

"But what if something goes wrong? What if the border patrols catch us, and we're arrested? Then everything we've done is for nothing. They'll turn us over to the Germans, for sure." Her voice trembled.

Christiaan thought he caught the driver glancing in his rearview mirror and spoke softly. "You can see Switzerland over there. You can almost touch the mountains, right? We're going to make it. The people taking us there do this every week. This time tomorrow, we're going to be in Geneva." Lisa looked at him curiously, as if she was trying to gauge his confidence. He placed his hand on hers. "Come on, Lisa, have a little faith."

The bus continued on for a good half hour until they suddenly pulled over. They were still the only passengers when the driver opened the door and shouted something at them. The man was waving his arms for them to get off the bus. Christiaan and Lisa disembarked and found themselves seemingly in the middle of nowhere.

"Are you sure we're in the right place?" Lisa asked, looking around.

Christiaan had the same thought but then spotted a small dirt road leading up a hill a little way back. "That must be the road to the seminary," he said. "Mademoiselle Meunier said we wouldn't be able to miss it."

Since leaving Annecy, they'd passed many similar hills, but Christiaan thought he could make out a small tower pointing out between the trees at the top of the hill. *If it's not the seminary, at least being atop that hill will give us a good view of our surroundings.*

They followed the winding road and half an hour later reached a large whitewashed building. The tower Christiaan spotted earlier turned out to be a modest steeple placed on top of the main portion of the building.

"This must be it," Christiaan said confidently as they approached. "It looks like a school, doesn't it?"

"One without any students, though. It's awfully quiet," Lisa said as her eyes scanned their surroundings. A curious chicken poked its head out from the side of the building, then quickly retreated.

They reached the front door, and Christiaan knocked. There was no answer, and he knocked again. Lisa tried to peek inside, but the curtains were drawn. They listened, but apart from some distant clucking, they heard nothing.

"Let's try around the back." Christiaan was already at the corner of the house and almost bumped into a woman coming from the other direction.

"*Mon Dieu!*" the woman exclaimed as her hand went to her chest. Even though she was a lot smaller than Christiaan, she didn't shrink away. She spoke in rapid French, and he held up his hands. "I'm sorry, I don't understand what you're saying," he said in Dutch before realizing she wouldn't have understood a word of that, either. He was searching for the right words in French when he noticed the woman looking at him with interest; she didn't appear surprised that he spoke in Dutch.

"I'm sorry," he said in French. "Is this the seminary? We were sent from Annecy." He pointed at the road behind him.

The woman didn't immediately respond but walked over to Lisa instead. She ran her eyes over her without a word, then turned back to Christiaan. "Who sent you?"

"Mademoiselle Meunier. She told us to look for the seminary." He pointed at the steeple. "I'm hoping we're in the right place?"

The woman pursed her lips, giving him a stern look before nodding. Then, to Christiaan's surprise, she switched to broken Dutch. "You're in the right place. I could tell you were the couple Marie told me about: your French is horrible. Good thing I've heard enough of your countrymen butcher my language recently not to worry about doing the same to yours."

Christiaan let out a sigh of relief, and when he saw a thin smile appear on Lisa's face, he relaxed even more. The French woman extended her hand. "My name is Amy Mae. My husband runs the seminary, but he's in Paris now. Come inside, you must be thirsty from the climb."

Christiaan and Lisa spent the rest of the day in the seminary. As no students were present—Amy Mae told them they had the week off to study—they were free to explore the many rooms. It was a welcome change after hiding in confined spaces for over a week now. Amy Mae had left soon after they arrived. She would check on their guide for the crossing. She said they would leave tonight, barring any complications. When Christiaan asked her about the kind of complications, she had simply smiled.

They sat in Amy Mae's living room, located in the back of the seminary. She said they could stay there, as they hardly ever had any visitors other than their students, and the local gendarmes weren't interested in their little school. Despite her assurances, Christiaan kept pacing between the window and couch.

"Come, Chris, sit down," Lisa said, patting the spot next to her. "You're making me nervous. She'll be back soon."

"Sorry, a force of habit, I guess," he said as he put his arm around her.

She rested her head against his shoulder, glancing at his face sideways. "What's the first thing you're going to do when we get to Geneva?"

He thought for a moment. "I've heard they have real coffee there. I wouldn't mind some of that." He reached out for his glass of water and took a sip. "What about you?"

"I don't know. I think I would simply be happy getting a real good night's sleep without worrying about someone breaking down the door." She looked pensive. "And then I want to find other people like me."

He stroked her hair and felt proud. Despite the dangers of his work for the resistance, he had never had to hide, he never had to live in the shadows. For Lisa, that had been her reality for over two years now, never knowing when that knock on the door would come, constantly questioning if the people she had no choice but to trust would one day turn on her. "I'm sure we'll find your people. And they're my people, too, now."

"I know," Lisa said, taking his other hand and placing it in her lap. "When we make it to Switzerland, I want to do everything I can to help our people back home."

They sat in silence as they considered their future until the front door opened. Christiaan could tell it was Amy Mae from the soft footsteps, and their host appeared a few seconds later. They sat up and looked at her inquisitively; her face was serious, but she spoke in an upbeat manner. "Everything is ready. You're leaving tonight."

It was dark when there was a soft knock on the back door. Amy Mae opened it, and a man around the same age as Christiaan stepped into the room. He had a sharp jawline and his narrow eyes made it look like he was constantly squinting. He shook their hands and introduced himself simply as Roger.

"Roger will take you across the border tonight," Amy Mae said as she handed them their backpacks. "He's done this many times."

Christiaan buttoned up his jacket and slung his backpack across his shoulder. "How far is it?"

Roger responded in surprisingly good Dutch. "The border is about two kilometers from here, and the first part is downhill. It should take us about an hour, as long as we don't run into any border guards."

"How often does that happen?"

He shrugged. "Every once in a while. I usually spot them before they see us, and we wait for them to pass. They have a lot of ground to cover, and we have multiple places where we can cross the border.

Don't worry too much. The weather is in our favor tonight. It's cloudy, so there's hardly any moonlight."

Christiaan looked at Lisa, who wore a thick scarf and dark hat covering most of her face. Only her eyes were visible, and Christiaan was relieved to see the look of determination. He turned to Roger. "We're ready."

"*Bon*," Roger said. "Once we step outside, we talk as little as possible. Just follow me."

Amy Mae led them to the door, and Christiaan was surprised when she hugged him and then Lisa. "*Bonne chance*," she said as she opened the door. "You're in safe hands."

The mountain air was crisp, and Christiaan took a deep breath—his lungs stung in a good way.

Roger took the lead as they avoided the road and went straight down the hill on the other side. The slope was gentle, and it hadn't rained for a few days, which made it relatively easy to climb down. Christiaan and Lisa kept pace with Roger easily, and it took them only fifteen minutes to make it to the foot of the hill. They headed west, and Christiaan was at first confused. The dark silhouettes of the Swiss mountains were to the north. He didn't say anything as Roger led them through a field parallel to a road about 50 meters to their left.

After fifteen minutes, they entered a small town. Roger turned to them and signaled for them to come closer. "This is Archamps, and we need to cross through there." He pointed at a small railway over-pass in the distance as he kept his voice low. "We'll keep to the side of the road until we get to that tunnel, and then we'll run through it and straight into the field on the other side, okay?"

Christiaan and Lisa nodded. Christiaan felt his heart rate increase; they would have nowhere to hide if anyone spotted them there. "Keep moving once we get to the tunnel. It's only a hundred meters. Just run as fast as you can." Roger didn't wait for a response as he turned and continued down the road.

They reached the tunnel within minutes without running into

anyone. The windows of the houses they passed remained dark, the French adhering to the curfew and blackouts. Christiaan thought how ridiculous that was in this area; there was absolutely nothing of interest for British bombers here.

Roger glanced back at them, and as they made eye contact, the Swiss man mouthed "now" before bolting down the tunnel. Christiaan looked back at Lisa, who was sprinting in Roger's direction. Together, they ran into the darkness of the small tunnel, their footsteps echoing like thunderclaps in the confined space.

As he exited the tunnel, Roger crashed down into the field on the other side, and Christiaan did the same. Lisa landed next to him, breathing heavily as they crouched in the low grass for a few seconds in their quiet surroundings, the darkness of the night enveloping them. Christiaan's heart rate returned to normal as no border guards sprang from the darkness.

"Ready?" Roger whispered as he got up and headed for a small forest ahead of them. As they walked between the trees, Christiaan breathed a little easier—the forest gave him a sense of security. He chuckled at the thought; the closer they got to the border, the more dangerous it became, never mind the trees. He looked back at Lisa, who followed him silently. She had no trouble keeping up with Roger as every step took them closer to freedom.

The trees cleared, and they heard a gentle burbling sound—they reached the stream Amy Mae had told them about. Roger stopped and pointed ahead at the water glistening in the faint moonlight. "The water level isn't very high, but it will be icy cold and reach up to your waist," he said. "Cross quickly as you wade through. We'll then climb that hill right there."

The hill on the other side was lined with neat rows of trellises. "We'll cross through the vineyard and then reach the border. There's barbed wire there, but I'll take us to a spot where we can crawl through."

"And then we're in Switzerland?" Christiaan said, excitement building up in his stomach. The hill wasn't too high; he could almost see the barbed wire at the top.

Roger nodded. "*Oui*, we're almost there."

"Then let's go," Lisa said with a hint of impatience.

Their guide stood and ran into the stream, Christiaan and Lisa following closely behind. As Christiaan's feet hit the water, the icy cold bit into them—Roger hadn't exaggerated. Christiaan gasped but gritted his teeth as he followed Roger, who was only a few steps ahead of him. He ran on, the water now up to his waist. Lisa was beside him, rushing as they splashed through. Christiaan soon felt the incline on the other side, and they were out of the stream moments later. There was no time to catch his breath as Roger quickly continued up the hill.

They were about halfway up the hill when a bright light illuminated it from behind them.

"*Arrêtez!* Stop!"

Christiaan and Lisa froze as they turned to the source of the light. A bundle of lights bounced toward them, but it was hard to make out how far down the hill it was.

"*Merde!*" Roger cursed as he ran back to Christiaan and shook him. "Keep running! We're almost there! Come on!" he shouted, his eyes full of urgency. "Lisa, come on!"

Christiaan snapped out of it and grabbed Lisa's hand, pulling her up the hill. Roger was about five meters ahead of them, shouting at them to go faster. Out of the corner of his eye, Christiaan saw the border guards closing in on them—they appeared in good shape and certainly more used to the terrain. *We're not going to make it!*

He heard Lisa coughing as her breathing became more labored. He pulled harder but felt resistance—she couldn't go any faster. Roger also noticed. "Lisa, only fifty meters left! Come on!" he shouted as he neared the top of the hill. The border guards' shouts became more urgent.

Lisa's grip slackened, and Christiaan stopped, looking her in the eyes. She breathed heavily, puffs of vapor coming through her scarf. "I ... I can't make it, Chris," she said.

He grabbed her shoulders. "You can! You have to! We're almost there. We can't give up now!"

"What are you doing? Keep moving!" Roger shouted. He had reached the top of the hill. The border guards were only a few meters below them—there was only one way to get Lisa over the border. Without another thought, Christiaan dropped his backpack and picked her up, slinging her legs over his shoulder. He clenched his jaw as he struggled to climb the final meters. Roger ran down the hill, and when he reached them, grabbed Lisa by the arms. With Roger's help, Christiaan pushed his legs a little harder. They were nearly at the top.

The French border guards were panting behind him, but Christiaan didn't dare look back. Just a few more meters. His legs were burning, but he gritted his teeth, ignoring the pain.

As they reached the top, they put Lisa back on her feet.

"Quick, over here." Roger was already on the move, running along a thick coil of concertina wire, Lisa following closely. Christiaan took a large gulp of air and stepped in their direction when he felt something on his ankle. He looked down and saw the face of one of the border guards, his hand on Christiaan's ankle. Time slowed down as Christiaan and the guard locked eyes. He heard muffled voices in the distance, and as the guard reached out with his other hand, Christiaan acted on impulse. He shook his leg as hard as possible, ready to kick out at the guard. It wasn't necessary. The man lost his balance and tumbled down into the path of the other guard, who was a meter or two behind.

"Chris! Come on!" Lisa's voice pierced the sky as all his senses returned. He turned and ran to where he saw two faintly illuminated silhouettes. Lisa and Roger stood near a large pile of sticks and leaves. Roger removed the pile, revealing a shallow ditch underneath. "Crawl through here," he said.

Behind them, the border guards had also reached the top. The beam went left and right before it focused on them again, the light blinding Christiaan as the guards sprinted forward.

"You go first," Roger said to Lisa. She dropped to her knees and crawled underneath the concertina wire. It took her only seconds to make it to the other side. Christiaan followed quickly after, the heavy boots of the guards meters away now. The wire cut into his jacket, but he struggled through, losing fabric to the metal teeth. He had only just cleared the ditch when Roger followed as the border guards reached them. His legs were still on the other side, and Christiaan grabbed his hands and pulled him through just before the men could seize him.

Christiaan had already turned to run, but—to his surprise—Roger made no move to do so. He stood and brushed the sand off of his jacket as he looked at the border guards on the other side of the wire. They stood motionless, their flashlight pointed at the ground, providing enough illumination to make out the faces of the escapees, as well as their own.

"Well done," they said in French, nodding at Christiaan, Roger, and Lisa.

Christiaan wasn't sure he'd heard that correctly, and he looked to Lisa, who seemed just as confused. "What's going on, Roger?" he asked with trepidation. *Something's not right.*

Roger slowly turned around, a smile on his face. "They're congratulating you on making it across."

"They don't care that we crossed?" Christiaan said.

The border guard shone his flashlight on Christiaan's face, blinding him. He looked away, and the guard chuckled as he did the same to Lisa. "*Bon voyage*—safe travels." The men gave them a wave before heading in the other direction.

"I don't understand," Christiaan said. "That's it?"

Roger was still smiling, white teeth visible in the darkness. "They did everything they could, wouldn't you agree? They just weren't able to catch us in time."

It suddenly dawned on Christiaan—they were no longer France's problem. He followed them as the light faded down the hill, the roll of barbed wire the only tangible marker of the border. It didn't matter. They were on the right side.

He felt a hand on his shoulder and looked into Lisa's eyes—her face was wet with tears. But her eyes shone brightly, and she wore a smile wider than he'd ever seen before. He put his arms around her waist and pulled her toward him, holding her tightly.

After a few seconds, they heard Roger softly clearing his throat. He held out his arms and with a twinkle in his eye said, "Welcome to Switzerland."

EPILOGUE

C hristiaan's coat flapped around loosely as he crossed the Rhône River using the narrow Pont des Bergues. Even though it wasn't the quickest way into town, he enjoyed taking the detour using the small pedestrian bridge, avoiding the busier, larger bridges. It reminded him of crossing the IJ River in Amsterdam.

Taking a minute to admire the view of Lake Geneva in the distance, he quickly walked on and reached the other side, crossing into the Old Town. Even though it was February, locals were undeterred by the cold temperatures, enjoying their late-morning coffee and pastry on the outdoor seating of the cafes in Geneva's city center. On days like these, the war really felt a world away.

He enjoyed his walk through the city's narrow streets, and he used some now-familiar alleyways to reach Café du Centre, its iconic green signboard proudly advertising the establishment. Before opening the door, Christiaan double-checked his inside pocket and was relieved to feel the smooth paperwork. It had become second nature to check for his refugee papers several times a day and anytime he entered a building. He couldn't imagine what he would do without them.

It had been nearly four weeks since they arrived in Geneva in the middle of the night. From the border, it had been another hour and a half's walk through the darkness. Roger had warned them to be very quiet, as they still needed to avoid the Swiss border patrols. He made it clear that if they ran into them, they would be sent back to France. Christiaan and Lisa had followed Roger closely, and he'd only allowed himself to relax once they reached the outskirts of Geneva.

Roger had taken them to a small house, where a woman was waiting for them. She hadn't said much, but Roger had introduced her as Elisabeth Cartier. She was already in touch with the Dutch embassy to arrange their refugee papers, but it could take a while. They had spent four nights at the house, and even though they were now safe from the Nazis, Christiaan and Lisa still needed to stay out of sight. Despite their long journey, they arrived in Switzerland to go straight into hiding again.

When Elisabeth had come through with their papers, everything had changed. They were now free to go wherever they wanted. She had arranged a small flat for them in the city. It was nothing more than a shoebox, but Christiaan and Lisa couldn't be happier—it was *their* shoebox.

For the first few days, they walked around the city and its environs. The absence of constant checkpoints had been odd at first to get used to, and Christiaan was still looking over his shoulder. However, that slowly faded as they became more comfortable in their new surroundings.

A modest bell rang as Christiaan opened the door to the cafe. It was lunchtime, and every table was occupied. He looked into the large dining room and spotted Lisa at a table in the back. She was reading, and he crossed the room, indicating to a waiter he was with her. Café du Centre was their favorite spot in the city. They discovered it on one of their walks, and the exquisite coffee meant they kept coming back. The chandeliers and the white linen tablecloths brought something classy and worldly that they weren't accustomed to in Amsterdam. Despite the upper-class looks, the service was friendly and the prices reasonable.

Lisa looked up as he hung his coat on a small hook next to the table. She smiled. "Everything went well? You're a bit later than I expected."

"Sorry about that. I couldn't resist taking a small detour with this weather." He sat down across from her.

"Pont des Bergues?" She put the book down.

"Feels a bit like home," he said, looking up as a waiter appeared. "Two coffees, please."

The waiter disappeared, and Christiaan put his hands on the table, leaning a little closer to Lisa. "I have news about Nora."

Her face turned serious. "And?"

"She's safe. More people came through over the weekend, carrying messages from Amsterdam and Brussels." As he spoke the words, he felt the same relief he'd felt when their contact at the embassy had told him an hour earlier.

Lisa reached across the table and squeezed his hand. There were tears in her eyes. "I'm so happy to hear that, Chris. I know how worried you were."

He nodded, blinking hard. "When we didn't hear anything last week, I feared my brother must've found out and somehow gotten to her. I almost gave up."

"I know. What about your brother?"

The waiter arrived, and they were silent as he placed two porcelain cups in front of them. When he left, Christiaan said, "He has disappeared."

She frowned. "Disappeared? How?"

He took a sip of his coffee, savoring the bitter taste. "They didn't say. The only thing they said was that we no longer need to worry about him."

"That sounds ominous." Lisa looked pensive as her eyes scanned the room. Christiaan did the same, still marveling at the normality of the situation around them. "How do you feel about that?" Lisa asked, her cup clanging a little as she replaced it on the saucer.

"I'm not sure. If it means he can longer harass innocent people, I'm happy. I always wondered if he truly believed in what he was doing?"

To his surprise, Lisa scoffed, and then immediately put up her hand. "I'm sorry, I didn't mean that. But from everything you've told me, your brother sounds like he knew *exactly* what he was doing."

"Don't apologize. You're right. He believed he was doing the right thing. I just wonder if there could've been some way to make him see his wrongs."

Lisa shook her head. "He was about to arrest you, Chris. He would betray his own blood. Whatever happened to him, he deserved it. Think of all the people he handed over to the Germans, all those people he robbed."

He looked at her and knew she was right. Her fierce eyes shone brightly, and he remembered she had lost her parents because of people like his brother. There was no need to feel bad about Floris disappearing. "There's no excusing what he did, Lisa. I'm sorry."

Her face softened. "I understand, he's still your brother."

Christiaan had mixed emotions as he finished his coffee. Knowing Nora was safe was overwhelming, but so was the realization that his brother had disappeared.

"Something's going on in that head of yours," Lisa said, interrupting his thoughts. "Want to tell me about it?"

"I feel odd about it all," he said. "Even though Nora is safe from Floris, it doesn't mean everything is okay now. Our country is still occupied. The Nazis are still deporting innocent people."

"You feel Nora is still in danger."

Christiaan nodded. "I know her. She might not be able to share information from Floris anymore, but she will still rescue those children from the crèche. And when she can't do that anymore, she'll find something else. And meanwhile, we are sitting here, having a coffee." Lisa looked at him without speaking, her eyes urging him on. "I can't sit here and wait for the war to end, Lisa."

"I understand, Chris," she said, holding his gaze as she leaned forward. "What do you want to do?"

"At the embassy just now, the man who told me about Nora and Floris asked about our plans, now that we are here. I told him we hadn't decided yet. He asked if we would want to help other people make it south as we did. He said they are looking to extend the route."

"Extend it where?" Lisa frowned.

"To Spain, to take people to England," Christiaan said. His hands shook a little as he spoke. "To join the fight from there."

Lisa's face remained calm as she nodded slowly. "Is that what you want to do? Go to England?"

"I don't know. I haven't thought that far ahead yet. But I would like to do something, at least. And this man seemed to know what he was talking about. He said we could make a difference from Geneva, even. He said he will be in town for a few more days and to find him if we want to help."

Lisa took his hands. "Listen to me, Chris. If it wasn't for you, I wouldn't be here today. In fact, I *know* I wouldn't be alive." He opened his mouth, but she shook her head. "No, let me finish. I will forever be grateful for what you've done for me and what you did for my parents." She closed her eyes and swallowed before continuing. "I will be by your side always. I love you."

Christiaan's heart beat faster as the warmth of her hands and words flowed through his body. "And I love you, Lisa," he said softly.

"You've protected me and looked after me since the first day we met. We've crossed half the continent to be here, to be safe. If we now have a chance to help the people we've left behind and somehow make things better, we have to do just that." She reached into her purse and placed some coins on the table, reaching for her coat as she stood. "How about some fresh air?"

They stepped out of the cafe, and Christiaan took her hand as they headed north. When they approached the riverfront, the Rhône glimmering in the bright sunlight, Lisa pulled him toward the Pont des Bergues. They crossed the small bridge, and Christiaan enjoyed the sound of the water gently sloshing beneath them.

Lisa turned to Christiaan, her eyes distant at first, then focusing on him. "You said this man isn't going to be here long, right?"

"Until tomorrow or the day after, I believe."

She nodded. "Then we better go talk to him. Do you have an address?"

"I do. He's actually Madame Cartier's husband. I think you'll like him." He nodded to the other side of the water, and they walked on with a little more urgency.

As they reached the other side of the bridge, he looked at Lisa, with Lake Geneva and the mountains in the distance. He decided that no matter what happened, he would always keep her safe.

No, they would keep each other safe.

AUTHOR'S NOTES

When people ask me how I come up with ideas for my books, the answer is easy: I read and listen to what happens around me. I know that sounds odd coming from someone writing about World War II, but I love to read, and I often find random articles giving me insight into something I'd never heard of before. That's where the spark of inspiration ignites, and I look to connect different people and events to create a new story.

For *Orphans of War*, I was triggered by a conversation with a good friend when we talked about the role of the NSB in the Netherlands. We like to focus on tales of heroic resistance, where ordinary people upset impossible odds to beat a clear enemy. In the case of European WWII stories, this enemy is often Nazi Germany. It's easy to forget that plenty of local collaborators were happy to assist the occupying forces. It's also clear to see why they did so; apart from being the path of least resistance, plenty of people believed in the new ideology. They thought they were joining the winning side.

I explored this angle as I dug into my own country's history of resistance and collaboration. To say I was shocked to find the rampant corruption and collaboration present within the Dutch police force would be an understatement. One of my main characters was going to be a bounty-hunting police officer, and Floris created himself.

On the other side, the Dutch resistance had so many more layers than just the well-known practice of hiding Jews. The most prevalent passive form of resistance in the Netherlands was sheltering these unfortunate people in basements, attics, and farmhouses across the country. And even though the resistance was not as partisan as those in Poland or France, the complications of hiding and smuggling people shouldn't be underestimated. Many heroes were operating in the shadows, taking great risks to keep those in hiding fed and alive —people much like Christiaan and Nora. But also real people like Bet van Beeren and Henriëtte Pimentel played their part.

The crèche at the Plantage Middellaan was real, and Ms. Pimentel oversaw the smuggling operation, along with her connection at the Jewish Council, Walter Süskind. Together, they saved an estimated 500 to 1,000 children from certain death. The crèche was closed by the Nazis in July 1943, after which Henriëtte Pimentel was deported to Auschwitz, where she was murdered on 17 September of the same year.

Apart from providing shelter for Jews in hiding, Bet van Beeren provided the Dutch resistance with a place to store their weapons. Her bar, Cafe 't Mandje, was located within the red-light district, an area off limits to German troops. The scene where Christiaan and Lisa overhear her keeping the Grüne Polizei at bay actually happened. Bet wanted to avoid them coming upstairs, where she presumably had weapons hidden. I took some creative liberties with her exact words, but she did kill all the lights to create a diversion and pretend to support the German occupation. And yes, they apparently did deliver the schnapps she requested. Even though Bet is no longer alive, her bar is still in the same location; Zeedijk 63 in Amsterdam.

The route to Switzerland Christiaan and Lisa took existed and was run by the Dutch-Paris network. As they made their way to Geneva in early 1943, it was still in its early days, with lots of uncertainties. When Christiaan meets Elisabeth Cartier's husband in Geneva in the epilogue, he met Jean Weidner, the founder of this network and route who was hard at work on improving the route's logistics.

Finally, I know there's one thing I need to address: the ending.

I'm sure you have questions. All I can tell you is that I'm not done with these characters just yet. At the time of finishing this story, I've never written or promised a sequel to a book. I like to wrap up a story and start a new one. But for this one, I can already tell you: this is likely not *the end*, but a *to be continued*. Let me know if you're keen to see the story continue; it's extremely motivating to know these characters resonated with you.

All my very best,

Michael

A NOTE TO THE READER

Dear Reader,

I want to thank you for picking up your copy of *Orphans of War* - readers mean everything to authors, and I appreciate you more than I can say.

As an author I depend on you to leave an honest review on Amazon, Goodreads, or your favorite (online) bookstore. If you've got the time to do so, I would be very grateful.

If you would like to reach out to me with questions or comments, please feel free to contact me via my website – michaelreit.com or reach out to me on Facebook – www.facebook.com/MichaelReitAuthor. I love hearing from readers, and look forward to hearing what you have to say about *Orphans of War*!

Warmly and with Gratitude,
Michael Reit

ALSO BY MICHAEL REIT

Made in United States
Orlando, FL
11 May 2024

46713256R00178